FATHER

CLARISSA WILD

Copyright © 2017 Clarissa Wild
All rights reserved.
ISBN: 978-1545293959
ISBN-10: 1545293953

© 2017 Clarissa Wild

This is a work of fiction. Names, characters, places and incidents are either the product of the author's imagination or are used fictitiously. Any resemblance to actual events, places, organizations, or person, whether living or dead, is entirely coincidental.

All rights reserved. No part of this book may be reproduced, transmitted in any form or by any means, electronic or mechanical, including photocopying, recording, or by any information storage retrieval system. Doing so would break licensing and copyright laws.

MUSIC PLAYLIST

"Nobody Speak" by DJ Shadow ft. Run The Jewels
"Till It's Gone" by Yelawolf
"Get Away" by DJ Paul ft. Yelawolf & Jon Connor
"Daylight" by Yelawolf
"Devil In My Veins" by Yelawolf
"Shadows" by Yelawolf ft. Joshua Hedley
"Iron" by Woodkid
"About Her" by Malcolm Mclaren
"Ooh La La" by Goldfrapp
"Get Some" by Lykke Li
"Cold Cold Cold" by Cage The Elephant
"Ain't No Grave" by Johnny Cash
"Going UpState" by Ritual Howls
"Get Up" by Dorothy
"Raise Hell" by Dorothy
"Black Ajax" by Locksley
"Boots Of Chinese Plastic" by The Pretenders
"BLKKK SKKKN HEAD" by Kanye West
"Voodoo In My Blood" by Massive Attack
"Kiss It Better" by Rihanna
"Deep Six" by Marilyn Manson
"Personal Jesus" by Marilyn Manson
"So Sophisticated" by Rick Ross ft. Meek Mill
"Hustle Hard" by Ace Hood ft. Rick Ross, Lil Wayne
"Believe Me" by Lil Wayne ft. Drake
"Shit Just Got Real" by Die Antwoord
"Toccata and Fugue in D Minor" by Johann Sebastian Bach
"William Tell's Overture: Final" by Rossini

AUTHOR'S NOTE

THIS STORY IS ENTIRELY FICTIONAL AND NOT ASSOCIATED WITH A REAL CHURCH OR RELIGION. IT DOES NOT FOLLOW ANY RULES OR MAKE ANY SENSE FROM A RELIGIOUS PERSPECTIVE. FRANK IS NOT A PRIEST BUT A PREACHER. THIS STORY IS PURELY WRITTEN FOR FUN.

This book is not for everyone.
It's filthy. It's vulgar. It's downright offensive.
But it's *oh so damn delicious with a capital D*.

If you are easily offended, please do not read this book. If you're prudish or extremely religious, definitely don't read this book.

But if you like a bit of dark humor mixed in with raunchy sex and fisticuffs, then read on.

You've been warned.

PROLOGUE

A druggie, a criminal, and a preacher walk into a bar. I know you're expecting a joke here, but there is none. Well, at least not yet.

With a smirk on my face, I sit down on a stool and nod at Chuck, the bartender, who shakes his head at me when he notices me. "Save it; I don't wanna hear it," I growl. "Gimme a whiskey on the rocks."

"Hi to you too," he growls back, chewing on a toothpick as he turns around to grab the liquor. "You know, I could save you time and just give you the bottle."

"No, I'm good. I prefer booze when it's slow and painful," I retort.

He snorts and shakes his head again. "Sometimes, I really wanna tell you to get the fuck outta here." He grabs a glass and tosses in some ice cubes then pours my drink.

"But then you'd be missing all that sweet cash," I reply.

He slides it my way. "You found my weak spot."

"That's my job," I muse, taking a sip. The kick immediately hits me in the guts, but it only makes me want to take another. I'm a sucker for pain.

"Maybe you should go easy on yourself tonight," Chuck says.

"You don't have to look out for me." I put down my drink and look at the cold moisture gathering on the outside of the glass. "I'm a lost cause anyway."

"That ain't true, and you know it."

I shrug, taking another sip. I fucking hate talking about this shit.

"Everybody needs someone to look out for them once in a while."

"Yeah, well, I got it covered," I say, blowing out a sigh. "You want my money or not?"

He nods. "You know I damn well do."

"Then stop talking and pour me another." I shove my glass forward and stare at him until he grabs the bottle again and starts pouring. "Keep going."

"You got anyone to drive you home tonight?" he asks.

"No. But I know you'll get me a cab."

He smiles when he realizes I know him all too well.

Right before the whiskey hits the edge of the glass, I hold up my hand, and he stops. I take a big gulp of the whiskey and let out a breath. "Fuck, yes. Exactly what I needed."

"What you need every damn day of the week, you mean." We both laugh. However, the smile disappears from his face the moment two shadows block the light.

"Hey, you there."

I don't reply. My name isn't fucking 'You there.'

"You deaf or something?" one of the guys behind me says, but I just keep drinking.

Meanwhile, Chuck turns and starts washing the dishes like he doesn't know who they are even though he damn well does. They come here every other Friday, trying to start a fight with a random guy so they can shake him for cash.

This time, they picked the wrong one, though.

"Hey, motherfucker. Turn around." One of them taps my shoulder.

Frowning, I put down my drink and glance over my shoulder, still not answering their catcalls. "Got something to say?"

Two ugly fucks stand in front of me. One with a bald head covered in swastikas and the other covered in pimples that are bursting as he talks.

"Yeah, who the fuck are you and what are you doing here?"

"None of your fuckin' business," I reply, taking another sip of my whiskey.

The little pimpled one mutters, "Jesus, isn't he some kind of pri—"

"Who cares," the bald one growls. "He can't be here. This place is ours ..." the bald one growls.

"Is your name on the sign?" I ask, raising a brow.

"The what?" the pimpled one says.

"The sign. Outside." I point at the door. "You're welcome to go look if you need some help."

"Fuck you," the bald one curses, showing me his gold teeth.

"Well, aren't you a pretty lady," I muse.

He presses his thick thumb against my chest. "Shut your fuckin' pie hole, you Bible thumper. Now give me your fucking money or else …"

"Or what? You're gonna hit me?" I say, unimpressed.

"Yeah … and worse," the pimpled one threatens.

I gaze at Chuck who seems to be hiding his laughter in his sleeve while he tries to dry the dishes. "Hey Chuck, did you hear that? They're gonna hit me. *Me*."

Chuck makes a face and rolls his eyes, and I burst out laughing. "Good one."

The bald one gets so mad, he grabs my collar and almost pulls me off my stool.

This is a point of no return for me.

Normally, I would let them off with a warning, but he crossed a line right there.

No one, and I mean no one, touches my collar.

That thing is sacred.

"Chuck …" I mutter.

"Frank"—he sighs—"can ya not—"

"Go," I interrupt.

"Money or pain. Choose," the bald one growls while Chuck slowly backs away into the supply room.

Grinding my teeth, I say, "Neither."

He lifts his fist ready to attack. Right as it comes close to my face, I lean sideways and narrowly avoid it. I quickly grab his wrist and hold him in place as I jam my knee in his face. Then I kick him away fast enough to protect myself against the knife the pimpled one just pulled.

He tries to slash me with it, but I block it and grasp his wrist, twisting it hard enough to break. He screams, and I punch him in the jaw, making him fall backward.

The bald one gets up and grunts as he tries to bulldoze me. I jump away from the bar just in time, and he rams his head straight into the wooden bar, knocking himself out. I laugh as the other one gets angrier by the second, his face so red I'm almost worried it might explode. That'd be a sight to behold.

"You motherfucker! You'll pay for that!" the pimpled one screams, grabbing his knife again.

He thrusts it at me, slashing along my cheek. The blade leaves a small slit, and blood seeps down my face, but I don't even notice the pain.

All I can focus on is grabbing him by the back of the head and shoving his face down onto an empty glass on the bar. He squeals as the shards enter his skin while I slide his face along the bar like I'm serving up some arrogant little shit with a side order of bald scum.

"Think you can pull that trick on me? Not today, bitch," I whisper into his ear, ramming his face against the wood again.

He fights back by throwing punches into the air, so I quickly grab his hands and force them behind his back.

"Didn't expect that, did you?"

The asshole under my grip whimpers from the pain, and as I tighten my grip, he begins to cry. "I'm sorry," he squeaks.

"Sorry, my ass," I hiss, holding him down firmly. "Who else did you steal from this week?"

"No one," he says.

I twist his pinky until he squeals like a girl. "Didn't your mother teach you not to lie to a preacher?"

"I'm sorry, I'm sorry! We only stole two dollars from

Chuck."

"Chuck!" I yell. "C'mere."

As Chuck scurries back from the supply room, I hiss into the boy's ear, "Where's the money?"

He sniffs. "In my back pocket."

I glower, not wanting to get my hands anywhere near his ass, but I need to make a point here. Guess every once in a while, I have to sacrifice myself for the greater good.

I reach into his pocket with disgust and take out two one-dollar bills, placing them on the counter. "There you go, Chuck. They're yours."

"Thanks," he says. "But that won't cover the broken chairs."

He points at the mess behind me, and I make a face at him. "C'mon, Chuck, work with me here."

He shrugs and holds up his hands. "Whatever." Then he goes back into the supply room. "Tell me when you're done."

"Tell him you're sorry," I growl at the crying little shit.

"I'm sorry!" he shrieks as I twist his other pinky.

For a second there, I wonder if I should take it one step further, but that would make me just as bad as they are. I need to set an example. That's what preachers do. Or so I've been told.

I'm not a priest, and I don't pretend to be one. I'm just your average joe preaching to the people. However, I won't stand for bad behavior.

"Good," I growl, lifting him off the bar and throwing him near his buddy. "Now get the fuck outta here and don't come back. And take that sorry-ass racist with you," I spit, grabbing my drink.

"We won't," he mutters, grabbing the bald one by the shoulders. Being a shrimp himself, I know dragging a bull of a man outside is a tough job. Especially when no one gives you a hand.

I don't even give a shit. I just watch, mildly amused by the silliness, while I sip on my whiskey.

"You done now?" Chuck calls out.

"Yeah," I reply, still staring at the door until the two have disappeared.

"Fucking hell, Frank. Why? Why do you always have to mess up this place?"

"I'm sorry, Chuck. I know I'm shit 'cause I attract a lot of flies."

He snorts while shaking his head then grabs a broom and walks to the front of the bar, holding it out to me. "Here. Help me clean."

I nod a few times and take another sip of my whiskey.

"You've got something," Chuck says, "here," and he points at my cheek.

Without looking away, I grab a napkin and wipe the blood off my cheek, throwing it down on the floor with the rest of the trash.

"Really?" Chuck raises his brow at me.

I shrug. "What? It's getting cleaned up anyway."

He pushes the broom into my hands and says, "You're one weird-ass motherfucking preacher, you know that?"

I laugh and take my last sip then put down the glass.

"You never change," he adds.

I grin as we get to work on the broken tables, chairs, and glass. "Nope. Never have. Never will."

CHAPTER ONE

I run. Faster than my legs can carry me. Faster than the air my lungs can breathe. Faster than the speed of light. But no matter how fast I try to be there, I'm never on time.

In the distance, I hear a scream.

The sound reverberates in my ears, over and over again, until I hear nothing but her voice screaming my name.

"Frank! Frank! Help!"

Faster, faster.

Seconds feel like minutes, and when I finally arrive, I'm too late.

Two men have her arms locked in their grip. They're dragging her to a car.

Another scream comes from the car, this one much higher and louder.

It pierces my heart, crippling me, but I won't give up.
I'll never give up.
I run toward them as fast as I can. But before I can catch up, the two men have already pushed her into the car and jumped in after her. Right as I touch the back, they hit the gas, and the car shoots away right from under my fingers.
The last thing I see is the faces of the people who put their trust in me. And I failed them.
Everything fades in front of my eyes, and I black out ... only to wake again in the darkness covered in sweat. Rain pours down from above as I stare at the woman lying on the dirty ground underneath my feet.
Her limbs twisted.
Her body broken.
Her face shattered.
Blood spilled everywhere.
I hold my breath, and it feels like forever until I breathe again.
But no matter how hard I try ... I can't get her voice out of my head. She keeps whispering my name.
Frank.
Frank...

"Frank!"

I open my eyes and blink a couple of times, unsure of where I am or what time it is. My vision is blurry, and my face feels like it's been inside an oven. I wait a few seconds, and she yells my name again. Only now, it's a completely different voice.

"Frank, get up!"

I lick my dry lips. "Mother ..." I mutter.

I take a deep breath and close my eyes again, trying to forget about what I just dreamed. My head throbs like a hammer struck it several times. And my stomach constricts like someone sucker punched me. God, I hate waking up like this.

"Christ, look at you," she mumbles, wiping my shirt with something, probably a wet cloth.

I'm way too out of it to even care.

"Get up," she snaps, patting me like I'm some kind of dog.

"What?" I grumble.

"You look despicable. Wash yourself."

"What did I do now?"

"Look around!"

I open my eyes and lean up on my elbows. Only now do I see all the empty bottles lying on the floor along with some socks, shoes, and a belt scattered around the room. A splash of liquor stains the carpet … and I think a bit of puke as well.

"Look at you …" Mother wipes a cloth along my forehead and cheeks. "You look miserable."

"Thanks," I say with a laugh, but even that hurts.

"I can't believe you did it again."

The disappointment in her voice really cuts deep. I hate when she talks to me like that. She's my mother. Well, sort of. Technically, she's just the woman who raised me because we're not related by blood. Her real name is Margaret. I call her Mother because everyone here does. She's the one who organizes everything at the church, and she's been my caretaker for all these years. Even though I'm thirty, I still need her more than anything in this fucking world. She's the only thing that keeps me tethered to this place.

"C'mon, get up," she nags, pulling on my arm.

I do as she asks and sit up in my bed. I place my hand against my forehead to stop the headache, but it's no use. Mother walks to my sink and fills a glass with water. She rummages in her pockets and takes out a few pills. "Take these." She holds both out to me.

I know she won't leave me until I do what she says, so I just take them.

"Where were you last night?" she asks.

"I guess that's obvious," I muse, grinning a little, but she smacks me with my own Bible.

"Frank Romero! How many times do I have to tell you to stop drinking!" With every word, she gives me another slap. "You drunk!"

"Okay, okay, I get it!" I hold my hand up to stop her from slapping me again. "I'm not drunk anymore." That's a lie, but I don't care. Anything to get her to stop.

"Then man up and get your filthy ass cleaned up," she growls, looking at me with those deathly eyes. They always terrified me when I was young. They still do.

If anyone ever told you old ladies were timid and gentle, they were lying.

I let out a long-drawn-out breath and get up from the bed, only just noticing I'm still wearing yesterday's pants.

"You have ten minutes to get dressed," she says firmly, putting the Bible back on my nightstand. "And not a minute more."

"Why? I haven't even had breakfast yet." I scratch the back of my neck and yawn.

She puts her hands on her hips. "Frank. Did you even

look at the time?"

Now that she mentions it … no, I haven't.

She frowns. "It's nine 'o clock."

"So?" I shrug. I still don't get the point.

"On a Sunday."

It takes a while for it to click.

My eyes widen as I say, "Oh …"

"Exactly." She taps her feet on the floor. "The church is filled with people already. They're all waiting. The only thing missing is you, Frank." She opens the door.

Flustered, I reply, "Sorry."

"Save it," she spits. "Just make sure you're"—she looks me up and down—"presentable." Then she walks out and closes the door behind her.

I quickly wash my face with water, rinsing off the puke and stench. I look like a mess, and I'm not talking about all my tattoos. No wonder people think I'm a hack. I act like one, so that's what you're gonna get.

I dry my face with a towel and take off all my dirty clothes, almost stumbling over them. Snatching the clothes off the hook, I comb my hair and slap myself to wake the fuck up.

I'm still so damn hammered that I can barely walk straight, but I finally manage to dress. Right before I walk out the door, I put on my robe and make sure the white piece of my collar is visible. One last look at the mirror has me blowing a kiss and winking at myself. Damn, I'm so hot I could bake an egg on myself.

Speaking of, I'm gonna grub out on some bacon and eggs when I finish.

I'm tempted to skip town so I can have a proper

breakfast instead of doing this sermon, but I know Mother would never forgive me. And boy, do I love her to death.

Before I walk out the door, I snatch the small bottle of liquor I saved underneath my nightstand and tuck it into my chest pocket. Call it a good luck charm. Or a fuck-it charm. Whatever floats your boat. As long as I have my drink, I'm good.

As I open the door from the chancel, all the people sitting in the pews look up at me, and I pause. Their eyes fall on me like spikes piercing my body, and it's at this moment I feel most judged.

Some would say not to let this feeling overwhelm me, but sometimes, the voices in my head need to shut up for a moment.

I make my way to the pulpit while fiddling in my pocket, looking for the small piece of paper I scribbled on yesterday. I remember writing down a sermon or something of the sort. But when I get to the pulpit and place the paper on it, all I find are random words and gibberish; sentences that don't make any sense. Well, so much for a great sermon.

"Uh ... good morning, everyone," I say with a half-assed smile.

Some people shuffle around in their seat, some cough, and others look bored.

It's the same shit every day, only worse. Every time I'm here, I see another empty seat. People just don't care anymore.

And me? I feel like shit, and looking at them, I honestly don't know why I'm still here.

Why I'm even trying to put up a front.

I clear my throat and try to ignore my raging headache

and starry eyesight.

"So … hope you're all having a great day so far," I say, the speaker slightly squeaking on me. I adjust it a little and continue my babbling. "Or I hope at least one of us is."

People look annoyed.

I guess that's only natural because I am too.

"Let's talk about God. We're all here for God, right?"

Of course, no one answers.

"Yeah, thought so." I chew on my lip for a moment.

"God. God. God. They say He's all around us. Everywhere. Anytime. Looking down upon us to keep us safe. To watch over us. Or so they say."

Everyone's still staring at me, so I guess I'll continue.

"God. You know … I haven't found Him lately. And I bet a lot of you haven't." I pause. "Have you ever wondered if He abandoned you?"

No one answers, but from the looks on their faces, I can tell half of them agree. The other half I prefer to ignore.

"If God wasn't the One looking out for you? Who do you turn to?"

No one answers, which I expected.

"No one," I say. "No one but yourself. You are the only one who can save yourself."

Some people clutch their purses tight, and others cover their mouths in shock. Like what I'm saying is so strange. Like none of them have ever thought it. Of course, they have. They're just afraid to admit it.

"And you know what? God doesn't care about me. Or you. Or about any of us."

Some jaws drop.

"Why else would He make us suffer so much? Why

would He give us so much pain? Why wouldn't He just take it away?" My nails almost dig into the wood. "He wouldn't. Because God doesn't do easy. God doesn't give us anything we need. God wants us to fight for it. God wants *us* to do the work. He's not here to have pity or make your life better. That's your job."

"Frank!" I turn my head to see Mother whisper-yelling at me from the side, but I ignore her.

"I'm not here to tell you what to do. Nor is God. I can only tell you that life will never be easy. It's always going to be tough, and shit's going to come at you and ruin your goddamn life."

More audible gasps.

"And you know what? That's okay. Because life is about pain. And suffering. It's about repentance."

As I speak, my eyes fall on a girl sitting in the crowd. A beautiful girl with wavy, dark brown hair just past her shoulders, sharply defined cheekbones, and thick eyebrows topping big blue eyes. She looks like she's in her twenties ... pretty, and definitely eye-catching. So much so that I can't even remember what I was saying.

All I can think of is her ... and then I notice the little boy sitting next to her, watching his feet dangle below the pew. She grabs his hand and squeezes.

Her eyes ... I can't stop looking.

For some reason, my brain stops functioning.

Even if only for a second, the worries disappear. And I don't know why, but somehow, someway ... she feels familiar to me.

Which is strange because I've never seen her here before.

A cough from another churchgoer pulls me from my thoughts, and I clear my throat and continue.

"We go through life because we must. All for the sake of the afterlife. For heaven, we do it all. Heaven … Boy, I think we'd all love to be there right now." I look at the girl and wonder what she's thinking. If she's ever thought of heaven. If she realizes right now that when I picture her naked in front of me, that would be heaven.

Luckily, no one can see inside my head.

Instead, everyone's gone quiet now.

I mutter, "And as far as I see it … you can live out your life to the fullest or give up. God doesn't give a shit anyway. He just wants you to make a choice. And whether you choose to accept is up to you. We're all going to die anyway."

Mother suddenly barges up to the pulpit and turns off the microphone then glares at me profusely. She doesn't need to say a word. I turn around and stumble off, grabbing the small bottle of liquor in my pocket and drinking it down in one gulp.

I don't give two shits that everyone in here can see me drink.

I'm already going to hell anyway. Might as well make it a fun trip.

CHAPTER TWO

I rummage underneath my bed and take out two *Playboy* I've been hiding from Mother. With a grin on my face, I plop down on my bed and sift through the magazine until I find a pretty picture of a naked lady and start rubbing myself.

What?

I never said I was a saint. Far from it, actually. I've done some very bad shit in my life. People would be afraid of me if they knew. But that all happened before I became a preacher.

Not in the official sense, of course. I'm not ordained. I just like to give back to the people, and I do it by preaching.

However, preachers have needs too.

And boy ... my needs have been piling up since I saw

that girl in church on Sunday. Something about her electrified my body. Like it suddenly came alive again after a long sleep.

For some reason, I can't get her off my mind.

No matter how many days pass, I can't stop thinking about her, wondering who she is, and why she's started visiting my church. Why she's here. If she ever has the same naughty thoughts as I have about her.

I admit it. I'm not ashamed to say I'm infatuated with the very thought of having her right here in my bed.

Is it wrong? Hell yeah, but I don't care.

Right now, I just wanna blow off some steam, and beating my meat seems like the perfect way to do it.

So I grease the pipe with some gun oil from my nightstand and start to rub one out.

However, the longer I stare at the pictures on the magazine, the less in the mood I'm feeling. I don't know what it is, but random nude chicks just don't do it for me anymore. And whenever I think of *her*, my cock springs right back into action.

So I close the magazine and my eyes and focus on the image I have of her in my mind; her sultry eyes focused solely on me as she strips down, removing her clothes piece by piece. So sensually, so sexually that I touch myself.

I groan from the thought of having her bounce on my dick, her tits jiggling in my face, and I come so damn hard it spurts all over.

"Fuck …" I hiss, biting my lip.

God, oh God.

You and I both know I needed that more than anything.

I grab some tissues and pat myself down to clean up the

mess. Right then, the door opens, and Margaret's eyes widen at the sight of my sloppy joe.

"Oh, God," she mutters as she slaps her hand in front of her eyes.

She's never sworn before, so I can't help but laugh.

"Lord Almighty," she mutters, turning around and slamming the door behind her.

"Sorry," I say, hoping she can still hear.

"Pray to God I forget this as soon as possible."

I laugh again. "I'll beg him for mercy, I promise."

"Of course, you will."

I don't even have to see her roll her eyes because I know she's doing it.

"Can't you just not do that?" she asks.

"No," I reply, grinning like a fool as I get up from the bed and throw away the tissues. "Preachers have needs too."

"I don't wanna hear it!" she quickly interjects, making me shake my head.

"I came to tell you someone's waiting for you in the confessional. Multiple people are waiting, actually."

"Great," I huff, grabbing my pants and pulling them on.

I hate that fucking confessional. It's too ... official, and I'm not a priest. But since the people asked Mother specifically to put a confessional in the church, she couldn't refuse, despite my hesitations. The people wanted this, so she gave it to them.

Maybe the people in this neighborhood like the privacy the confessional offers. And if that's what people want, we'll give it to them. Anything to help, right?

"They've been waiting for a while now," Mother adds.

"Yeah, yeah, I'm coming," I reply, staring at my sexy,

tattooed body in the mirror as I put on my shirt and collar right. "Don't get your panties in a twist."

"My what?" she scoffs.

I open the door and see her standing with her arms folded. "Nothing," I say. "Let's go."

"I'm not going in there with you," she says, frowning.

"Like I'd want you in there," I retort. "We're not stuffing a clown's car. This is a church."

Her eyebrows are so low I swear they're permanently stuck. "You know, half the time I really don't know what you're saying."

I smile and pat her back as we both walk through the corridor. "That's a good thing; trust me."

"Well, I'll see you when you're done, okay?" She raises her brow. As if keeping tabs on me is anything new for her.

"Yeah, yeah," I mutter. "I'm going."

We each go our own way. I straighten my collar before I go up to the main area and look around. A few people are in the pews, praying or silently sitting there, overthinking their sins. For those who glance my way, I give them a fake smile and a nod as I walk past and enter the confessional.

The wooden bench underneath my ass feels so damn hard that I find it hard to stay seated, but I guess we all make sacrifices for the greater good. Besides, I've got to keep up appearances of being a semi-okay preacher.

But dammit … I hate how confined this space is and how ancient it makes me feel to look at the latticed wood between me and the other side.

Especially when an older lady sits down and closes the curtain then stares at me profusely like she can gape straight into my soul. Scary shit.

She makes the sign of the cross and begins her talk. "I've been doing a terrible injustice toward one of my boys," she mutters. "I should've punished him harder, but I just couldn't. Not because I didn't want to, but I felt so disgusted; I didn't even want to confront him even though he'd earned it."

"What has your boy done?" I ask.

"He's been ... well, how do I say this ..." She smashes her lips together and frowns, looking down at her feet.

I lean in closer. "Done what?"

"He's been doing ... inappropriate things."

"Like what?" I ask, cocking my head because I can't believe where this is about to go.

"When he's in the shower or in his bed, I've heard him make noises." She looks away in disgust, her eyes clearly in despair.

And I honestly don't know how to respond.

"Like dirty noises. And he's still a boy. He shouldn't be doing those things."

I snort, trying to hold back the laughter, but I just can't.

"Are you ... are you laughing?" she asks after hearing my sniffling.

"You're confessing about not punishing your boy hard enough because he was jerking off?"

Her eyes widen, and her face tightens. "Excuse me?"

"Is that seriously what you came here to do?" I ask, raising my brow at her. "You do realize wanking is absolutely normal for boys his age?"

Her jaw drops and nothing comes out of her mouth, which I'm thankful for.

"Ma'am, you don't have to confess something that

trivial."

"Trivial? Trivial?" She repeats it like she didn't hear what I said. That or she's very, very mad. Crazy mad indeed.

"That sort of thing is disgusting!" she hisses. "I can't believe you would say such a thing, Father."

"Well, you came to me, not the other way around."

"Oh!" She makes this squeaky sound that makes me wanna reach into her cubicle and slap the shit out of her just for coming in here with that ridiculous shit. Wasting my time.

"Are you for real?" she sputters.

"Realer than you," I quip.

She grimaces. "You're supposed to do your job."

"I'm supposed to listen to real confessions here. Things that matter."

"Are you saying my boy doing filthy things to himself doesn't matter? That I should just leave it?"

"That's exactly what I'm saying."

She sighs out loud. "But you're a preacher. You're supposed to carry out God's will."

"So?" I shrug, trying not to let her get to me, even though I really wanna say something about that shitty comment about 'God's will.' Fucking hell. "If you wanna know, I sent out the troops this morning too."

"Troops?" She looks really confused now.

"Yeah, you know. Spank the monkey. Rope the pony. Milk the bull."

She looks at me like I've got peanut butter stuck on my face.

"Rubbed one out."

"Are you implying …"

I cock my head. "My dick was hard this morning."

Another soft squeal leaves her throat.

"Don't worry; it's not anymore." I roll my eyes. "Not by a long shot. Although I did have a very long shot this morning." I grin to myself.

"I can't believe this." She shakes her head in disbelief. "A preacher, out of all people. You should be ashamed of yourself."

"Ashamed? Far from it. Everyone has needs," I reply. "My point is, if you want to stop feeling guilty, you gotta stop thinking everything is a sin."

"The Bible says you can't—"

"The Bible also says you can't mark your body." I pull down my sleeve and show her my tattoos. "See this? Think God hates me now?"

"Oh, my Lord …" She clutches her chest. "Why did I ever come to this church?" she mumbles to herself. "I should've stayed with my regular one."

"They were tired of your whining there, weren't they? That's why you left."

"What?" A scowl appears on her face. "How dare you? I'm leaving." She gets up from her seat, clutching her dress like she's afraid I'll see something. As if I'd ever wanna see her cooch.

"Good, and stop complaining. Maybe your son will stop wanting to play whack-a-mole then."

"It's because people like you rot his mind and make him sin!" she yells, the curtain already opened. Everyone can hear us now.

"He'll never stop being an ass because he's living with you, and that's the worst kind of hell anyone can have. But you know what? I'm going to forgive you because I'm a nice person. And nice people do that kind of shit for other people, you know?" I get up from my seat and wave her away. "Just go … And thank the Lord for His mercy because I know you ain't getting it anywhere else."

As her self-righteous, scorned ass turns around and struts away, I look out at the people staring at me and yell, "Next!"

Then I go back inside the confessional and slam the little door shut.

CHAPTER THREE

After I've listened to everyone's sins, I go back to my room and grab one of the bigger bottles I hid in the bookcase and take a large gulp. It always lessens the severity of the headaches, strangely enough.

Suddenly, my door bursts open, and Mother comes waltzing in.

"Frank," she barks.

"Oh, God …" I mutter, putting the bottle on the small kitchen cabinet in the corner. "Not now, please."

She marches to me and snatches the bottle away. "You're drinking again."

"Yeah. No shit." I shrug. "You would too if you had to listen to that nonsense."

"Listening to people's confessions is not shit, Frank." She grabs my arm. "I don't understand. What's wrong with you?"

"What's wrong with me?" I scoff. "Nothing. Absolutely nothing."

"You never used to act this way," she says.

"Yeah, well … people change." I clear my throat and sit down on my bed.

"You've got to stop drinking like this." She shows me the bottle like I don't know I'm a fucking drunk.

"You know why I do it," I reply.

"That doesn't make it okay. Don't you think you should stop?"

"Nope." I lean back and let out a breath.

"Frank …" She sighs again in the same way she always does when she's disappointed with me. "It's enough. You've suffered enough."

"Don't," I growl. "Don't go there."

She slams the bottle down on my nightstand. "You know as well as I do that you're wasting your potential."

"Does it look like I give a fuck?"

"Frank!" She looks pissed and rightfully so. "Doesn't this church mean anything to you?"

"Of course, it does."

"Then how can you treat it this way? Your sermons have turned into doomsday predictions. Your presence is making people turn their cheek on their faith. You ruin their days by not giving them proper advice during confession." She folds her arms. "You're chasing people away."

I turn to face the wall, so I don't have to look her in the eyes. It's humiliating.

"Look what you're doing. Look what you're doing to yourself. To us. The church. Shame on you."

I take her mental beating because I must. Because I know I'm fucked up and that I'm doing everyone a disservice. I feel guilty ... but at the same time, I know I can't do shit about it. I'm stuck in my own torment.

The only solace I've found lately is in the alcohol.

And that girl who I saw.

"Think about your sins. We'll talk later." Mother turns around and leaves, the sound of her closing the door reminding me of myself when I closed off my heart.

***

I saunter across the pebble path, clutching my drink close to my heart. The sun shines brightly, but it doesn't warm the coldness deep in my soul. Looking at all the headstones makes my body feel heavy and my head weary, but I still continue walking. I don't stop until I finally see the little stone angel perched atop the stone. Each step I take feels heavier before I finally halt in front of the grave.

"Kaitlyn ..." My breathing is shallow and ragged. Just whispering her name makes the tears well up in my eyes.

I quickly take a large gulp from the bottle. The burning sensation in my throat makes the pain even more real, and I *want* to feel it. Every last drop. It's not enough.

Staring down at the ground, I wonder when it ever gets easier. If it's supposed to.

From this place, I gather the strength I need to fight, but the effect is waning with every passing day. I don't know how long I can continue.

Another big gulp down the gutter. The more time I spend here, the more I wanna get drunk in the middle of the day. I don't care that I'm on public property. That I could be seen by anyone. I just don't care anymore. Not about any of it.

"Hi."

A squeaky voice makes me turn my head only to see a young boy standing on the pebble path. He's clutching a few blades of grass, pulling them apart with his fingers as he looks up at me.

"What do you want?" I ask.

"Nothing," he muses.

Frowning, I put the bottle to my lips while he stares me down profusely.

"What are you drinking?" he asks.

"Something for grown-ups," I reply, tucking it away into my secret pocket. I don't want to give him the wrong idea. I know I'm a shitty-ass preacher, but I don't wanna expose a kid to my fucked-up life. I don't want them to think this is normal, so if I can prevent it, I will.

"Can I have a taste?" he asks.

"No," I scoff, shaking my head.

He cocks his head. "Why not?"

"Stop asking so many questions."

I fish my pack of cigarettes from my pocket and take one out, lighting it in my mouth.

"Are you a priest?" he asks.

"No," I reply, taking a drag and blowing out smoke.

"But you have that thing …" He points at his neck, probably meaning my collar.

"Yeah."

"What are you then?"

I chuckle. Kids ask so many strange questions. Like they're oblivious to the world. Gotta commend them for it. I wish I was still that innocent and ignorant.

"Whatever you want me to be, but most people call me Preacher. Or Father. Whatever. I don't care." I take another drag.

"So you do belong in church."

I tilt my head and fold my arms. Can't believe that little shit just told me off like I'm not supposed to be here. "I can go wherever I want to, kid. I'm also a human being with a life outside the faith."

"Okay ... but why are you smoking?"

I look at the cig in my hand and then back at him, and I shrug. "It relaxes me."

"I thought preachers weren't allowed to do that."

I snort. "Yeah, well, there's a whole lot more we're not supposed to do. Doesn't mean we actually listen to the rules."

He nods. "So you're like my brother?"

"Your brother?" I raise a brow. "How so?"

"He doesn't listen to anyone either."

I don't think I wanna know what this is about. However, the more I look at the kid, the more I have the feeling I know him from somewhere. And I do ... because I suddenly remember his face. He was at the church the other day with that beautiful girl.

A smirk spreads on my lips. "What's your name, kid?"

"Bruno," he says with a big fat smile.

I take another long drag of my smoke and chuck it, blowing out the smoke into the air. "You have a sister, right? Or was that girl I saw at church your mother?"

"Sister, but she's at work. We go to your church every Sunday."

"That's good, kid. Keep that up." I smile when he grins. "But hey … You're not alone here, right?"

"No." He shakes his head. "My brother's here too, but he told me to go for a walk, so I did."

"Ah-ha." No wonder he's stalking me. "Where's your brother now?"

"There." The boy turns and points at a young guy, maybe ten years older than he is, sitting at a picnic table with his head bent over his arms to hide something, but when I see a tiny whiff of smoke, I know exactly what he's doing.

"Wait here," I tell the kid, and I pass him to go to his brother.

I approach him from behind and watch him heat a spoon filled with liquid.

When he finally notices my presence, I quickly snatch his spoon, chucking the liquids out onto the grass before grasping the syringe and snapping it in two.

"Hey!"

"Are you crazy?" I yell. "Doing that in front of your own little brother?"

"And who the fuck are you?" he growls, getting up from the picnic table, but before he has a chance to get up in my face, I push him back down.

"Sit down."

"What the fuck, man?"

I grab his jacket and force him to look at me. "Are you stupid or something? Trying to get yourself killed?"

"Fuck off, man. I didn't do nothing."

"You were trying to shoot heroin. I know what the fuck that looks like," I spit. "And you're doing it in a fucking cemetery. With your little brother standing watch. How dare you."

"Mind your own fucking business, all right?" He swats me away.

"You're his brother. You're supposed to take care of him."

"So?"

"Does this look like taking care of someone to you?" I growl, and I point at the little kid whose standing far enough away he won't hear us. "That kid looks up to you. He loves you. He needs you. And you're sitting here trying to ruin your own goddamn life."

He's not responding, but from the look in his eyes, I can tell it's beginning to sink in.

"Don't you see it? That look in his eyes." I grab his face and force him to look. "Look at him. Look at your own brother and tell me you don't see it."

He sniffs. "I'm sorry, okay?"

"If you do this, there's no going back. He will lose you, and you will lose him. Either you end up in jail, or you're dead by the end of the year."

He swallows the lump in his throat as he looks at me with scared eyes. I can tell he's a newbie.

"Is this your first time?" I ask.

He nods. "Some of the guys gave it to me."

"What guys?"

"Friends. From the block. Said they'd help me get more money if I tried out their shit."

I grind my teeth, trying not to boil over when I'm a

raging volcano inside. I know exactly what this means. This neighborhood is notorious for its drug problems, and now the dealers are recruiting again by first getting them hooked and then forcing them to work.

"Don't," I say. "Even if they do give you money, it won't ever be enough. And it'll keep getting worse. Whatever they told you, it's a lie. That money is not worth it, trust me."

"How do you know?" He makes a face at me. "Aren't you some kind of—"

"Preacher, not a priest."

"Whatever. What do you even know about me?"

"Enough to tell you that your brother will die too if you continue with this."

He looks at his little brother and then back at me like he's waiting for an explanation.

I place my hand flat on the picnic table. "Once they get their hands on you, it's only a matter of time before they try to persuade your little brother too. Do you want that to happen to him?"

"No, of course not." He rubs his arms and lowers his sleeves, covering up the spot he was about to inject.

"What about your sister, huh?"

He raises a brow at me. "How do you know I have a sister?"

"I've seen her and your little brother in church. But that's not the point. Do you or do you not want to see her turn into a druggie? Or worse, have to sell her body on the streets?"

"No, of course not." He snarls in disgust. "Do you think they'd do that?"

"I've seen it happen so many times. I live and breathe this neighborhood. I see everything. I've seen girls wasted on drugs, sucking every dick they can just to pay for their next hit. And I've seen guys like you come and go like bodies at the morgue."

He bites his lip and looks down at his trembling hands.

I place a hand on his shoulder. "Just promise you'll find another way to make money. I know this seems like the easy way, but it isn't. And do you wanna do that to your little brother? Who believes so much in you? Who trusts you to do the right thing?"

We both look in his direction now and watch him throw small stones into a pond up ahead.

"I love him; I swear, I do," the guy says.

"Good." I pat him on the back. "Leave all this junk behind."

He nods and gets up from the picnic table.

"Go to him. Take him out for something to eat. Whatever. It'll make you feel better," I say. "And if you ever feel like shit, come to my church. Okay?"

"Okay." The dude smiles, and I pull him in for a bro-hug. Everyone needs a little bit of support sometimes—even dudes like him who are at rock bottom and looking for a way out.

As he walks toward his brother, I ask, "So I'll see you in church with your sister next Sunday?"

He glances over his shoulder and nods stiffly, which is good enough for me.

Besides, the mere thought of seeing her again heats me up.

But that was not the point of this conversation.

I needed to do this. For me. For him. For the boy. For the world to have one less criminal in it. Even if it means so little because it's a blip in the entire scheme of things ... every little thing can make a difference.

Fuck me.

Guess I've got some good in me after all.

CHAPTER FOUR

With a bottle in one hand and a cigarette in the other, I traipse around the church, wistfully staring at the paintings on the wall. I don't know what I'm doing, but I can't stay in my room while I get drunk either. It feels so damn dark and damp in there. Besides, it's not like anyone's going to see me. It's almost ten p.m. at night. Mother's already fast asleep, and everyone else has gone home. And who the fuck would visit a church this late at night? Exactly.

Especially not this church. My notorious reputation is spreading like a disease, and soon, there won't even be a soul left during the day. It wasn't always this way. There was once a time I was actually a great preacher, but it all went to shit. It's all my fucking fault.

Maybe I should've never become a preacher. It would've saved everyone a lot of trouble.

Sighing and wallowing in my own misery, I lean against the stone pillar in the corner as I take a swig from the bottle. It's then that I notice a girl standing in front of the big cross hanging on the left side of the church.

My eyes widen, and I blink a couple of times to make sure I'm not dreaming.

A girl in this place? This late at night?

The more I stare, the more I realize I've seen her before.

She's *that* girl … the one I've been consumed by since I first saw her. The one consuming every inch of the little bit of positive space in my brain. The one girl who gives me that buzz I need to survive.

What is she doing here?

Her lips move, and she mutters some words under her breath. I'm too far away to hear, but I can see make the sign of the cross on her chest as she looks up at the statue of Jesus. I can't stop looking at her elegant posture and the graceful way she moves.

But then she turns her head … and looks straight at me.

I'm captivated.

Completely mesmerized by her pristine eyes.

And I realize she's caught me standing here with a bottle of vodka and a cigarette. Me, the preacher of this church.

I quickly hide them behind my back and turn around to hide behind the pillar. Like that will magically take away the fact she's seen me in my most shameful moment.

"Father? Is that you?"

Her voice.

It rings through my ears, making my heart stop and start

all over again.

The sound of perfection.

I want to hear her say it every day. Is that wrong?

I take a deep breath and turn around to face her. "Hi there."

She walks toward me with hesitation.

I quickly place the bottle on a small table standing in the corner and put out my cigarette in a potted plant after taking one final drag.

"I'm sorry if I'm bothering you," she says, clutching her fingers.

"Oh no, it's fine," I reply, smiling awkwardly. "I was just taking a nightly stroll."

"With a bottle?" she asks, peeking over my shoulder.

"Ahh ... it makes me sleep easier." I'm having a really hard time coming up with excuses.

"You were about to go to sleep? I'm sorry; maybe I should've come at a better time." She averts her eyes, almost as if she's ready to leave again, but I don't want that.

"No, no, it's fine." I place a hand on her arm, and the moment I touch her, a hot flash shoots through my veins.

We stand in front of the pulpit as she gives me her first smile.

I don't know why I need to memorize this moment, but I do.

Like it's important. Something I will remember for the rest of my life.

That smile is a smile of one in a million.

So beautiful.

She clears her throat. "I just wanted to say thank you."

"For what?"

"Bruno told me he talked to you yesterday at the cemetery. You left quite an impression on him."

"Oh, yeah?" I smirk.

"He said you helped Diego rethink what he was doing." She bites her lip, and my eyes hone in on it, and I can already imagine sucking on it. God, I'm such a horny bastard when I'm intoxicated. No, screw that—I'm *always* a horny bastard.

"Look, I know my brother's hanging out with the wrong people and doing things he shouldn't be doing. But you changed his mind. So I wanted to thank you for that. You didn't have to do that."

"Oh, it was no problem. I'm here to help people." There I go again, being smooth as fuck when I'm the world's worst preacher.

"Well, thank you for that. At least someone is looking out for the people," she says.

I smile and scratch the back of my head, not knowing how to take the compliment. I don't get them often. "Thanks."

"So what's your real name?" She chuckles. "Other than Father, of course."

"Frank," I answer. "And yours?"

She holds out her hand. "Laura."

Laura. I like the sound of that.

We shake hands. "Nice to meet you," I say.

"Yeah …" Her smile really makes my brain numb.

It's quiet for some time, and I wonder what else I could say to make her stay.

I don't know why I feel this way, but I want her close. Her presence alone causes all the pain in my mind to fade, just like when I smell the grass after a thunderstorm.

"So ... praying, huh?" I mutter, trying to break the ice.

She looks up at the statue of Christ and nods. "Yeah, sometimes you just have to. For the sake of your own wellbeing, you know?"

"Well, if you need someone to talk to, I'm here."

"Hmm ..." She looks at me briefly before glancing back up at the cross. "I don't know. It feels so wrong."

From the way she smashes her lips together, I can tell something's bothering her. "Is it something you want to confess?"

"Isn't it too late for that?" she asks.

"No, any time is fine. The church is always open."

"Oh, that's good to know." She smiles. "It's hard to wait when things weigh down on you."

"I definitely understand. When life gets you down, it can be hard to trust yourself to work through it. Sometimes, you need a little bit of an extra push. Someone to tell you things will be all right. A nod from up there." I wink.

"Yeah ... I feel like ... I owe it to Him or something. Is that weird?"

"No, not weird at all. Everyone feels like that sometimes."

"Even preachers?"

"Yeah, even me." I grin, and the way it makes her smile sets my heart on fire.

Hot damn, Frank. Keep your head straight, and your heart buried.

"Is it ... I want to ..." She starts and stops several sentences. "Could we? Is it possible to confess?"

I frown. "Sure."

"I mean … in the confessional?" She seems flustered, and I'm flabbergasted for a moment but then compose myself.

"Yeah, of course." I hold out my hand, gesturing toward the confessional. "Ladies first."

She chews on her lips again as she turns and walks toward it, tentatively sliding aside the cloth covering the entrance. I open the little door and go inside, sitting down on the wooden bench. Her face now hides behind the lattice screen, the design forming an intricate pattern on her face. Just like the ink etched into my skin. Stunning.

"So … tell me what's on your mind," I say.

She breathes out a sigh and makes a quick cross symbol. "I … have been keeping a secret for some time now, and I don't know if I can ever tell anyone about it. I am so ashamed."

"Feeling shame is natural. It helps us learn the difference between right and wrong."

"I did something so wrong …" she continues, her voice softer than before. "So … indecent."

"If you want to feel better, you have to admit to yourself what you did."

She nods, mulling it over. "I … I …" She briefly glances at me, her face turning completely red, before she looks away again. "A few days ago, I felt this incredible urge to … to …"

"Say it out loud. It's the only way to confront your fears."

"Masturbate."

My eyes widen, and I find it hard to take down the gulp of air I just breathed.

My dick just grew an inch.

She drops her face into her hands. "Oh, God ... I'm so ashamed."

"No, don't be." I clear my throat, exercising a pure force of will to get my dick to go down. "Feeling urges is normal too."

"Not in church," she whispers.

"Why? I ... do it too sometimes," I mutter.

"You do it too?" She frowns at me like she can't believe what I'm saying.

"Of course. Every human has needs. If God didn't want us to make ourselves happy, why did he make it so pleasurable?"

She looks confused. "Well, that's one way to put it."

"The church is here to make you feel welcome."

"Not like that." She shakes her head.

"Not like what?"

She leans in closer, whispering, "I masturbated ... in the bathroom ... here."

"Here?" I look her straight in the eyes.

"In *church*."

Fuck. Me.

The mere mention of her fingering herself in this place makes me picture all kinds of unholy acts. More specifically ... catching her in the act. Oh God, how I would've loved to have seen that. To have been there myself and enjoy the sight of her touching herself. That's what I've been fantasizing about—her naked body ready for the taking—and now she's telling me it could be a reality.

Well, not yet. But close enough.

And for some reason ... I want her to tell me all her

dirty sins. I want to know every filthy little detail.

"When?" I ask.

"Last week. Does it matter?"

"Yes." I blink a couple of times. "God needs to know the precise truth … otherwise, your sins can't be forgiven." I made that up on the spot. Hey, a dude's gotta do what a dude's gotta do.

"I just … couldn't control myself anymore. I don't know why. Probably just a weird day."

"Oh no, nothing weird about that," I muse. Probably should've kept that to myself, though, because she keeps looking at me like we're both being immoral.

Well … maybe we are.

But I really don't care.

I mean I'm a half-drunk, half-assed preacher in a small wooden cubicle with the most attractive girl I've seen in a long time, and it's turning me into a horndog. See, it's not like I can get any worse.

She swallows, visibly unsettled. "I … I'm done. I'm sorry, Father Frank."

"It's okay … but only if *you* forgive yourself."

She nods. "Thank you."

And suddenly, she's up from her bench and out of the confessional.

And I'm left with a boner as high as Mount Everest.

Damn.

I clear my throat and take a deep breath before I step out. When I look around, no one's in sight. She disappeared. Maybe she was so ashamed she couldn't bear to look at me any longer. I can imagine—as it's not something you'd want to tell *anyone*, let alone your preacher. But she felt the need to do so, and I was there to listen. That's all that matters.

And now, I gotta go take care of this boner.

I casually stroll through the church back to my room and grab the first magazine underneath my bed, flipping it open on my bed. I throw off my robes, pull my dick out, and then start rubbing one out.

It feels so wrong, but I can't control my urges anymore.

Like I said, it's natural.

I just hope God will forgive me for having these filthy thoughts. For wanting to fuck her brains out.

I mean who can forget about a girl saying she masturbated? No one.

Not a man on this earth wouldn't picture her touching herself, fantasizing about watching her do herself.

Not even a preacher can resist.

I turn the page and continue to jerk off, my veins pulsing with greed as I imagine her sitting right in front of me with her pretty mouth opened wide, ready to receive my blessing. God, I'm such a filthy fuck, but I can't help it. This is who I am, and nothing will change that.

I'm so drunk on arousal and alcohol that I moan out loud; the thought of having her ready and willing to take me was too much to handle.

I close my eyes and picture her rubbing her pussy while also pinching her nipples, licking her lips in anticipation of my cum. And I come.

I come so hard it squirts all over the pages of the magazine and my bed. I groan and rub myself until every last drop is gone and my bed is a giant mess. Breathing out loud, I open my eyes again. From the corner of my eye, I spot something. No, someone ... gawking right at my naked, flexing butt.

I glance over my shoulder, and the moment I realize Laura caught me in the act, I know I'm fucked.

Big time.

Her eyes zoom in on my still rock-hard dick, slowly trailing across my tattoo-covered body before widening as she looks me right in the eyes. She slaps her hand in front of her mouth as I rip the sheets off the bed to cover myself up.

"Fuck," I hiss.

If I'd known she was still here, I would have never done this.

And why didn't I lock my fucking door?

I'm so infatuated with her that my head doesn't work anymore. That, or the booze is clogging up my brain.

The fact of the matter is … she saw the preacher jerking himself off to a couple of magazine tits. If that isn't unholy, I don't know what is. Did I just scar her for life?

"I'm so sorry," she murmurs through her fingers.

But before I can tell her it's okay, she turns around and runs.

CHAPTER FIVE

It's been days since I last saw her, and I'm not sure if she's ever coming back.

The moment she ran from the church was the moment I knew I fucked up real good. I tried running after her, but by the time I'd dressed, she was already long gone. More than anything, I wish I could find her, but with only her first name as a clue, I don't have a chance.

I just hope and pray to God she doesn't tell anyone what she saw.

If Mother finds out, I'm screwed.

She'll probably throw me out on the street right away.

I've already given her so much trouble; this could be the last drop in the bucket. She's told me so many times before it was the last time she'd forgive me my sins. A man can only break the rules so many times before it catches up with him.

Still, I feel like I need to make something up to Mother. Because she, of all people, deserves better. She deserves a better me.

So with that thought in mind, I go visit an old friend who's been having trouble lately. He hasn't come to church in ages, and Mother's worried about him. Rightfully so, I'd say, because, in all the time I've known him, he's always hung out with the wrong people. Same as Laura's brother—gang business.

However, this morning he called for help, and since Mother picked up the phone, she obviously said yes the moment he asked if I could come to his home. I don't like it, because I already know he's going to try to hand me his problems instead of dealing with them himself. But Mother doesn't know him as well as I do.

Sighing, I knock on his door and tap my foot until he finally opens.

A screaming baby is the first thing that greets me. Then his ugly mug.

"Dude, finally." He tries to hug me, but I stand there awkwardly, cringing from the screeching going on right next to my face.

"Hey, Ricardo, nice to see you too."

"Come in, come in," he says, opening his door further to allow me in.

It's a mess inside. Pots and pans lie scattered on the kitchen counters, and stains mark the furniture while flies fly through the room.

"Jesus, Rick, ever clean this place up?"

He shoves aside a few of the dirty cups and baby toys and tries to make room for me to sit on the couch. "I know, I know. It's a mess. I'm a mess."

"I can see why you haven't come to church lately," I say, sitting down.

He sighs. "It's not because I don't want to. I just can't." He puts the baby in a makeshift crib while it still cries, shushing it with a blanket. It won't stop.

"Because of the baby?" I ask.

"Not just that. I mean yeah, but I've been busy with the gang too. You know how that shit goes."

He looks at me like I'm supposed to understand.

I don't.

It's been ages.

Literally.

"That, and Nadia left me with that *thing* so she could go to *work* or something. Like that's more important." He scratches his head nervously. "She seriously fucking left me with that fucking baby."

"Calm down," I say. "It's not a thing. It's a baby. Boy or girl?"

"How should I know?" He reaches for his pack of cigarettes and lights one up.

I make a face. "How do you *not* know? It's not that hard to find out."

"Like I don't know that!" He blows out the smoke.

"Calm. Down," I repeat. "Is this why you called me?"

"Yeah. Why else would I call you?"

I sigh again. "And here I thought this would be some gang shit or something." I shake my head. "Rick and a baby

… how about that."

"I didn't plan this. We broke up. We weren't even together, dude. And all of the sudden, she comes out of nowhere and flops this baby in my hand, saying it's mine and telling me I should take care of it. She even demanded money, dude. Fuck!"

He kicks the trashcan, which falls over, causing garbage to tumble out over the floor.

Meanwhile, the baby is still screaming like a firetruck.

"Dude, calm down," I say. "This ain't gonna go any better if you don't stop screaming."

"Tell that to that *thing*!" He points his finger at the baby like it's some kind of monster. "It hasn't stopped screaming since she dropped it here. And why? Because she thinks her job is more important than mine is. Like I don't have anything better to do than to take care of some stinking, screaming baby all day."

"Her job *is* more important," I remark, raising a brow. "Because hers isn't illegal."

"So what?" He shrugs. "I make cash."

"And you seriously think that's going to be enough to support a baby?"

"Hey, I didn't ask for this, okay? If I'd known she'd do this to me, I'd have never stuck my dick up her snatch."

"Yet you did." I roll my eyes. "Do you even know how babies are made?"

"Of course, I do." He glowers. "I had school. Junior high. Top dog."

"Top dropout, yeah," I retort. "You know it takes two people to make a baby."

"She was on the pill."

"Maybe she forgot one. It happens," I say.

"Who gives a shit how it happened. The point is I cannot take care of that thing."

"Stop calling it a thing. What's the baby's name?"

"I don't know ... Sofia or something."

I get up from the couch and approach the baby. "Sofia, huh?" I pick her up from the cradle, and I put her on my shoulder, patting her back while soothing her. "It's okay. Shhh. Mommy's going to be back later tonight."

I look at Ricardo for the answer to that.

"I don't know; she said she'd be back when she was done with work."

"When was she last fed?" I ask.

"I dunno. I tried to give her Cheerios, but—"

"You gave a baby Cheerios?" I interject.

"Yeah ... with milk, of course, so they were soggy."

I close my eyes and sigh out loud, rubbing my temples. "You can't feed a baby Cheerios. They need baby formula."

"It was milk. I thought it was okay."

"Cheerios ..." I shake my head. "Goddammit, Ricardo." I immediately apologize to God in my head for using his name in vain.

"Dude." He picks up the box and shows me the back. "It says right here. Nutritional."

"What do you think she's going to chew those up with? Imaginary teeth?" I open her mouth and show it to him. "Look at that. She needs liquids."

"Milk is a liquid." He shrugs, which makes me roll my eyes again.

"Buy some baby formula." I pull her up so I can smell her, and the stench immediately makes me gag. "And some diapers while you're at it."

"What? Now?" he asks.

"Yeah, now." I stare him down until he gets the message, picks up his keys, and leaves the apartment.

Fifteen minutes later, he's back with a whole truckload of Pampers and three brands of baby formula.

"I didn't know which one to get, so I grabbed 'em all."

I chuckle. "Well, at least you know how to bring home the goods."

"What now?" he asks, looking at me like it's my kid.

I place Sofia on a table and say, "C'mere with some diapers."

"Aw, hell naw, I ain't doing that shit."

"Come. Here," I growl.

He sighs and stomps but eventually comes closer, and I show him how to pull off her clothes. "Go on," I say. "I'll help if you need it."

He frowns while glaring at me then rips off her diaper. The stench that greets us makes him yowl and pinch his nose. "Jesus Christ."

I chortle. "Better get used to it."

While standing as far away as he can, he pulls it away from underneath her, and I hand him some napkins so he can clean her.

"Put on a clean one," I say.

He does what I tell him to although it takes him three tries to get it on right. When it's done, we quickly dress her again, and he jumps away with the dirty diaper, dumping it in a plastic bag like it's a toxic hazard he wants to contain.

"Lord, help me get through this," he mutters, grabbing some of the baby formula. "How does this work?"

"Follow the instructions. Put it in the microwave. Test it on your wrist, so it doesn't burn her tongue."

He grabs the bottle the baby's mommy left him, fills it as instructed, and then puts it in the microwave. When it's heated, he tests it and brings it to me. I contemplate having him feed her, but I'm convinced he'd only make a mess, so I decide to do it myself.

I grab her and hold her in my arms while putting the bottle to her lips, and she greedily takes it, gulping down the milk.

"Good girl …" I whisper. "You were just hungry, that's all."

"So, is she gonna calm down or what?" he asks.

"If you take care of her, she will," I say, hinting that it's his fault.

When she's finished, I put down the bottle and pat her back, hoping she'll burp. She's still crying, which isn't a surprise at all, considering how he took care of her. Or rather, not.

He sits down on the couch again and rubs his face. "What am I supposed to do, Frank?"

"What are you supposed to do? And you ask me that? You're the dad." I try not to look at him as I hold the little girl tight and rub her back, trying to calm her down.

"Fuck, Frank. You always know … everything. And you're a fucking priest."

"I'm not a fucking priest," I hiss, trying to keep my voice down. "I'm a preacher."

"Preacher, priest, Father, whatever. It's all the same to me."

"Like you'd know. You barely come to church."

"I know. The boys won't let me."

"Then try harder," I retort. "Who gives a shit about them anyway?"

"I do."

"No, you care about the money. You wouldn't lie awake one single day if one of them died right now."

He's silent, so I guess my rant is working.

"I know because I felt it. I've been in the same position you're in now, and you know it. They're not your friends."

"But they give me what I need." He pulls out a tiny bag of cocaine and draws a line on the table in front of the couch. I set the baby down in the makeshift crib. Right before he snorts it up, I swipe my arm across it.

"Fuck! Dude, why—"

"You should know better." I grab his collar and pull him up. "You have a fucking baby."

His eyes turn red. "Let go of me."

"No, listen to me," I growl. "See that little girl there?" I point at her. "She's yours, whether you like it or not. That little soul counts on you to do the right thing. She didn't ask to be born. You created her by being a selfish little shit. And now you think you can run away from your responsibilities?"

He shakes his head. "I don't fucking know how to take care of a kid!"

"Then start learning!" I shove him back on the couch and stare at him. "Stop the drugs. Now."

"What? Forever?"

"Yes!" I ball my fists. "You wanna call yourself a man? Then act like a man. Be a daddy to that little girl."

I walk over to her and grab her, cradling her in my arms

to show her to him. "See this? Her blood runs in your veins. You caused this. Now you have to deal with the consequences."

"But I can't ..." he mutters, his eyes turning red.

"Look at her," I yell, forcing him to look at her tiny face. "That's your daughter."

He begins to cry. And now the baby too.

"Stop crying," I tell Ricardo. "And man up."

"I'm only nineteen. I'm not a man."

"No. You're a kid who did adult things, and now he realizes the world ain't as easy as he thought it would be. Time to grow up, kid."

"Frank ... how do you do it?"

"One step at a time," I say, and I gently rock the baby back and forth until the screams become less and less.

"What about the money?"

"Get a job. A *real* job." I look him directly in the eyes, so he knows I'm serious. "Stop drinking. Stop smoking. And clean this place up, it's a fucking mess," I say.

"But I can't do it all—"

"Yes, you can!" I growl. "Dammit. That's what it means when you create life. You do everything and anything to take care of it. Even if it means sacrificing your own goddamn soul."

He shakes his head and laughs a little, wiping away a tear. "Look at you. A swearing preacher."

"I don't give a fuck. God doesn't give a shit if I swear or not. He gives a shit whether I take care of His children. That's what matters."

"Like her ..." he mutters, looking at little Sofia.

"Yeah. And you."

"Me?" He raises a brow at me.

"Yeah. Believe it or not, we're all important, including you. It's time you fought for the right things. You deserve better than this. *She* deserves better than this."

It's quiet for some time. "You're right …" he says, looking into the distance. "I've fucked up."

"Everybody fucks up from time to time. It's about seeing it, and learning from it, and doing it better this time around."

"But what about you? Are you doing any better?" he asks, his gaze penetrating mine. It's like he can see straight through me.

"This isn't about me. You know my past. I'm doing the best that I can. Are you?"

I know he can't answer that question, and he doesn't.

He sits there silently while I tend to his kid.

This sweet little child, sucking on my thumb. She's an angel. And holding her like that brings back memories I tried to keep buried for so long.

I don't want to remember them.

And as soon as she's fallen asleep, I bring her to him and place her in his arms. "Hold up her head."

He holds her like I tell him to, and for the first time since I came here, I can see a flame burning in his eyes. A smile slowly creeps onto his face. "Okay, I admit, she is kinda cute."

I take a deep breath and nod. "Yeah, she is."

"What now?" he asks, looking up at me.

"Now, you get your shit together and raise that baby."

CHAPTER SIX

When I'm finally back in my home, the church, I collapse on my bed with a roaring headache. Ricardo's unkempt apartment kept me busy all day, trying to help him out. I couldn't walk away; not with that little girl stuck with him. She's the victim in this story. She has no choice, and I wanted to give her the best I could, even if I barely know her. It's the least anyone can do.

But the more time I spent with her, the more depressed I became. Every time I looked at her, I could feel my heart shrivel up and die a little more.

I curl up into a ball and pull the sheets up to my neck, cocooning myself in my own warmth as I try to forget about Sofia.

At one point while I was there, I even contemplated

taking her away from him. But what would that accomplish? Another kid in the foster system. There's no way they'll allow a baby to be under the care of a preacher like me either. It makes no sense. It's a bubble I had to quickly burst for myself.

I want every kid to have a good life, and only the parents can give them that. As long as Ricardo mans the fuck up and starts acting like a dad for her, it'll be okay.

And I'm sure he will … Today was a wake-up call for him. I could see it in his eyes. All he needed was a firm hand and a push. My words did just that for him. He immediately threw away all his coke and started cleaning up, just like I told him. I hope he realizes he can't go back to where he used to be … for her sake.

Enough thinking about someone else's kid.

I twist and turn in bed until I slowly fall asleep. It's a tough one, but I close my eyes and force myself to sleep.

Soft jazz fills the room with life. I blink a couple of times and open my mouth to speak, but nothing comes out. I walk through my house, light bulbs lighting my way like fireflies. Warmth covers me as I watch her dance in the middle of the living room. She smiles at me and holds the baby close to her chest, waving its little hands around as she spots me.

I smile as I approach her, grabbing her shoulders to dance along with her. I press a kiss to her forehead and imprint this feeling onto my brain, so I can remember it forever.

Forever. And ever.

That's what this is supposed to be.

Everything fades. The red wallpaper turns lime green. Wooden tables make place for larger ones. Chairs are added, and more plants suddenly appear. The room is light, but my body feels weighed down. The more I try to move, the less my body reacts.

It's like I'm frozen in place.

Frozen ... while everyone and everything around me continues to change.

It's like time has sped up while I'm still me ... forever.

And in the midst of it all, a boy runs around the house with his toys ... but his image is so unclear. The more I try to look, the more he fades away. Until everything in this room has disappeared, and all that's left is an empty house with moldy wood and spider webs in every corner.

I shoot up in bed and turn on the light.

Panting loudly, I feel my face. I'm so damn hot and sweaty ... and tears are running down my cheeks.

I pull off the sheets and sit on the edge of the bed, burying my head in my hands. I rub my face, trying to shake the images from my mind, but nothing I do works.

It never works.

So I do the only thing I know.

I get up, put on my casual clothes, and go out.

***

Four hours later, it's the middle of the night, and I'm drunk again.

Yep, like that's so much of a surprise.

"Pour me another one, Chuck," I say, sliding my glass to him.

"I think you've had enough." He slides it right back.

"Oh, c'mon. I'm a paying customer." Now it's my turn to slide it again.

"I care more about you than your money. Sorry." He picks it up and tucks it into the soapy water.

"Fucking hell …" I slam my hand on the bar. "What's a man gotta do to get some liquor around here?"

"How about not being a drunk fuck?" Chuck retorts.

I laugh. "Like you know me any different."

"I wish I did," he says, washing the glasses.

"I'm not fun to be around when I'm sober; trust me."

"I doubt it's any worse than this."

"Keep pushing me, Chuck, and I might start giving you a personal sermon."

"Fuck no. I'd rather you drink yourself to death." He grabs a bottle of whiskey and slams it down in front of me. "Have at it."

"Aw … thank you, Chuck. If I didn't know any better, I'd almost think you like me."

"I don't. I just want you to shut up."

I laugh again and put the bottle to my lips. "There's the Chuck I know."

"Yeah, well, the Frank I know took better care of his church."

"Oh please, like you know." I let out a burp. "You never show up."

"You know I hate church."

"Exactly."

"But you and I both know *you* don't," he says. "You used to love your job."

I laugh again because it's really funny. Or ironic. I don't

know any more at this point. I'm too drunk to care.

"Yeah ... I remember a Frank who actually cared about the church. Gave it all he had. And now he's a sad slob getting drunk every night."

I slam down the bottle. "You're g-goddamn right." I fish in my pocket and take out a few bills, slapping them on the counter too. "There you go."

"Going already?"

"I'm d-done listening-g to your w-whining," I reply with a half-assed tone. God, I'm so drunk, I can't even talk straight.

"Want me to call you a cab?" he asks.

"Nah, I'm good. I'll w-walk," I mumble.

He shrugs and takes the money off the counter, and I turn around. But before I go out the door, he still opens his mouth. "See you tomorrow."

Goddamn motherfucker.

He knows me too well.

I don't respond. I don't think I could even if I wanted to. If I think about it, all that comes out of my mind is a bunch of gibberish and mumbo-jumbo that I can't even understand, let alone him.

So I walk out and stroll across the street, wandering aimlessly. Rain pours down from above, drenching my clothes, but I don't give a crap. The chill makes me shiver, but I don't seek shelter. Instead, I stumble along the sidewalk, almost hugging the wall while I try to find my way home.

Now that I think about it ... I don't even know where that is.

Or where I am.

Or what I'm doing.

And before I know it, one small pebble makes me tumble and fall face-first into the mud.

I don't bother trying to get up. This sad slob has lost his will. It's dripping down into the gutter along with my soul.

Guess today really did a number on me.

I can't get up. My muscles won't work, and the longer I lie here, the less they respond. My eyes slowly open and close, and I find myself drifting in and out of consciousness.

In the distance, I hear a voice.

It's calling for me.

Beckoning me to get up and walk.

I blink and look up, and in front of me is an angel. Her silhouette illuminated by blinding light. Her voice so pure, I swear I've died and gone to heaven.

"Frank. Frank!" Someone slaps me, and the more it happens, the more I wake up out of my trance. "Frank!"

It's the voice. But it wasn't an angel. Or maybe it was.

"Laura," I mutter, my voice hoarse.

"Oh, God ..." She clutches my body and tries to lift me up, but I'm too heavy for her. "Get up, Frank. C'mon."

With the power of her voice alone, I manage to crawl up from the ground. With her support, I can stay upright without falling down. I can't think. I can't talk. All I know is that warm hands wrap around my waist and lead the way.

CHAPTER SEVEN

Matthew 11:28 – "Come to me, all you who are weary and burdened, and I will give you rest."

When I wake up again, my head roars with pain.
I immediately clutch my face and roll around to stop the light from entering my eyes. God, I wish someone hadn't opened the blinds.
"Morning ..."
I squint and see that beautiful angel again, her body glistening in the light of the sun with the rays dancing on her skin. I only now realize it's Laura ... and that I'm completely and utterly infatuated with her.
"Did you sleep well?" she asks.

I nod, but when I try to answer, my throat dries up, and I cough.

"Here, have some water." She hands me a glass, and our fingers briefly touch during the exchange, causing sparks to shoot up my veins like fireworks.

God … I can't remember the last time I touched a woman who gave me these feelings. Please forgive me.

I swallow and gulp down the water in one go, thirsty for more. "Thanks."

She takes back the glass and pours me another until I'm sated, and I place the glass on the table beside me.

I look around and notice the room isn't what I'm used to. The walls are a salmon color, in the corner is a small wooden chair and a wardrobe, and the blanket I'm lying under feels ruffled. It's much more somber than my room, which I didn't think was possible.

But the point is … it's not my room. I'm in somebody else's house.

"Where am I?" I mutter, squeezing my eyes to make the light less painful.

"My home. Sorry, I had to bring you here. It was closer, and I couldn't carry you all the way back to church."

"Carry me?" I mutter. "Oh, God." I rub my face and blow out a breath then sit up straight. "I remember now …"

"I found you out on the street. You seemed intoxicated."

I look down at my hands, ashamed of myself. How could I look her in the eyes? I'm the son of a bitch she had to take care of. A fucking preacher being taken in by a girl because he was too drunk to walk back home.

"I … I'm so, so sorry." Words cannot explain how

terrible I feel right now.

Literally, I feel like I've been struck with a hammer.

"I shouldn't have put that on you," I add.

"No, it's okay ..." She smiles so sweetly that it tears up my heart. God, what did I do to deserve her? Nothing. I did nothing, yet she still crossed my path like it was meant to happen.

"If you hadn't found me, I don't know where I would've ended up." I try to laugh it off, but it's as serious as can be. "I could've died."

"No, don't be silly." She chuckles, but from the look in her eyes, I can tell she knows it was serious.

I was way beyond drunk. I was hammered. Completely wasted to the point of blacking out.

"But you're here now. Alive." She smiles again. "How do you feel?"

"Like someone smacked me with a table."

She grins. "Sounds like you had a lot to drink."

"Tell me about it ..." I mutter, slapping my face to wake myself up properly.

"Well, I hope it was fun," she muses.

"Not really." Wait. Did I just say that out loud? Guess I did, because she's looking at me all weird and shit.

"But ... why drink then?" she asks, but then she holds up her hand. "Wait, don't answer. I'm sorry. That was kinda rude to ask."

"No, it's okay. I know I drink too much. It's a habit."

"Is it because of ...? I'm sorry ... um ..."

"What? Because of you ... Oh ..." I look away, smashing my lips together as I'm thinking about how to accurately put this without making it sound dirty as fuck.

"About that… I just had an off day. I'm sorry you had to see that."

"An off day?" She repeats me like she doesn't believe me.

Of course, she doesn't because I'm lying. Why can she see straight through me? Dammit. "I mean, I was drunk, and I was stupid." I slap my forehead again, just thinking about her seeing me naked and jerking off.

"It's okay. I ran because I panicked and I didn't know what else to do, but now that I think about, it really doesn't matter." She swallows, grabbing my hand. "I get it. We all have needs."

"Yeah, but most of us don't expose ourselves to other people," I say. "Let alone preachers."

She struggles to hide a laugh. "Well, yeah, you are the last person I expected to do that."

"I'm not your average preacher."

"I could tell …" She struggles to hide a smile.

Was that a dick joke or an ass joke?

Or am I imagining things now?

Whatever it is only makes me like her more. Girls who aren't afraid to enjoy the good side of life. And judging from her confession the other day, she sure seems to be enjoying herself from time to time.

"Hmm … Maybe I shouldn't have spoken about that … *thing*. In confession." She looks away, but I can clearly see the blush on her cheeks.

I place my hand on top of hers. "Like you said, we all have needs."

She nods, dipping her tongue out to quickly lick her top lips then rub her lips together. God, what I wouldn't give to lick them too.

Contain yourself, Frank!

I clear my throat. "I wanted to apologize to you for seeing that. I should've locked the door." I look her in the eye as I speak, not wanting this to feel fake to her, even though I'm going to ask her something very personal. "Can we ... keep this a secret?"

"A secret?"

"I'd prefer if Margaret didn't find out."

"Margaret?"

"Yeah, the old lady at the church. You've seen her, right? She's basically the one who organizes everything there."

"Oh." She frowns. "Yeah, of course. But ... only if you keep my confession a secret too."

"Done." I hold out my hand, and she shakes it. "That's an easy one since confessions are strictly between the confessor, the preacher, and God."

"What?"

I burst out into laughter. "Relax, I'm not going to tell anyone about your little sexcapade in the bathroom."

Her whole face turns red again. "Shh ... not so loud. We're not alone." She looks at the door, which is opened slightly.

"Oh, sorry." I smile, and somehow, that makes everything right again.

She picks up a wet cloth and holds it to my forehead. For some reason, it feels really intimate. It's been a long time since I had someone take such diligent care of me. Since I last felt feminine hands touch me in such a delicate way.

"Thanks," I say as she slowly wipes the cloth along my

forehead and cheeks.

"You're welcome." She smiles back. "You were sweating so much last night. But you look a little bit better now."

"You stayed with me all night?" I ask.

She nods and gestures to the makeshift bed on the floor, which consists of a pillow and a blanket. "Slept over there."

"Oh, no … you shouldn't – I took your bed?" A pang of guilt stings in my stomach.

"It's okay. It's not the first time. "Bruno sleeps here often when he's sick. He doesn't like being alone."

"Bruno … your little brother, right?"

She opens her mouth and then closes it again, containing whatever she was going to say.

"We don't have a lot of rooms, but it's cozy. We like it this way. And we're happy," she muses, making me smile because she's content, even with what little she has. I wish I could say the same.

She continues to pat me down, the cold water giving temporary relief to my overheated body. God, what I wouldn't give for an entire wipe down of my body right now. Everything. But I'll take a cold shower too.

When she's about to pull away, I grab her wrist and murmur, "Thank you."

"Don't mention it. It's the least I could do."

"So … you're not mad at me?" I ask.

Her brows draw together, and it's the best angry face I've ever seen. I could look at this all day and still feel completely at ease.

"No, of course not." Her smile is so bright … it makes me forget everything I was thinking. And for some reason, my hand automatically reaches for her face, wanting to get closer to divinity, to whatever it is that makes me feel this way about her. With the back of my index finger, I brush her cheek, her hair flowing past my hand smoothly. My eyes focused solely on her. I can't take them off.

But then I realize what I'm doing is incredibly awkward, and I clear my throat and pull my hand back before it gets even more awkward.

It's quiet for some time, and I know she can sense the awkwardness too.

Luckily, she breaks the ice before I blurt out something stupid. "Do you ... Would you like to stay for breakfast?"

"Uh ..." I think about it for a second, but I can't find any excuses not to. Especially not with the way she's looking at me right now. "Sure, why not."

"Cool." She gets up and grabs something off the cabinet in the far corner. "I washed and dried them. I couldn't get the stain out, but this is as good as I could get it." It's my clothes from yesterday, and she hands them to me.

"Whoa ... thank you so much. You didn't have to."

"Yeah, I did," she insists. "You were a mess."

"Thanks, I guess." I frown.

"You're welcome." She winks, and it sets my heart ablaze.

Fuck me; I like a woman who knows how to taunt me.

But she'd better be careful with that.

"I'll see you in a minute then?"

"Sure." I nod and throw the blanket off me.

It's only then I realize she took off my clothes ... and I'm sitting here in bed in only a pair of boxer shorts. Great.

She snorts and covers her mouth with her hand, to which I immediately reply, "Like you haven't seen that before."

"I'll just go." She shows herself out before I embarrass myself any further.

I quickly put on my stuff, which smells so damn fresh; like lilies ... or any other fresh flower. Like I can fucking tell. The point is it smells good, and I like the feel of it. So smooth. Maybe I should ask her to wash my clothes more often in exchange for payment. Would that be weird? It probably would.

As my internal monolog rambles in my head, I fluff up my messy hair in the scratched mirror hanging on the wall and straighten my collar, making sure I look pristine before I go out. Can't let anyone else find out I'm an alcoholic ... I mean, she's got brothers and shit. Gotta keep up appearances for her sake. I don't want to embarrass her too.

When I'm ready, I pop out of the room.

I'm immediately greeted by Bruno and Laura's grumpy brother, Diego, who slams his coffee down on the table. "What's he doing here?"

"Diego!" Laura hisses from the kitchen, giving him the evil eye.

"What?"

"He's our guest," she explains as she stops cooking the eggs and turns to face him.

"I never invited him."

"Well, I did." She taps her foot and puts her hand on her side. "Stop being such an asshole."

"Tell him that." Diego eyes me now, and I feel like I've walked into something so personal, I'm about to excuse myself.

"It's okay, Laura," I say. "I'm not hungry anyway."

She immediately marches over to the table, grabs a chair, and points at it. "Sit."

"Really, it's not needed," I say, trying not to get between them.

"I'm not taking no for an answer," she declares, glaring at me and the chair until I finally sit down. "You're my guest, and we feed our guests properly ..." She looks over at Diego. "*And* we treat them with kindness."

"Fuck off," he mutters with his mouth still on his cup.

She grabs his plate and brings it to the kitchen.

"Hey! I wasn't even done yet."

"Can't be nice?" she spits. "Then you don't eat."

He rolls his eyes while scooting his chair back. He stands and then saunters out the door, slamming it shut behind him.

Laura sighs and rubs her forehead. "I'm sorry."

"Don't apologize to me. You didn't do anything wrong."

"I know." She puts a fork and knife in front of me along with a plate. "I hate when that happens."

"He's a stubborn kid. But he'll grow out of it."

"I pray to God he will." She sighs. "He's so hard to handle."

"I can imagine," I say. "Diego just needs a bit of a push, that's all."

"Yeah, well ... leave that up to his dad. He'd smack some sense into him if he could." She chuckles awkwardly, but her laughter dies out as quickly as a snuffed-out flame.

"Is he around?" I ask, hoping I'm not out of bounds with my question.

"No ... and I don't want him to be," she declares. "We

live on our own."

"So you're like their caregiver or something?"

"Yeah, I rent this place, and they stay with me. I'm the only one they've got, so I have no choice. Family, you know."

"I get it," I say, nodding. "And your mother …?"

"I prefer not to discuss my family," she says, adding a smile while setting some spices on the table. "If that's okay."

"Yeah, of course." I clear my throat. "Sorry, I didn't know. I wouldn't have asked otherwise."

"It's fine," she says. "Anyway, want some milk with your coffee?"

"No, I like it black," I answer, and she sits down with me.

I'm flabbergasted by the amount of food she puts on the table. Eggs. Biscuit. Muffins. Sweet rolls. Coffee. And even some homemade fruit salad.

It's quiet for some time until she breaks the ice again. I don't know why I always grow silent with her. I can't help but stare, and then I completely lose my words when I'm around her.

"Well … eat!" The big smile on her face snaps me out of it.

I grab a sweet roll as she pours coffee into our cups. "Bruno! Breakfast," she yells down the hall.

"Coming!" the little boy yells back.

Laura grabs a glass of water and takes a pill, which I recognize as birth control. Well, you can never be safe enough. Especially when you intend to fuck a guy like me because I fuck often and I like pussy a lot.

I'm in the middle of spreading butter on my roll when

Bruno strolls in without pants and with one finger in his nose while the other one is smashing buttons on what looks like a handheld video game device.

"Bruno! Why are you naked?"

"Naked? I'm not naked," he replies, flicking his booger into the air.

"Ugh, Bruno, stop doing that, please." She closes her eyes and lets out a long-drawn-out sigh.

I chuckle to myself. The kid's a lot like me—walking out of his room without any care for how he looks, what he does, and with his addiction right there on display. No fucks were given.

"And put on some pants," she says. "Or you'll permanently scar Frank."

"Scars? He's got scars?" The kid's eyes glow with excitement, and I laugh at the sight.

"No, kid, but I do have some ink on my skin and invisible scars."

"Invisible scars?" He lowers his gaming device and focuses on me, his eyes glimmering with enthusiasm.

"Scars of the soul ..." I say, making silly hand movements like it's magic or something, which makes Laura chuckle.

"What's ink in your skin?" he asks.

"You know, like tattoos," I answer.

"Tattoos? You've got tattoos?" He seems genuinely thrilled. "Can I see them?"

"No, Bruno. Stop asking so many questions. You're bothering him," Laura insists, drinking her coffee.

"Aw ..." He looks disappointed.

I rub his head until his hair is messy. "Maybe some

other time, kid."

"Put on some pants," Laura says. "He doesn't wanna see your naked ass."

"It's fine," I whisper to Laura. "I've seen so much ass in my life, nothing will faze me at this point."

She makes a face and shrugs. "All right, if you say so."

Bruno smiles as he sits down at the table and places his video game beside his plate. "What's that?" He points at my cup.

"Coffee. Want some?" I hold it out to him, after which Laura gives me the death stare.

"No, thanks. I already took a sip a week ago, when Laura wasn't looking, and I didn't like it."

I snort as Laura's jaw drops, but she doesn't make a sound, which makes it even better.

I love this little squirt already.

I take a bite from the sweet roll and groan a little. Fuck, that's good.

"Like it?" Laura asks.

"Mmm … so good," I answer.

"Her eggs are good too," Bruno says, picking one up. "I love them."

"Not much to mess up there," she muses.

I grab an egg and peel it, taking a bite. "Delicious."

"See?" Bruno grins. "Told you so!"

"You're a smart little man. Eggs are good for you, did you know? They make you grow and become strong."

"Laura says the same thing," he muses.

Laura gives me a coy smile as she takes a grape from the fruit salad and stuffs it in her mouth.

"So are you her boyfriend?"

She spits out half the grape. "Bruno!"

I laugh and take a sip of my coffee. "Nope."

"Are you sure?"

"Take a biscuit" Laura growls, stuffing it into his mouth to stop him from talking.

"Oh, wait," he says, munching on his biscuit. "You can't. You're a priest, right?"

"Preacher. And I can," I answer.

"So you can marry someone?"

"Yeah," I answer.

"Hmm ... Odd."

The kid's so curious. I wonder if he even knows what a preacher is.

"So you work for the church then?" he asks.

"I don't work for the church, but I do give sermons."

My eyes widen.

Sermons. I was supposed to give one today.

"Shit!" I jump up from my chair.

"What?" Laura asks.

"I'm supposed to be at church. Shit!"

Bruno chuckles. "He's swearing."

"Shhh ..." Lauren shushes him, and then she looks at me. "So you have to go?"

"Yeah, I'm so sorry. Breakfast was real nice though. Thanks."

"Take it with you," she says, and I take the opportunity to stuff a roll into my mouth.

"Thanks so much for everything," I mutter through the biscuit, sounding like an idiot.

"Don't mention it."

"So we'll see you in church then?" Bruno asks as I make

my way to the door.

I pause and look over my shoulder at Laura. "Ask your sister."

Then I leave the house.

And it strikes me. It's the first time in ages when I've actually felt guilty over not being where I'm supposed to be. That I know I messed up and have to make it right. It's like somehow, someway, Laura turned the switch inside my brain that forces me to come face to face with my demons.

And conquer them all.

CHAPTER EIGHT

"You're late!" Mother hisses at me as I walk into a church filled with people.

"I know," I whisper back. "Sorry."

"Where were you?" she asks, stopping me in my tracks.

Everyone's looking at me, but I try to ignore the gazes as I whisper, "Out."

"Drinking again?"

I nod. There's no use in denying the truth.

She sighs out loud and then pats me on the back. "Go on."

I take it as her approval to give the sermon. I was almost afraid she'd kick me out right here, right now, but she's giving me another chance, and I'm grabbing it with both hands.

I make my way up to the chancel and stand behind the pulpit. I realize I didn't prepare anything, so I guess I'll have to wing it … again.

I clear my throat. "Good morning, everyone."

Crickets.

Not surprising, considering my last speech.

"I know last time I wasn't the brightest star in the sky … but let's focus on something positive today, hmm?" I look into the congregation, hoping they agree, but they all seem to be staring ahead like I'm not even there. Like I'm talking to zombies or something. Well, one granny does seem like she's wilting away in her seat. Wouldn't surprise me if she died.

I snigger to myself, but then I see Laura and her two brothers sitting in the pews again. And somehow, I can't think of anything else than seeing her pretty face after waking up from my drunken night. Like crawling up from the pit of hell and coming out in heaven.

I swallow away the lump in my throat and clutch the pulpit.

"Today, I wanted to talk to you about joy. Fun. The riches of life and earth."

People shuffle in their seats like they're finally waking up.

"As we all know, a long, long time ago, God created the earth and then mankind to enjoy its riches. God created us in his own image, and we, in turn, worship him as the one and only truth."

The intense look in Laura's eyes is so distracting; I find it hard to focus.

"God teaches us to love each other and to love

ourselves. To be happy with what we have and to enjoy this life he gave us on this earth."

Some people nod, but I can't look away from Laura. There's something about her ... something that changes my entire mood. Something that makes me wanna be a rebel again. Makes me wanna be bad.

"So then why do we not allow ourselves a little enjoyment once in a while?" I ask.

Margaret's eyebrows furrow as she stands in the far left corner of the church, watching me like a hawk.

I hold my head up high. "God creates us exactly the way he wanted us to be. To deny that would be an insult to his name. So that means he created us *with* all the needs we feel. And if you feel that goes against your belief, then answer this question: How is it possible for someone to love another or themselves, if something they do or think isn't right? And do you think that loving yourself is more important than following a set of arbitrary rules? Or do you think that God intends for us to experience everything there is on this earth? Because I think it's the latter."

Laura shifts in her seat, biting her lip as her fingers slide through her hair. I imagine it's my hand running through her hair, my hand touching her face, my teeth biting her lip.

Fuck me.

I grip the mic a little bit harder. "To trust in God means to trust in His plan for us. To trust in His ideas of what it means to be human. He created us exactly the way we were intended to be. So enjoy this life you have. Go out. Live a little. Do some things you never dared to do."

I grin, seeing all the confused faces.

"Party out loud. Live on the edge. Go skydiving. Go

crazy. Smash something you don't like. Go skinny dipping. Make love to your partner in the car or on the table."

And there go all the jaws again, dropping like stones in a lake.

"Sex is nothing to be ashamed of, people. It's a natural function of the body, the way God made it. If he didn't want us to enjoy it so much, he wouldn't have made it so enjoyable to begin with. So live a little."

"Frank!" Mother hisses from the sidelines, but I ignore her.

"And whatever you do … don't judge yourself or others. That's exactly what God didn't want you to do. Love thy neighbor as yourself, remember?" I smirk. "And if you think it's weird to have these feelings, it's not. I have them too. Everyone does."

Audible gasps follow.

"What, you thought a preacher didn't have needs? Wrong." I laugh. "Like I said, we're all human."

Mother storms up to the chancel again and snatches the microphone, shoving me aside. "The sermon is now over, everyone. Thank you for coming. We'll see you next Sunday." Her voice is unhinged. "Hopefully."

She releases the mic and pulls me back with her to her room in the back of the church, slamming the door shut behind us. "Frank. Explain yourself."

"What?" I shrug. "I wanted to tell them the truth. Isn't that what faith is all about? To make the people feel better?"

"Not about their sins!"

"Maybe you and I just disagree on what a sin actually is."

She picks up a Bible and shoves it into my arms. "I

suggest you re-read this because you've obviously forgotten what it's about."

"Or maybe I've learned to take it to the next level."

"Frank." She sighs and rolls her eyes. "You're testing my patience here."

"Look, I'm sorry, all right? I know I've messed up a lot in the past."

Her laughter interrupts me. "That's putting it lightly."

"My point is I'm trying, okay?"

"Not good enough."

"This is who I am. Who I wanna be. Who I feel comfortable being."

"Oh please, you're only acting this way because you were drunk and didn't prepare anything. You used to be so good at this, and now look at you. A bumbling mess." She places a hand on my shoulder. "It's time you got your spirit back."

"And how do you propose we do that?"

"Do a little soul searching. Talk to God. Go to the chapel and pray. It's the only way to find the answers for *you*, Frank."

I sigh. "Do I really have to?"

One stern look is all it takes to get me to relent.

"All right, all right." I hold up the book like it's the only truth there is. "I'll talk to God. See what he has to say about my awesome personality."

She rolls her eyes again as she grabs the door knob and opens it for me. "Please. Next time ... do me a favor and don't show up."

I shrug it off as I walk out. "Fine."

But I can't even say bye because she's already closed the

door on me.

Damn, she really is disappointed in me.

I hate that look on her face, but what can I do? I am who I am.

Or at least, I became this way a long time ago …

Some days, I wish I could undo everything I did in the past. Maybe then I would've been a better preacher. Too bad God never invented time travel.

***

I stand at the image of Jesus in the small chapel on the far right side of the church and make the sign of the cross on my chest. I close my eyes and pray like Mother told me. I don't just do it because she wants me to. I do it because I want to. I need help.

Like so many times before, I seek His guidance when I've lost my way.

God only knows how many times I've begged for his help. His mercy. For this pain to end.

Yet I still live. It's like He wants me to suffer.

Maybe He thinks it will make me a better man, but so far, I don't see any of that yet.

I should try more. Fight harder. Defy the odds even though they're stacked against me.

Because He must be keeping me alive for a reason.

"God … please show me Your way," I plead, as I stare up at the beautiful fresco on the ceiling. "I don't know what to do with myself. I used to love this job so much, and now, look at me. I'm a mess. I'm drunk all the time just to cope with my life. And now … now, I've even fallen for a girl who comes to church."

I sigh out loud and lower my head, feeling the shame hit hard.

"Is it wrong? Is it wrong to want someone to the point of it becoming an obsession? It can't be healthy to fantasize about her so much. It feels like a disservice to the memory of ..." I can't even say the words without choking up inside.

"Is it cheating? Am I morally corrupt when I want that girl? Even if only for just a day? Could I have that without feeling guilty? Without feeling like I'm sacrificing the vow I made?"

I shake my head, knowing no one can answer these questions except me.

But it still helps to talk to someone about it, even if He won't talk back.

"I will do my best, God, to serve you as I always have. I promise I'll do better. I promise I'll make this right, someday. But first ... I need to fix myself. Please guide me. Amen."

I nod and let out another breath. A small fragment of the weight has been lifted off my shoulders. Not enough to completely forget, but enough for me to be able to smile again.

Until I turn around, that is.

Because guess who's standing in the small opening to the chapel area?

Laura.

"I'm sorry ... if I'm interrupting," she mutters.

"It's all right." I wonder if she heard me speak ... and if so, what part.

"I was looking for you, and then I found you here

talking, and I was a bit … mesmerized." She smiles briefly, looking down at her feet.

"Is there something I can do for you?" I ask.

"I was wondering if you … would be able to take my confession again?"

I rub my lips together from the thought of being alone again with her. The last time was already so fucking hard … literally, I was hard. I bet it's going to be even harder this time. My dick, of course.

Fuck.

"Yeah, sure."

I think my cock responded there. Definitely not my brains. Or maybe my brains are under her influence like my whole entire body just drifts to her. As they say … like moths to a flame.

I follow her out into the main area. Silently traipsing behind her, I'm still thinking about what I said in there … and if she heard the whole damn thing. But if that's the case, she'd probably be running right about now, and she isn't, so that's a relief.

We both enter the confessional, and I sit down on the wooden bench while she closes the curtain.

"Thank you for seeing me."

I make the sign of the cross on my chest and say, "Of course. Tell me what's bothering you."

"My sins …" she mutters. "I can't stop them." Her eyes flicker with mischief. I wonder if she's thinking about her time in the church bathroom. If she did it again.

Her hand moves to her chest, and she pulls one of the buttons of her shirt loose. "I feel bad for feeling this way."

Fuck. Am I dreaming?

What is she doing?

I can't believe this is happening, so I pinch myself, but it doesn't work.

Another button pops. "I've been thinking about this for a while now."

With a sultry look in her eyes, she pops another, and her hand slides in. My mouth salivates from the sight, and blood pumps to my dick.

What the fuck is happening here?

"I don't know why … I just can't contain myself sometimes." She starts rubbing her tits right in front of me, and even though they're still hidden behind her shirt, her nipples are clearly peaking. And fuck me, does it make me hard.

"What are you doing?" I ask, unsure of what to do with this.

Should I walk? Should I defy temptation? I have to say; she's making it really hard now. Both the decision and my cock.

"What I want to do …" she whispers, leaning forward so I can look into her shirt.

I swallow away the lump in my throat, trying to resist the temptation to look, but she's making it difficult, and that's an understatement.

"This is my sin," she says, and she licks her fingers and rubs them across her nipples. She moans, and my dick bounces up and down in my pants.

"Is it wrong?" she asks, biting her lip.

I blink a couple of times to try to keep my composure, but I'm burning up with desire. Fuck me; I want to reach through the gaps of the lattice partition so badly.

"It feels wrong," she whispers, and her hand travels down her body. "Tell me to stop."

"Only God can tell you what to do," I answer.

What kind of answer is that? Fuck.

"I can't speak to him the way you do," she says, eyeing me. "So … intimately."

So she did hear *everything* I said.

Damn.

Her hand dives between her legs, underneath her skirt, and my cock bursts with need. "I believe you, Frank. You said needs were okay. And I have a lot of needs."

I lick my lips. "Oh, I can definitely believe that."

"And I feel … like I need this." She rubs herself while she looks at me. It's like she's not even ashamed anymore. And it's all my fault. "Like *you* need this," she adds.

I frown, rubbing my lips together because I don't know what to do or say. I can't admit it. But fuck, do I want her badly. However, I'm a preacher. I shouldn't even be thinking about this.

"You snooped on me," I say. "In the chapel. How much did you hear?"

"Enough." The left side of her lip tips up into a smile. "Was that bad?"

For some reason, it makes me wanna smile too. Guess the cat's out of the bag. "Maybe."

"Bad … I like bad," she murmurs, biting her lip again while she spreads her legs. "I like it when it's wrong."

"Is that why you did this before? In the bathroom?"

She nods, and her hand dives down her panties. "I know this is what you want. What you've been thinking of all this time … *Me*," she says. "C'mon, say it."

I shake my head. "You know I can't. We're in a church."

"No one has to find out ..." she whispers, pressing her fingers to her lips. "It could be our dirty little secret."

I try to ignore the voice in my head telling me not to cave in, but it's already too late. My hand rests atop my dick, and I start rubbing it through my clothes.

She closes her eyes and leans her head back against the hard wood, and I take the opportunity to let my eyes glide up and down her body, enjoying the view. She touches herself so seductively that I immediately find myself rubbing faster and faster, trying to keep up the pace. I imagine how her body would look naked. How slick and wet it would be when I brushed my dick along her lips. I can picture it all, and that makes this all so much more frightening. Because ... if I already gave into this, there's no telling what I'll do next time I see her.

"Fuck ..." she murmurs, licking her lips. A soft moan escapes her mouth, and she adjusts herself so I can see her even better. My hand dives into my pants because I'm unable to stop myself any longer.

When she briefly opens her eyes and sees me jerking off, she purrs, "Do you like this?"

"I'd be lying if I said I didn't ..." I mutter, stroking my length. "But it's wrong, and you know it."

"Then why are we doing it?" she asks.

"Because this is our dirty little secret," I hiss, feeling the veins in my dick throb with excitement. "And I need to see just how naughty you can get."

She grins and slides her panties to the side with her index finger, showing me her naked pussy. And fuck me, it makes me one hungry motherfucker. What I wouldn't give to be able to suck on her clit.

"Is it wrong that we're doing this?" she asks. "Because I'm so damn wet right now."

"Do you even care people are just a few feet away from us?" I ask.

She shakes her head, grinning even more. "That only adds to the excitement."

God, this fucking woman … she sure knows how to make a guy's heart throb. And his dick too.

At this point, I really don't care anymore.

Screw the consequences.

Fuck morals.

I've thrown every rule out the window.

I rip down my zipper, unbutton my pants, and pull my dick out of my boxer shorts.

Her eyes widen and immediately focus on my length; her lips parting as if she's preparing to receive it.

"My eyes are up here," I muse, smiling.

She winks and then continues to rub her clit right in front of me. She doesn't even look remotely scared of discovery, and I love it. With long strokes, I pleasure myself to the sight of her. Each time a soft whimper escapes her lips, my dick reacts, hardening under my touch. Fuck, I wanna come so badly.

Holding my shaft, I picture her hands running along it instead of mine. I imagine shoving her down on my bed and ramming my dick into her pussy, finally fucking her brains out.

With squinted eyes, I watch her be filthy. Her clit looks so delicious; I wanna lick it, but this damn lattice panel is in the way. God, what a tease she is. Especially when she rubs her tits too. We're both reaching an epic climax soon, and I don't think I wanna stop it.

She moans, and her eyes roll into the back of her head. My breathing is rapid as I watch her come undone, her body quaking from the powerful shocks. And it's so fucking sexy that I come.

"Fuck," I hiss through gritted teeth, unloading myself.

My cock shoots all over the wood, coating the confessional with cum. I furiously beat my length to release every last drop, squirting it everywhere. By the time I'm done, I'm completely out of breath, the entire confessional is covered in my jizz, and Laura is grinning at the scene I left like a motherfucking vixen.

She's already corrected her panties and buttoned her shirt like nothing ever happened. "Impressive," she mutters under her breath, and I wonder if she's referring to my size or my load. Either way, I'm happy.

She reaches into her pocket to take out a few tissues. "Here." She tucks them through the lattice, and with a frazzled look on my face, I grasp them. "Thought you might need these."

"You think of everything ..." I mutter under a heavy breath as I wipe the cum off and then try to wipe it off the wood. No pun intended.

"I'm always prepared," she muses, winking again.

"What about your confession?" I ask.

"You know we didn't come here for that ..."

As she gets up, I ask, "Why?"

She shrugs. "Because I saw you struggling ... and I know you needed this."

"So it was all a lie?" I frown.

"No …" She smiles. "But everyone needs someone sometimes …"

"I don't need a pity fuck," I reply.

She raises a brow and shakes her head. "It's not." Then she opens the curtains.

"So you wanted this?" I ask before she goes.

She doesn't answer. All she does is smile and close the curtains, leaving me here with my dick out. I'm completely wiped out by one girl and her fingers.

With what remaining energy I have, I make the sign of the cross on my chest. "Jesus Christ, I beg your forgiveness … because, by God, this woman will make me commit more sins than I ever have."

NINE

In my tank top, I sit on the bench in the park, enjoying the breezy wind. For the first time in ages, I'm completely sober, and it feels so damn ... strange.

Like I can see the world through a much clearer lens. And I'm not sure if I like it yet.

Still, it's something I think I can be mildly proud of. I may be a shitty preacher, but at least now I'm not also a drunk one.

It's sunny outside, the perfect day for a random visit to the park.

Except for the fact it's not so random that I'm here.

You see, in the middle of the park, a group of women is having a yoga session that involves lots of stretching and downward dogs. Now, you might be thinking I'm a giant perv, and on that, I would have to agree, but there is one clear difference from my normal routine.

Yes, I've done this before, albeit with a different group

of women in an entirely different park. And I mean, what man doesn't like perky lady butts in spandex? A gay man.

No, I'm not ashamed.

Today, I don't give a shit about any of those women … except one.

Laura.

She's been on my mind ever since that spicy encounter in the confessional, and I've wanted to talk to her since. But one doesn't just casually stroll up to a woman and discuss dirty sex, now do they?

No.

However, I'm not letting this slide either.

She did something to me that can't be undone.

When she stepped into that confessional and touched herself right in front of me, she opened a door neither of us can close.

Now that I've had a small sample of what she has to offer, I want more. So much more.

She makes me unable to control myself, and for a man with needs like mine, that's a dangerous thing.

I've followed her all the way from her home to this park just to watch her. I don't know if that's creepy or not, but I just grasped any opportunity I could to see her. I have yet to think of an appropriate moment to approach her, but for now, I'll be content with gawking at her juicy spandex butt.

Fuck me; the way she tightens them as she bends over to touch her toes makes me wanna put my dick in her ass.

Is that wrong?

Yeah, it probably is.

But so help me God, I will do it. It's only a matter of time before she comes to me again, and we have sex like mad rabbits. One thing's for sure, though ... I won't let her run off with a tease like that again.

"Hi."

Frowning, I turn my head only to see Bruno standing next to the bench where I'm sitting. "Uh, hi."

Shit.

I knew he was here, but I never actually expected him to approach me.

He's been playing on the kid's playground while Laura exercises, and I honestly completely forgot about him even being here.

Why would he come over to me? I'm not interesting. Not even remotely.

God, this is so fucking awkward.

"What are you doing?" he asks me, crushing a leaf he just picked from a tree in his hand.

"Uh ... just relaxing in the park," I answer, trying to laugh it off like it's no big deal.

"Are you here because my sister is?"

My eyes widen, and I laugh again. "No, of course not! Why would you think that?" My voice sounds so ridiculous; I'm such a bad fucking liar, it's unbelievable.

He shrugs. "Well, I know you followed us from our home."

Mortified, I close my eyes and sigh.

"It's okay. I can see why you like her. She's nice to people."

"Yeah," I agree. "Very nice."

He smiles at me in such a cute way that it's hard for me to maintain my badass composure.

"So whatcha doing?" I ask him.

"Nothing," he says, letting the crushed pieces of leaf in his hand fly away. "I was playing in the sandbox, but I got bored."

"Why? You can create so many things with a bit of sand."

"I know, but it's no fun if you don't have any friends to play with."

I nod, feeling a bit sorry for the little guy. "I see."

The awkward silence returns, and I feel like this is some kind of invite for me to come play with him or something. But I'm not sure I want to let Laura out of my sight. What if she sees me in the sandbox with him? She might think I'm some kind of weird-ass stalker.

That's because I am, but still.

"Father Frank," Bruno suddenly begins, "why aren't you in your church clothes?"

I shrug. "Because it's hot outside, and I'm just a regular person now."

"So you're not a person in church?"

I snort. "Of course, I am. But in church, I need to look like I work there. But I'm not working right now, so I get to dress however I like."

"And what are those black things on your skin?"

Frowning, I look at where he's pointing, and I realize it's my back, which is covered in tattoos. "Oh, those are the tattoos I mentioned, remember? They're drawings but on the skin."

"Cool! Can I have them too?"

"No," I say sternly, but then I soften my voice again because I don't wanna sound like a dick. "Tattoos are for grown-ups only."

"Why?" He seems disappointed.

"Well ... because they're permanent. They can't be erased."

"Really?" His eyes glow. "Awesome."

I snort and shake my head. "You're a funny one, kid."

"Thanks," he says. "You too."

I'm not sure if that's a compliment, but I'll take it.

"But ... I thought priests weren't allowed to have tattoos?"

"I'm not a priest, Bruno," I reply. "I'm a preacher. And who told you that?"

"My brother," he says, making a figure-eight in the dirt with his shoes.

"Well, your brother was wrong."

"How come?" He cocks his head.

"I'm a special preacher. A bad one." I turn to face him and squint, trying to look as menacing as I can. "You don't wanna mess with me, kid. I'm wicked." I make a scary face, and the kid bursts out into giggles, which makes me smile.

That's when I notice Laura walking our way.

I clear my throat and sit back again, trying not to look like a perving creep, but here I am... being a perving creep.

She cocks her head when she recognizes me and smiles deviously. "Hey, don't I know you from somewhere?"

"He's Father Frank, sis!" Bruno says. "He was in our house eating breakfast! Did you forget?"

"No, silly, it was rhetorical." She rubs his head, messing up his hair.

"What's rhet-rhet-orca?"

She chuckles. "It means it wasn't really a question."

"Should I even answer then?" I muse.

She turns her attention to me as she rubs her forehead with her towel. "Well, well, what a coincidence."

I smile and enjoy the view. No point in denying anything, especially since there's been no allegation. Yet.

"So Bruno already found you. Are you stalking us or something?" she asks, raising a brow.

Ah-ha, there it is.

"Nah." I grin. "Just your friendly neighborhood preacher patrolling the area."

She rolls her eyes, but I can tell she's barely able to keep the laughter inside.

"Got something to confess?" I ask.

She snorts. "Like you don't already know *everything*."

"I do!" Bruno raises his hand.

"Oh, yeah? Tell me then, what'd you do?" I inquire, inching closer.

He closes his mouth and freezes, so I lean in even closer and pat the bench. "Sit."

He does what I ask, and then I turn my ear to him so he can whisper.

"I peed in the sandbox."

My grin turns into a full-on outburst of laughter.

"What?" Laura asks.

I turn my face to Bruno and whisper back into his ear, "Is that the real reason you didn't wanna play in the sandbox anymore?"

He nods.

"What?!" Laura's voice is even louder this time, and she's even thrown her towel over her shoulder like some kind of statement.

Bruno looks at me as if he's pleading me not to tell

her—probably because she'd get mad and rightfully so. But I think I'll play along with this game.

So I twine my fingers and smile like a motherfucker. "I'm sorry. Confessions made to a preacher are strictly confidential."

Oh, that look on her face right now.

Blood-boiling rage.

Magnificent.

"Frank ..." she hisses.

I shrug, still smiling as I lean back.

"He did something; you gotta tell me. This isn't a joke," she grumbles. "What if it's something embarrassing or wrong?"

"You mean like that thing we did in church?"

Her eyes widen, and the shock on her face is amazing to see.

"What thing?" Bruno asks.

"Nothing!" Laura hisses. "Frank ..."

I look at Bruno and say, "Bruno. If you say you're sorry, your sins will be forgiven."

"Does that mean God forgives me too?"

I nod. It's hard to explain these things to a kid as young as he is.

He draws a cute cross on his chest and mumbles, "I'm sorry."

"Good." I pat his back and then look at Laura. "See? He's repenting, so he's forgiven of his sins."

She narrows her eyes and snarls at me. "You are so bad."

"I know." I grin because I consider it a compliment.

I get up from the bench and dust off my pants. "Well, I

guess this is my cue to run."

Bruno jumps off too, saying, "Thanks, Father Frank!"

"Don't mention it, kid."

I start walking even though I wasn't done with Laura yet. However, I can't talk to her in private with Bruno around. It's just not happening.

"What did Bruno do?" Laura yells.

I glance over my shoulder. "You'd like to know that, wouldn't you?"

"Yes!"

"Guess you'll have to come to church then because that's the only place we'll talk confessional business." And with that, I give her a thumbs-up and walk out of sight, leaving a flabbergasted and annoyed Laura behind.

CHAPTER TEN

I'm outside the church at night, leaning against the building as I put a cigarette in my mouth and light it. Only after being alone for a good five minutes, Carl, who's the church's pianist and general handyman, walks out and sees me, and he walks right to me. Not a day goes by when I don't look at his malformed ear and nose. Damn. No wonder people don't come to our church anymore. They're either shocked by me or scared of him. We're like the ghosts at a haunted house at the fair or monsters in Frankenstein's mansion.

"Hey," he says, perching himself beside me. "Got a smoke?"

I glare at him, wondering when he started smoking. Even though he's only four years younger than I am, I feel like I need to protect him from bad shit or something. Not that I'm such a great influence.

I sigh and rummage in my pocket, handing one to him. He puts it in his mouth, and I light it for him. We both blow out smoke and continue to stare at the busy streets in front of us.

"So uh … can I ask you something?" Carl says out of the blue.

"That depends," I say.

"Do you still have some of those old contacts?"

"Old contacts?" I lower my cigarette and eyeball him.

"Yeah, you know … with the dealers and shit."

I tap my cig and ask, "Why?"

He shrugs and takes another drag. "I dunno. Been thinking about doing some side business."

"What? Is the church not enough for you?" I growl, putting my cig back into my mouth.

"I just … Look, I don't want this to be awkward, but I really need to earn more. So I thought, why not get another job? I mean it can't be hard right?"

I snort and shake my head. "You have no fucking clue what you're talking about."

"But you were part of that—"

"Stop," I interrupt.

I can't believe we're talking about this.

"What? Why? I just wanna earn more."

"Not that way. Not with them."

"Look, I know they're bad people, but I need the money more than anything." He chucks the cigarette away. "My medical bills are stacking up, yo."

I think he's referring to his apnea as a result of his nose, and maybe even the continued use of medicine for the pain. I can't imagine what it must be like, and I really don't want to, to be honest. Too many bad memories.

"C'mon, dude, you know how long I've been working here. I wouldn't ask if I wasn't desperate."

"No," I reply. "Not happening."

"What? You're not even going to give me the contacts? I'm not asking you to vouch for me. I just wanna talk."

"Not. Happening." I flick my cig away and fold my arms. "You don't know what you're messing with."

"Don't treat me like a kid," he huffs.

"I don't give a shit how old you are," I say, tapping on his chest. "You're still younger than I am, and by default, that makes me more experienced."

"Fuck that logic."

"No, fuck you wanting to die."

"Die?"

"Did you forget what happened to you?" I grab his ear, and he screeches, after which I release him again. "Next time you get involved in that shit, you'll lose a finger or two."

Two days, he went missing, and when we finally found him on the steps of the church, he refused to discuss what happened. But I know ... you only need to look at his face.

"They're a different gang," Carl says.

"Who gives a shit? Exchange one motherfucker for another motherfucker and you still have shit."

"I'd have money," he says. "And how would you even know what they'd do or if it would happen again? Nothing like this ever happened to you." He points at his nose, which has been chipped away by acid.

"That's because I knew what the fuck I was doing. But make no mistake, kid, I paid the price."

"Maybe I'm willing to pay too," he says.

I grab his collar. "Don't you *ever* fucking say that again. I lost something precious to me. Something no one can ever replace. And all thanks to those motherfuckers you wanna work with." I shove him away and spit on the ground. "You should be ashamed of yourself for even bringing it up. How dare you? You know as well as I do what happened that day."

He swallows, visibly shaken by my honesty.

"I don't have anything important."

"Your life," I growl. "*Nothing* is worth giving that up."

"But you did it too …" he retorts. "And then you just gave up? After going through all that?"

"Too. Late. I gave up too late. And that's why you need to be smart now, Carl."

He swallows again, leaning away from me, his eyes still skidding around while he probably thinks about his options. If he should do it or not.

"Don't you even think about it, Carl. It's not fucking worth it. Not a dime in the world, trust me."

"But I can't pay …" he says. "The church … it's not enough." Tears well up in his eyes.

I place a hand on his shoulder. "Look. I will ask Margaret if she's got any more jobs for you, okay? Would that be good?"

He nods, closing his eyes.

I grab him with both hands and shake him softly. "Promise me you won't do anything stupid."

He sighs. "Fine."

"Good." I slap him on the back. "Now go back inside. You know they're waiting on you to fix the lights."

He nods. "You coming?"

I contemplate it for a second, wanting to stay out here for the fresh air, but I realize it's probably better if I support him while he's down, so I agree and follow him inside.

He goes to Mother's room where she asked him to fix a couple of things while I sit down on one of the pews in the church. It's empty right now; no visitors, no churchgoers. I love these days of peace and quiet. Even Mother is leaving in a few minutes; off to play bridge at the old ladies' club where she's a member. And when Carl's done with his work in her room, he'll also be leaving, allowing me to finally enjoy a nice bit of alone time in the church.

I wanna enjoy it, but that conversation I had with Carl really put a damper on my mood. It's not every day that I get confronted with my past. And I don't like it one bit. Mostly because of the memories involved ... the ones I try to bury so deep no one can reach them.

But now ... ever since Laura came into my life, those memories have been bubbling to the surface, and strangely enough, it doesn't even hurt as much as I thought it would. Or maybe I was stuck in my own little world of drunken pain until she came along and somehow quenched that thirst I felt.

But it doesn't feel right.

I sigh and lean over in the bench, clutching my face as the guilt washes over me.

I shouldn't even be thinking about her.

I should be repenting ... day in, day out ... praying to God for mercy.

Begging him to forgive me for what I've done.

For what was taken away from me.

Yet whenever I talk to him or plead with him to give me an answer, a reason for it all, I just get radio silence, and I'm left with empty nothingness.

The large wooden doors creak, but I stay put. I'm not in the right mood to help people right now.

However, when I notice a girl sits down next to me, I look up and a hint of a smile forms on my lips.

"Laura. What are you doing here?"

"I … saw you outside, so I thought I'd come say hi."

It's been minutes. "And you waited until now?"

She swallows, seemingly having trouble with her words. "Yeah … uh … Bruno, Diego, and I were playing soccer in the alley next to the church, and I happened to overhear your conversation. I wasn't sure if I should even come up to you or talk. And then you went inside and so … well, here I am."

"So you … eavesdropped?" I frown. I did not expect that from her. Then again … I didn't expect her to start rubbing her pussy in a confessional either. People can surprise you.

She rubs her lips together and smiles coyly. "It wasn't on purpose. I mean I was there, and I can't turn off my ears."

I sigh out loud and shake my head. "How much did you hear?"

"Enough to know you had a completely different job before."

"You can say it out loud," I say. "No need to hide it if you already know everything."

She licks her lips and takes in a big breath. "You were a

drug dealer."

I'm not saying anything, but I guess not denying it either speaks volumes.

"Or you did something with those drug dealers. What did you do exactly?"

"Anything and everything I was told."

"How long ago?" she asks.

"Long time ... Nine years."

"Wow. So you're like what ... thirty now?"

I chuckle. "Close enough. Twenty-nine," I answer, looking her straight in the eyes. "You?"

"Twenty-five. But I'm mature for my age."

Oh, yes ... that I already knew.

"So why did you become a preacher then?" she asks.

I take a deep breath, hoping this conversation won't go in the deep end. "Oh, you know. I just kinda rolled into it."

"How?"

I narrow my eyes at her. "You sure do ask a lot of questions."

"I'm just curious." She shrugs. "I wanna get to know the guy I showed my pussy to."

I laugh out loud from that comment. Can't help it. Her dark humor matches mine so well.

"On point," I muse. "But aren't your brothers waiting outside?"

"Nah, I told Diego to take Bruno home."

"Hmm ... so you've got plenty of time on your hands." I lick my lips at the thought of fucking her right here on this pew. I'm such a filthy pig.

"So ... talk." She winks, pulling me from my wicked fantasies.

"Well, if you really wanna know." I clear my throat, lean back against the wooden bench, and stare up at the large statue in the back. "I wasn't a good kid back in the day. I mean my parents … they were druggies, so they couldn't do shit for me."

I still have her undivided attention, despite sharing that dark piece of me, so I continue.

"Since they didn't take care of me properly, I took care of myself. And after a while … I ran away."

"Oh, wow …"

"Yeah. I ended up at this church, right here. Margaret, you know her. She practically raised me."

"Oh, my … I never expected that. No wonder I hear you call her Mother sometimes."

I nod. "She is my mother to me. The only one who truly cared about me."

"So you were prepped really well for the role as a preacher then?"

"Yes and no." I take a deep breath again. We're arriving at the part I hate the most. The part I regret more than anything. "When parents don't take care of their children, it leaves a mark on their lives. Like a scar. It never fades, no matter how much you scrub. When my parents brought me into this world, even though they never wanted me in the first place, it made me feel like I didn't belong."

"That must've been horrible …" She bites her lip but listens to my every word.

"It was but mostly because I couldn't deal with that sense of rejection. Still can't. I mean look at me. I'm a drunk, useless fuck because of it."

"Hey, you're not horrible. We all come with baggage,"

she says. "I mean my brothers and I ran away from our dad and went to live with our aunt because he was that abusive. And when she died, I was the only one who could take care of my family."

"That must've been hard on you," I reply.

"Yeah, but we all have a past that shapes us. It's not necessarily bad."

"I am ..." I sigh. "It was just never enough for me. No matter what Margaret did, she couldn't fill that void left by my parents. I became increasingly unhappy with myself and the world, despite the fact she tried to make it as joyful as possible. I still sought my worth somewhere else. I wanted to feel good. Like I was somebody. Someone people wanted around."

"You hung around with the wrong crowd." She fills in the blanks perfectly.

"Exactly," I say. "I joined a gang. Did whatever they asked. Loved the praise and hated the refusals but I went with it anyway. I knew I was disappointing Mother, but that didn't stop me from seeking out more. Her love just wasn't enough for me. And to this day, I regret that decision. I came back to her on my knees, begging for her help, and she still gave it to me. She let me back into her home, back into her life, back ... into her heart. She even let me become a preacher for this church. Why? I did nothing for her. I took and took without giving back. There's no way I can ever make it up to her."

"Why?"

"Well, how do you make up that you didn't appreciate the love a stranger gave you, despite the fact you had nothing to offer her in return? What she did was selfless ...

and what I did was selfish. There's nothing good about me."

I sigh.

It's tough to think about, but at least I've got some shit off my chest now. It helps a little.

"That's not true. I see how you are with people; you do want to help. You can be a good person; I know it."

"Hmm …" I wonder how deep she can see. There's much more she doesn't know … and I'd rather she didn't. Some things are better left hidden.

"Would you say that if I told you I once robbed a crippled lady?"

She keeps looking at me with those pristine blue eyes that make me wanna drown. Fuck. How can I ever say no to her? How can I ever deny her anything if she keeps looking at me like she would accept the most heinous parts of me?

"Would you still want to talk to me if I told you I once sold drugs to a homeless boy?"

I swallow away the lump in my throat, feeling more and more angry with myself over the awful things I've done. Reminiscing about these things is never good for one's self-worth.

"Would you ever want to see me again if I told you I'd killed someone?"

She gasps and blinks, and I look down at my hands that dangle between my thighs. "You can go if you want. I won't stop you." I pause. "But you need to know that's not who I am. Not today. Not anymore. I don't kill anymore."

It's quiet for some time, but she doesn't move.

Instead, she does the most peculiar thing.

She places a hand on my knee and says, "I don't judge people on their past sins. I judge them by their strength and their ability to do what's right in the present."

"My lips part, but I have no clue how to respond.

"You were threatened, weren't you?" she murmurs.

I nod, unable to discuss this subject.

"If you didn't do it ... they'd kill someone dear to you."

"Yes ... but I also did it to prove myself, and it was wrong."

"You did what you thought you needed to do. And you've already repented for that by preaching for these past nine years. You have to stop punishing yourself."

I close my eyes to stop myself from feeling too much. She reads me like a book, and her words slice through the tangled veins coiled around my heart like a knife through butter.

She squeezes my leg slightly and says, "I'm not leaving. I know you're struggling. That's why I came to you. I feel you ... You're like me."

Those words. I know exactly what she's talking about. From the moment I first saw her, I already knew we had a connection on a different level. Something you can't taste or touch, but something out of the ordinary. Something that makes us understand each other.

And I do the most irresponsible, stupidest thing ever.

In broad daylight, for every passerby to see ... I grab her face with both hands and smash my lips to hers.

CHAPTER ELEVEN

1 Peter 4:8 – "Above all, love each other deeply, because love covers over a multitude of sins."

Her lips are as tantalizing as I imagined them to be. Fiery, so damn delicious, and when she kisses me back, it only makes me want her more. Even though it feels wrong, I can't stop, and I won't. Her mouth is so sweet and everything I hoped it to be.

My tongue darts out to lick her lips, eager to find its way in. Her lips part, allowing me to slip through and claim her mouth as mine. And fuck me … does it feel good.

As I come closer, her fingers grasp my shirt and pull me in. Our mouths are locked in a lustful battle, needing more and more. Heated kisses make my body crave hers, and my hand instinctively reaches down her chest, brushing my fingers along her tits before letting my fingers slide up her blouse.

I lick the roof of her mouth, and when she moans, my cock responds with a thump in my pants, wanting out so badly. I groan when her hand travels down and grabs my dick.

"Fuck," I hiss against her lips.

She grins and kisses me again, rubbing my length through the fabric, and fuck me, does it feel good. I immediately reach for her tits, not caring about her blouse and bra still being in the way, and I squeeze them tight. The more I touch her, the more I can forget about my troubles, and the more I want to be deep inside her.

"You don't know how fucking long I've wanted to do this," I murmur as my lips travel along her neck.

"How long?"

"Since the first time I saw you."

"I know ... I've seen you looking ... that's why I did all those dirty things with you."

I lift my head and look into her mischievous eyes. "Then why did you ask?"

"I just like to hear how much you've been craving me," she teases with a smirk, and it makes me wanna smash my lips to hers again.

"You should be more careful, taunting me like that. Unless you're okay with committing the dirtiest of sins ... right here in church."

"Right here?" she moans.

"Yeah, did you think I'd let you go anywhere? Not a

chance," I growl, placing a few hot kisses on her neck and shoulder.

"Fuck … I don't think I'd be able to say no, even if I wanted to," she mutters as I massage her tits.

I chuckle and whisper into her ear, "So you want me to fuck you?"

"Is that wrong? Is it wrong that I've been fantasizing about being fucked by a preacher?" She rubs me so hard my cock is stiff as wood.

"Fuck no," I say, grinning against her skin as I give her another kiss. "I'm about to make both our fantasies come true."

I flick her bra to the side and let my hands roam free, brushing past her nipples until they harden. With my other hand, I grab her hair and pull her head back, grunting as I lick her skin. I feel like an animal, but I don't even care anymore. All I want is to bend her over and fuck her in every goddamn hole until I'm sated. Right here, right now.

Does that make me a bastard?

Maybe.

But this church has seen worse.

Much, much worse.

I know so because I was the cause. Just like I'm the cause to her sitting right here in my arms, waiting to be taken. My desires drew her in like a moth to a flame, and her willingness to be naughty only made me that much more interested in her.

But now I'm tired of waiting. I'm going to take it all.

Except for the moment I wanna rip her blouse off, a door opens to the left, and I scramble to take my hand out of her blouse. "Shit," I hiss.

"What the fuck?" she mutters, and I place a hand over her mouth, shushing her.

"Quiet. It's Mother." I place a finger on my lips, and she nods. "I'll take care of this."

I slip off the bench and will my dick to go down as I watch Mother walk out into the main area. I meet her halfway, and she gives me this peculiar look like I'm not supposed to be here.

"Still here?" she asks.

"Yes," I say with an awkward smile as I walk beside her. "I'm not interested in going out tonight."

"Well, that's a first," she scoffs. She briefly glances at Laura, whose face is completely red, and they both wave at each other.

"I'm going to meet the girls," Mother says.

Girls. I snort. They're not even close to young.

I guess she means the women she plays bridge with.

"I know," I say, accompanying her.

"I told Carl he could go, so he went out the backdoor. I've already locked it. But if you're staying here, I don't need to lock the front, do I?"

"No, I'll take care of that," I say. "You go out and have fun."

Right before we arrive at the big doors, she turns around and asks, "Are you sure? I mean... I'm a bit worried about you."

"Yes, it's fine! I'm feeling great."

"Are you sure?"

I roll my eyes and put my arm around her shoulder, opening the door for her. "Yes. Now go out and have some fun, will you? I'll watch over the church; don't worry."

"All right," she says as she scurries out. "Don't stay up too late. You need a good night's sleep. Maybe it'll finally be a new beginning for you."

"Uh-huh … I will," I reply, and I wave goodbye before slamming the door and locking it with the key I've got stashed in my pocket.

When I'm sure Margaret's gone, I turn around and see Laura standing in the middle of the hall, staring at me.

I don't wait.

I'm so tired of fucking waiting that I do the first thing that comes to my mind.

I run toward her and grab her, lifting her up, and I smash my lips to hers and kiss her like the hungry wolf I am. She wraps her legs around my waist as I take her bottom lip between my teeth and nibble, wanting to taste every inch of her. I can't get enough; that's how horny I am… or maybe I'm addicted to her.

Kissing her as I go, I carry her all the way to the front of the church until her back hits the altar. There, I set her down right on top of the white cloth. In one fell swoop, I manage to chuck almost all the items off, including a chalice and a few unlit candles.

"We're desecrating holy ground," she murmurs as I continue to steal kisses from her.

"If you're gonna do it, you'd better do it good," I growl back, grinning against her skin as I let my lips roam free. She moans out loud as I reach her tits and grasp her ass at the same time. Squeezing firmly, I assert my dominion over her body. With my teeth, I tear off the buttons of her blouse and spit them out, shoving it aside so I can finally touch her naked body.

"Fuck ... you're so fucking delicious," I whisper as I twist her nipples and kiss her on her stomach.

She squeals and giggles a little. "Jesus, you're horny."

"Jesus ain't horny, babe; it's all me." I smirk at her eye-roll, and in one swoop, I've ripped down her panties and lifted her skirt, exposing her bare pussy. Licking my lips, I slide my thumb down her slit, making her squirm on the altar.

"I'm gonna fuck that pussy raw," I growl, rubbing her clit. "But first ..." I bend over and kiss right above. "Lemme get a taste."

My tongue dips out to slowly slide along the edge, making her practically beg for it. Her fingers tangle through my hair as I roll around her clit. She pushes down, unable to stop herself from wanting more. And I definitely have more where that came from.

She tastes delicious ... and I like it a lot when she's a saucy vixen.

"How much do you want it?" I murmur against her sweet, delicate skin.

She mewls. "Fuck, I want you so fucking much."

I twirl around her clit, expertly avoiding it while watching her face scrunch up from desperation. "Beg for it."

"Oh, please, give it to me," she moans, biting her bottom lip.

I lick my lips from excitement, and her taste only turns me on more. So much so that I start rubbing my dick while I'm licking her.

"Call me by my name," I whisper, planting a kiss on top of her clit.

"Fuck, just give it to me." Her voice is heady and

feverish.

Another quick dip between her slit has her bucking.

"Who?" I muse, sliding my finger along her entrance until she practically leans in to receive it.

"Fuck me, Frank!"

Fuck me; I love it when a woman is so needy that she'd do pretty much anything for it.

What can I say? I'm a sucker for giving a woman everything she needs.

Pleasure. It's all mine, and I'm claiming her now.

CHAPTER TWELVE

I cover her pussy with my mouth and let my tongue roam free. Her engorged clit is so damn wet I can't help but suck and lick everywhere. Top to bottom, not an inch of skin is missed. She tastes so good, and all I want is more. So when she grips my hair and rubs her pussy against my face, I stick my tongue into her pussy and roll it around.

Her moaning squeals tell me she's close.

That and the fact she's as wet as a monsoon.

Fuck me.

I rub my dick even harder, wanting to feel every inch of her pleasure myself. I'm a greedy fuck.

I grab her waist tight, digging my fingers into her skin as my animalistic urges bubble to the surface. My tongue swivels back and forth across her pussy, licking up all her wetness until she begins to squirm underneath me. I know she's close—I can feel it—so I shove two fingers into her pussy and make her feel what I'm going to do to her in a minute.

"Come all over me; I wanna taste you," I murmur, sucking on her clit.

"Fuck!" she moans out loud, and then her body bucks. Her muscles tense, and she gasps, thumping against my lips. Exquisite heaven right there on my tongue.

When she relaxes and her breathing slows, I grab her body and twist her around on the altar. She squeals from my roughness, and I spank her ass.

"Told you I wasn't going to be the nice preacher."

"Well, that licking session you gave me *was* nice," she jests, so I spank her again.

"That was *my* present to me. And fucking your pussy will be the second one," I growl, slipping my index finger up and down her wetness. "After you've been parading your body around, I think it's time I gave it a good filling."

She giggles, and I slap her a final time for good measure before I rip down my zipper and take out my wood. Goddamn, how long I've been yearning for this moment. Too long. It's been too fucking long.

I rub my dick up along her slit, waiting for the noises she makes when she gets aroused, but the more I gawk at her butt, the more I want to have it too.

I wanna have it all.

So I rub my wet finger along her ass and push it in. As she raises her head, mewling, I grasp her hair and fiercely pull her head back. "Ever had your ass taken by a preacher?"

"No, but I'm more than willing to try …"

"Guess today's your lucky day," I reply, grinning.

I shove my finger farther up her butt, and then insert another one into her pussy, rubbing both along her walls. I can feel her tense up, and her moans only add to my own excitement. My cock bobs up and down as I watch her crave my fingers as much as she craved my mouth, and I imagine myself taking both holes. Maybe I will.

"Hope you've said your prayers because after I fuck your brains out, you won't be able to come to church and thank God for your perfect fuck for an entire week."

I pull my finger out of her pussy and push my cock in without warning, making her gasp out loud. My finger's still in her ass, and I slide it in farther with each thrust of my rock-hard dick. Every stroke is another pump, and soon, her body begins to move along with mine to the rhythm of my fuck.

She's perfect. Just fucking perfect.

Fuck me; I'm so fucking hungry for more.

And at this point, I honestly don't fucking care what's allowed and what isn't. I crossed any line by miles the moment I sucked her clit on the altar, so if I'm doing it dirty, might as well go all the way.

Biting my lip, I pull my finger out of her ass, pick up the only candle still left on the edge of the altar, and shove it up her ass.

She moans out loud, and I grasp the opportunity to fist her hair and pump into her harder, all while the candle is stuck inside her ass. I just love the sight of a willing woman doing all sorts of dirty things without regrets, even if it means defiling the most sacred things.

"Fuck me harder!" she begs, and I increase the pace.

I even twist the candle, pushing it in and out as I go, fucking her in both holes.

Maybe that makes me a filthy bastard but so be it.

Fucking her is my number one priority right now, and if I think of something good, I'll fucking do it because I want to.

I put my finger on her clit and flick it hard, wanting her to come again so I can feel her tighten around my cock. Her whole body starts to rock, desperately trying to get closer to me. Her pussy gyrates against my fingers, and she's so damn wet. I love every second of it, despite the fact I'm desecrating my own damn church.

And I don't give a damn.

"Fuck, I'm gonna come again," she mutters, out of breath.

"Fuck, yes," I groan, still twisting and turning the candle in her ass. "Come all over my dick."

Within seconds, her body quakes again, and the wetness pours out of her. Her muscles deliciously contract around my length, making me come. Roaring out loud, I fuck her so hard, my cock explodes deep inside her with all the pent-up energy. I thrust and thrust, my cum jetting into her and coating her warm pussy. One. Two. Three times, and I'm still not sated.

When I pull out, I'm still rock-hard, so I pull out the candle and replace it with my own stick. She squeals, probably surprised by my stunt.

"Fuck! Jesus, warn me or something?"

"I told you it was gonna be dirty. I need to have your pussy *and* your ass."

I grunt as I push farther, forcing her ass to adjust to my

ample size until I'm completely in. Our cum provides nice lubrication as I thrust in and out, claiming her ass too.

I grab her waist, my fingers digging in, as I take out all the pent-up lust on her. Maybe it's wrong, maybe I'm selfish, but at this point, I'm far beyond reason.

I just need to fuck.

Fuck.

Fuck.

Fuck!

That's all I can think of.

So I fuck her as hard as I can. I fuck her so hard that the altar screeches as I drive her against it. I fuck her so hard that a groan escapes from her mouth with each thrust. I fuck her so hard that she'll beg me to come and release her from my longing.

Beads of sweat pool on her back as well as on my body, which has heated up to the point of me breathing raggedly. So beastly, so utterly animalistic—it's fantastic.

I slap both her ass cheeks again for good measure, and the reverberations pulsate through my dick. My veins pulse with arousal; my cock ready to dispense its second load. I love the feeling—just like I love her ass and her pussy and my cock being right there inside them.

"You ready for me?" I growl, grasping her hair again so she looks up.

She turns her head slightly, whispering, "Come in my ass. Do it."

That right there … that pleading voice … is all I need to come undone.

And I do.

I fucking howl like a wolf as I fill her ass with my cum.

More and more and more. It's an endless stream. Like I haven't come in ages.

By the time I'm done and panting and my cock's slipped out of her, both her holes are creamed white. The color of heaven itself. Perfection.

If I may say so myself.

I slap her ass, and the cum flows down her legs. "Now that's what I call a good creaming."

"Oh, my … Lord."

That voice … makes all the hairs on the back of my neck stand straight.

Within the space of a second, I've turned around and faced the most horrible consequence of my actions already.

Mother is standing right there, in the doorway, with her jaw hanging wide open. A key tumbles from her hands to the floor as she bears witness to the full naked glory of my half-hard dick and a woman covered in my juices, rolling around on the emptied altar.

In a hurry, Laura scrambles off the table and pulls up her panties, which instantly soak completely through. Still, she tries to cover it up with her skirt by patting it down and then continues to pull her blouse together like it will hide the fact we were having sex here. On the altar. "Oops."

I don't think 'oops' describes this situation accurately.

We're fucked is more like it.

CHAPTER THIRTEEN

Mother wasn't supposed to be back yet. And here she is, standing right in front of me, gaping at my naked dick.

"Well, shit," I mutter.

The shocked look on her face turns into pure disgust as she barges over to me. Her lips are smashed together, teeth grinding as she stomps my way, and I quickly push my dick back into my pants and pull up the zipper before she sees any more of my junk and has a heart attack.

I mean I hate her for coming home too early, but I love her too much to be the cause of her death.

Behind me, Laura quickly knots her blouse together, trying to make up for the lost buttons as Mother approaches us. "She looks upset," she whispers.

I nod and focus on Mother, who's now right in front of me.

Clearing my throat, I say, "I thought you were at—"

"You filthy animal!" she screams, slapping my arms with a mini Bible she pulled from her pocket. "How dare you?"

"I'm sorry," I say, blocking my face with my arms to protect myself from her wrath, although I deserve everything she's giving me. "I didn't think you'd be home this soon."

"Really? That's your answer? After disgracing the church's altar with this … this …" She glares at Laura, who then mouths, "Okay," to me while squeezing my hand.

"Laura," she says, smiling awkwardly. "And I'm really, truly sorry you had to see that."

Mother keeps her mouth shut, but I can tell she's fuming. And when she turns her head back to me, I swear the look in her eyes is borderline murderous. Maybe I should back away slowly before she chokes me to death. It wouldn't surprise me, after all the shit I've done.

"You disgusting, dirty pig!" Mother smacks me again with the Bible.

Laura slowly slides away from me. "Yeah … I'll be going now …" she mumbles, quickly diving away behind Mother and rushing to the door.

That girl escaped a certain doom.

Wish I was smart enough to run. But now that I'm the only one left, she'll never let me leave.

Shit.

"I'm sorry," I repeat.

"You defiled the church," she hisses.

"I know, but … I thought you weren't—"

"I can come home whenever I *want*; that's *not* up to you to decide," she interjects. "You should be ashamed of yourself. Fooling around with a girl on the altar. Have you lost your mind?"

"No, I was just ... lost in the moment," I reply, sighing to myself, because I know I fucked up big time.

"Your pecker was lost in her snatch is more like it," she growls.

Her words make me chuckle, which I try to hide, but it's too late. The moment she sees it, she smacks the book against my arms again.

"Stop laughing!"

"I'm sorry; it just sounds so funny coming from your mouth."

"I don't care what words I use. What you did was wrong."

"I know, and I apologize. I couldn't control myself," I say. "I have urges. Needs. Mother, don't you understand?"

"Of course, I do, but those things are called 'beds,' remember?" She cocks her head. "And last I checked, you were sulking around, drinking yourself numb to forget your memories. Has that suddenly disappeared?"

The mere mention already makes me sour and any joy I still felt from my dirty fuck with Laura quickly dissipates.

"Rub it in, why don't you."

"Is this really who you wanna be?" she asks.

Grinding my teeth, I reply, "I don't know who the fuck I wanna be. I've lost track of myself."

"Then maybe you need to find out who you are before you go around fucking random girls in *my* church."

"She's not some random girl," I growl back, feeling the

rage coil around my heart.

"I don't care who she is. You did something unforgivable. You can say sorry all you want, but the only one who you have to seek forgiveness from is God." She points at the statue behind me, and my eyes follow, falling onto the statue of Jesus Christ and his merciless gaze as he judges me from above.

And I feel the sudden need to fall to my knees and beg.

"Why?" I ask, tears welling up in my eyes. "Why can't you give me this one thing?"

"I can't give you what you want," Mother hisses. "You need to accept what happened and move on."

"I was trying to! With her!" I shout.

"Screwing that girl won't change anything about *you*." She taps my chest with her index finger, but the pressure feels like a ton of weight bearing down on my heart.

I shove aside her arm and walk past her.

"Where are you going?" she yells as I walk toward the door.

"Out."

"You're going to see her again, aren't you?"

"Just leave me alone," I growl back.

"It won't help. You'll only end up lost again. Drinking yourself to death." Her words cut deep like a knife. Mother knows me too well … so well, she hurts me like no one else can.

The anger inside me comes to a boiling point, and I can't stop myself from turning my head and screaming, "Just shut up!"

She freezes, her lips parted, but no sound comes out.

A moment of complete silence passes, and I know I've

done something worse than fucking a girl on the altar. I showed Mother what real hatred looks like. And not just that. I handed it to her on a fucking platter like it was hers to begin with.

While regret pours in, I choose not to answer the immediate sting. I turn around and walk out the door, slamming it shut behind me.

***

Revelation 21:4 – "He will wipe every tear from their eyes. There will be no more death or mourning or crying or pain, for the old order of things has passed away."

With a bottle of whiskey in my hand, I saunter across the cemetery, grasping the occasional stone to stay upright. In the dark of night, two lamps light my way across the pebble path to the stone that crushes my soul each time I see it.

Still, it draws me here to this wretched place I'd never visit if it wasn't for her.

As I stand in front of it, the weight of her death pulls me to the ground, and I fall to my knees. I wipe away the snot dripping from my nose, sniffing as I stare at the stone in front of me and the ground beneath it.

"I fucked up. I fucked up so badly. It's all my fault," I mutter, sniffing again. "I've accepted that now. There's no going around it. I am the cause. I always was."

I slurp down more whiskey straight from the bottle and sit down on the cold, hard ground, not caring that my pants will get dirty. "I deserve everything. I had it coming. But you didn't deserve to die for it. I did." I slap my own chest like it will help. "I should've died instead of you."

I look up at the sky, wondering why this had to happen. "Why, God? Tell me why. Do you hate me so much? I know I've been a shitty preacher, but why did you take her away? Why did you have to make me suffer? Huh?"

Tears roll down my cheeks, and I wipe them away with the bottle still in my hand. "I'm a fucking mess. I never did the right thing. I don't understand. Why?" I yell at the stone like it'll suddenly start talking back to me. "Why the fuck did you ever marry me?"

Behind me, something snaps, and I turn my head toward the sound. Something behind a tree … or rather someone.

"Laura …?" I mutter, confused as to why she's here.

Her lips part and she licks them like she's thinking about what she's gonna say. "I … I didn't mean to sneak up on you. I was just …" She swallows. "I'm sorry if I'm interrupting."

I sigh out loud and turn my head back toward the stone, not knowing what to tell her. I'm a drunk fuck sitting in a cemetery. I mean it's pretty telling. Still, I wasn't prepared for her to see me like this.

"How did you know I was here?" I ask, my voice not strong enough to carry the words.

"After you stormed out of the church, I followed you. I was waiting in the alley. I thought since you had a fight with Margaret, I might need to … you know … apologize."

"Don't," I say. "You don't need to. I made a choice. I live with the consequences." I can't even look at her. That's how disappointed I am in myself that she has to see me like this.

"About that ... I'll help clean up the mess," she says. "If you want."

"It's fine. I'll do it tonight," I groan, rubbing my forehead.

It's quiet for some time. All I can hear are the crickets chirping and my own lackluster breathing while I wonder when it'll be the last time I'll hear those. Is it strange to wonder about those things? Maybe. Or maybe I'm too drunk to think straight.

Suddenly, I feel a hand on my shoulder. I flinch, my body uncertain what to do with affection like this. I've not felt a warm hand comforting me like that in a long time. And it makes the tears well up again.

"I'm sorry," I say. "I never wanted you to see this."

"It's okay," she says. "I understand."

I nod and place my hand on top of hers to show my appreciation. But now I'm beginning to wonder how long she's been standing there since she said she followed me.

Did she hear everything I said?

"I get it now," she says, interrupting my thoughts. "Why I found you passed out the other day. Why you seem so self-destructive. Why your speeches are ... riddled with rage."

"You heard ..." I mutter.

She squeezes my shoulder. "I'm sorry about your wife. If you want to talk about it, I'm here."

The moment those words slip from her mouth, my heart breaks open.

I feel so much, but I've never been able to let it out. So many emotions running amok and I've never found an outlet except for the liquor. Maybe it's time I started trusting someone else.

"She died … six years ago."

Laura sits down on her knees beside me and looks me in the eye, waiting for me to open my mouth and speak. She's not looking away, despite my awful, drunken stench. I know she can smell it coming from my mouth, and I know she sees the sorrow in me. I hate seeing the pity in her eyes.

"Was she sick?" she asks softly.

I snort and shake my head, wishing life was that simple.

My life has never been easy.

Never.

Not when I worked my ass off to find someone else's approval of my life.

Not when I finally found love when I thought I didn't deserve it.

Not when they took *everything* away from me.

Grinding my teeth, I reply, "She was murdered."

CHAPTER FOURTEEN

Ephesians 6:11 "Put on the whole armor of God, that you may be able to stand against the schemes of the devil."

Six Years Ago

I pick up my Bible and eat the last bite of my pancakes before bringing my plate to the kitchen and kissing my wife on the cheeks. "It was delicious. Thanks, hun," I say, winking as I tuck the Bible into my pocket. "See you later."

"Work hard, honey!" she yells as I run out the door, not even having the time to close it behind me.

However, I still make time to turn around halfway down the path and blow her a kiss, which she catches and holds close to her heart.

Just the sight of her warms mine.

It reminds me of the day we met. One year after I left behind the gang life and vowed to take care of the church, I went to buy flowers for Margaret. When I entered the shop and saw a girl … *my wife* … behind the cash register, I instantly fell in love with her welcoming smile.

I asked her out on a date, took her to a fancy restaurant, and the rest is history.

She knows about my past. About all the messed up things I did. And she accepts me anyway. Even knowing that someone's going to come for me one day didn't stop her from loving me, and I can't help but love her madly for it.

It's true what they say. Love knows no bounds.

With a stupid smile on my face, I make my way to the church, enjoying the nice weather outside. "Morning, Frank!" Margaret walks out to greet me as I come in, and I say hi to her too.

"Hope you're having a great day," I say.

"Sure thing. Can't wait for today's sermon," she says, smiling as I place my Bible on the pulpit and pull out my notes for today.

"I've prepared a great speech. You'll be amazed." I wink at her, and her smile widens because of it.

She quickly steps toward me and pinches my cheeks like she did when I was still young. "I'm so proud of you."

"Thanks," I reply. Even though I hate it when she squeezes my cheeks, I still love her. "I mean it. I'm eternally grateful you let me be here."

"Aww … Frank … you don't have to say it." She cocks her head as she places a hand on my arm. "You know I'll always accept you, no matter your past."

I nod, and after a short hug, we part because the church bells are ringing and people are pouring in.

Soon, believers fill the whole church, waiting for me to talk to them about their faith and give them encouragement in their daily lives. Just like I've been doing for the past few years.

I've come such a long way. From barely being able to form the words to performing complete speeches in front of entire crowds. All with Margaret's help. I couldn't have done it without her.

It's because of her that I'm here today.

Back where I belong. Back in the church. Doing good instead of evil.

Margaret made me swear that I would devote my life to God, so that's what I did. I turned my back on the gang life and focused on being a new me. A different me. A man worthy of the unconditional love she gave me.

She is the reason I've come so far. The only person who's supported me through hardship. Who held out her hand when no one else would.

She helped me become the person I was meant to be. It was a long road, but I fought hard, and look at me now.

A full-fledged preacher.

I sigh and stare at the note in front of me. While the crowd grows quiet, I look around, trying to find that spark to start my sermon.

Except what I find today isn't hope.

It's judgment.

The hairs on the back of my neck stand straight as I lay my eyes on the devil himself.

Time seems to come to a stop the moment I'm confronted with my past.

Or rather ... the one whose life I've ruined.

A top dog in a drug empire not far from here.

The rival drug empire of the gang I was a part of during my darker days.

The same gang that asked me to prove my worth to them ... and pay a visit to that rival to teach him a lesson and show him who's boss around this neighborhood.

That man is sitting right in front of me.

My throat clamps up as he eyes me down, and my fingers tremble with fear. I'm suffocating in my own memories, wanting to erase them from the planet, but I know I can never take back what I did. I wish apologizing was enough, but I know he'll never accept it.

He wants blood.

He licks his lips, tilting his head as he sees my slow demise. And right then, he gets up and walks toward the exit silently.

I can't help but stare at the door even though all these people are waiting for me to continue my sermon.

How did he find me?

Why is he here?

Before he opens the doors and leaves, the man briefly holds up what looks like pieces of flesh ... a piece of an ear and part of a nose.

I gape in shock and horror, unable to utter a word.

Flashes of memories pass through my mind of Mother telling me Carl didn't show up for work yesterday ... and it all suddenly clicks.

If he has Carl, then he knows ... *I took something away*

from him.

And now, he's going to take what's mine.

My notes blow off the pulpit as I take off as fast as I can after him. I rush through the church, past the people waiting in the pews, who look at me like I've seen a ghost. I don't care what they think, and I don't even care about Margaret screaming my name as I sprint for the door.

When I'm outside, the man is already gone.

As fast as I can, I make my way to my house. Faster, faster, faster, as fast as my legs can take me. The pain tears away at me, but not as much as the pain in my heart as I realize what's about to happen.

The ultimate revenge.

When I arrive at my door, almost tumbling over a toy on the driveway, I scream at the top of my lungs, but no one screams back. My hands shake as I search for my keys, my heart racing as I stuff it into the lock and turn it, slamming open the door.

The house is completely silent.

Unlike anything I've heard in ages.

But then a door bangs in the back, and I rush toward it.

I'm too late.

What I see rips a hole in my soul.

My wife being dragged away by two men toward a car with her hands tied behind her back. A piece of black tape slapped across her face. Her eyes filled with a terror that will haunt me forever.

She's pulled feet first into the car by another man who was already inside, along with a little boy.

My baby boy.

I howl like a dog losing its owner when the tires screech

as the car pulls away ... as I know that the look of pure horror on their faces will be the last thing I'll ever see of them.

***

Now

"Oh ... God." Laura covers her mouth with her hand in shock.

But then she does the most unexpected thing.

She pulls me in for the tightest hug I've had in years. Literally squeezes the life out of me while wrapping her arms around me like a warm cocoon. At first, it feels weird, but after a while, I just accept it and relax, letting her take me over.

Now that I've finally told someone of the horrors I've faced, it feels like a weight has lifted off my shoulders. Like I can finally breathe a little again.

"God, no wonder ... I'm so sorry ..." she whispers. "I don't know what to say."

"You don't have to say anything." I clear my throat to prevent more tears from falling. I've cried enough now. "It was a long time ago."

"Yeah, but you're still ... you're still ..."

Still messed up?

Still a drunk?

Yeah, whatever it is, it's not okay, and she's right. What happened to my wife and son does still affect me.

"I can't get that image from my mind," I say. "Her face."

"It must've been horrible," Laura says. "And it was the last time you saw them?"

I nod, but then I shake my head. "Alive, yes. I saw my wife after she died. They eventually found her body not far from this neighborhood. I had to identify her at the morgue, but what I saw wasn't my wife. It was a body, cut up in pieces."

"Oh, God …" She shudders, but her hands remain steady on my back. "What about your son?"

"I never saw him again. The police assumed him to be dead too, but they never found his body. I even searched … day and night for a whole damn year, but it was useless." I close my eyes and try to imagine his face, but no matter how hard I try, I can never get it right. "He was so young. Just a few months old. How could they do that to a kid?"

Laura hugs me even tighter. She's unrelenting in her support like she's willing to take up the world and more. A fighter, just like me … or at least, what I used to be.

"I'm here," Laura whispers, holding me close. "I'm not going anywhere."

Her support means the world to me. I never thought I'd be able to lean on someone else like this, but it feels good. I'm relieved I can finally tell someone my story without feeling guilty.

Even though I am.

I couldn't even go back to the same house where I once lived. Not after they were gone. It was too empty and loaded at the same time. So I went back to the church, and that's where I've been ever since.

Still, the shame never stopped.

"My wife died because of me. My son is gone because of

me."

"You didn't kill them," she says.

"No, they died because I took something from *him.*"

She puts her hand on my arm. "He chose to retaliate. That was not your choice."

"Revenge," I say through gritted teeth. "That's what it's all about, right?"

"It doesn't have to be." She grabs my shoulders. "Look at me. You are better than this."

"They took everything from me." I grab my bottle, but when I attempt to drink, she snatches it away.

"No. Alcohol is *not* the answer, and you know it."

"Maybe not the answer but definitely a great distraction," I muse, chuckling like an idiot.

She shakes her head. "Look at you. Getting drunk at your wife's grave."

"Pathetic, right?" I fill it in for her.

"No." She sounds upset, and then she shoves me. "Get up."

"Why?"

"Get up and walk, goddammit," she snaps, slapping my chest. "Get up and go on with your life."

"What's the point?"

"There's more to it than sulking and staying in the past," she growls, grabbing my arm to try to lift me up. "C'mon."

I sigh, looking at my wife's grave one last time.

"She would've wanted you to go on even though it's without her."

I frown. "How do you know?"

"Every woman wants her man to be happy even if she's not there," she replies.

That actually makes a lot of sense.

I close my eyes, take a deep breath, and then let her help me up.

"Steady," she says as she supports me.

I'm so drunk I can't even walk straight.

"I'm sorry I put this on you. But you didn't have to come, you know."

"And leave you here in the dirt?" she scoffs. "Not a chance."

At first, I'm still holding the bottle of liquor in my hand, but then I mumble, "Ah, fuck it," and I drop it on the ground, letting the alcohol spill out onto the soil.

"Good," Laura says. "It's time you said no to yourself."

"Someone's gotta do it," I jest, laughing a little even though it's not funny.

However, my smile dissipates the moment I see an old Chevy with darkened windows slowly driving along the cemetery. I stop walking. Goose bumps scatter on my skin. I can barely make out the two figures in the front, but I feel their intense stares as they drive by and disappear from view.

"What were you looking at?" Laura asks.

With furrowed brows, I look at her and then back at the empty road. It must've been my imagination. "Nothing."

CHAPTER FIFTEEN

We go back to the church even though I'm drunk as fuck and shouted at Margaret. I don't want to be an even worse person by not fixing it even if I'm only partially capable. Besides, the cold air of the night has done me good. My vision is much less hazy than it was at the cemetery, and since I left the bottle of liquor, my head feels much clearer. Although I am expecting a raging headache any moment now.

Laura smiles at me as she helps me up the steps of the church and I open the door. However, what I see inside is not what I expected.

The altar is completely clean again with everything back where it's supposed to be. Not an item misplaced. It's like we were never there.

Confused, I stumble inside and gawk at the scene in front of me.

Mother appears from behind a column, and when her eyes slowly fall onto mine, this innate sense of guilt and humility wash over me.

I fall to my knees and face the floor, unable to look at her.

"I'll ... let you two talk," Laura mumbles, and she quickly scurries toward the chapel.

I hear Mother's footsteps approach me, but I'm frozen to the floor, bowing my head as low as I can.

"I ... cannot apologize enough," I say softly, hoping she can hear.

"Look at me." Her stern voice can pretty much make me do anything even when I know she's upset.

However, I never expected to see the calm in her eyes. It makes the tears well up again.

"I'm sorry ..." I mutter. "For all the things I put you through since ... since ..."

Margaret goes to her knees and wraps her arms around me, pulling me into her embrace.

"What did I do to deserve you?" I murmur, hugging her tight.

"You don't have to do anything, Frank. I'll always be here. I'll always forgive you," she whispers, kissing the top of my head.

"I know I've been an incredible burden. Especially with the drinking," I say.

"You have to stop destroying yourself, Frank. It's the only way," she says, making me look at her. "You have to stop and love yourself."

I nod.

"I know you've been dying inside," she mutters. "I can feel your pain every day."

I sigh out loud as I realize what I've been doing to myself.

"But you have to stop now. You have to be better. And you have to love God. Trust in him to guide you even in the most difficult times," she says, turning her head to look at the statue of Jesus. "Go pray with him."

Inside me, a powerful current of energy directs me and forces my limbs into action, commanding me to get up and walk. And I do. I let go of Mother and let my body be drawn to the cross, an immense need to repent and do good being the driving force behind me.

It's like I've suddenly seen the light.

Felt the vindication falling in my lap.

The shroud of anguish lifting to reveal a new man.

I stand tall and look up, making the sign of the cross on myself. "God, I've mistrusted you. I've blamed you for everything that happened to me. I hated you for so long. But enough is enough. I won't live this life any longer. I won't continue to hurt those around me for the sake of hurting myself. I've been punished enough. No one but You can judge me now. God, please forgive me my sins. I put my life in Your hands once again." I draw another cross on my chest. "Amen."

Suddenly, someone rams on the big front door and smashes it open without regard to its value. It almost comes unhinged. I turn to see what the ruckus is. Two tattooed guys wearing dirty jeans and white shirts saunter in. It's the same guys from the bar who were looking for a fight not too long ago. One of them, the bald one, is holding a bat ... the other pimply one, a gun.

"Well, hello there!" the one with the bat yells, and he smashes the pew to his left. "Long time, no see!"

Mother slaps her hand in front of her mouth, shocked and completely frozen to the floor.

"Nice church you have here," the one with the gun says, swaying it around. "Be too bad if something were to happen to it, don't you think?"

The more I look at them, the more I'm starting to realize they were the guys in the car at the cemetery.

Did they follow me here?

"Back for a rematch?" I ask, cocking my head.

"Oh, yeah." One of them swings his bat again, ramming it into a pillar, and some stone flies across the room.

Grinding my teeth, I ball my fist and narrow my eyes at them. "Leave this church alone. Your fight is with me."

"Or what?" the one with the gun asks. "You gonna slap us with your Bible?" He laughs as he approaches Mother. "Or is she gonna?"

"Stay away from her," I growl, and I march to her, blocking her with my body to prevent them from hurting her.

The one with the gun cocks his head at me from afar, but he doesn't move an inch.

"Go," I whisper over my shoulder at Margaret. "Lock yourself in your room and don't come out until I say so."

"Yeah, go on, Granny," the one with the bat jests, and he smashes a vase in the corner of the church to smithereens.

"Come with me. I don't want you to get hurt," Mother murmurs, grabbing my hand.

All this time and she's still trying to protect me.

Now, it's my turn.

I let go of her hand. "I won't. I promise." I straighten my collar and crack my neck. Behind me, Margaret slowly slips away into the back of the church, and when I hear the door lock click, I know it's game on.

"You ready for a second round, pretty boy?" the one with the gun threatens, and he spits on the marble floor. "We've come prepared."

"Do you even know where you are?" I ask, tilting my head as I roll up my sleeves.

"Fucking churches." The one with the bat smashes another bench, breaking the wood in two.

"You'll pay for that, you know," I say.

He laughs. "Yeah, with what?"

The one with the gun grins and quips, "Yeah, tell us how we're gonna pay because as far as I know … we just came to smash shit up."

"You came to smash shit up," I repeat, nodding a little as I casually saunter toward them. "And you chose a church. Of all places to do it."

"*You* were here," Batboy says.

"Oh, so it *is* me you're after," I retort, narrowing my eyes. "You know, we could've taken this outside so the church would remain intact, and done it the easy way. No one would get hurt."

"No one?" Batboy laughs.

"Except you," Gunboy says, laughing too.

I smile at them. "Keep saying that to yourself, and you

might start to believe it. After I kick your asses into next week."

"Ha ... funny you'd say that," Gunboy says, pointing his gun at me. "Too bad only one of us is carrying a gun."

"Is that supposed to compensate for something smaller?" I jest, looking up and down his small frame. When I see his face contort, I grin, and he comes at me.

Guess I've gone and done it now.

They picked the wrong preacher to mess with, though.

Right when he's in front of me and his gun is in reach, I push his arm aside with a flat hand. The gun goes off, and a bullet ricochets off the wall before landing on the floor. I quickly grasp his wrist and force him to drop it.

He squeals in pain, and then his buddy rushes at me with his bat out like it's some kind of giant meat-stick.

Kicking Gunboy in his balls and then smashing his face against my knee, I push him aside and grasp the bat before it hits my face, holding him back with sheer will. I might be a little bit drunk, but that doesn't make me weak ... It only makes me more of an asshole.

I push it back so hard it smashes into his forehead, leaving him dazed.

Meanwhile, Gunboy gets up without his gun and starts punching the air, trying to hit me. I'm avoiding both easily, and I laugh while I do it.

"Too slow!" I joke, getting on their nerves.

I can tell. Their faces are bloating and turning red like a hot air balloon. Looks great.

Batboy tries again, and this time, I manage to snatch it away from him. I smack it right into his ankles, breaking one of them. He whimpers and falls to the ground, crying like a little bitch, while his tiny-dicked friend is still trying to punch me. This time, he even throws in some kicks, trying to hit me with all four limbs like he's some kind of martial arts expert. It looks silly, to be honest.

Like they saw some shit on TV and decided they could do it themselves.

No.

Real fighting happens on the streets. You don't learn it from a one-day course, and you certainly don't fucking learn it from watching it on TV.

You learn it by fighting.

Day in and day out.

We don't fight fair here. Rules don't apply to criminals. We fight while carrying our life on our sleeves. We fight with our heart out and with death breathing down our necks.

Just like I'm doing right now.

I throw away the bat because I hate using weapons. I'd much rather use my own fists.

With one quick punch to the gut and another one between his eyes, I manage to knock him to the floor. He tries to get up again, but I know he's dizzy because that's exactly what that move is for. So I stomp on his belly so hard he almost throws up.

Meanwhile, Batboy's crawling out on one leg, still whimpering like a little baby.

"Where you going?" I growl, marching toward him. I lean over and grasp him by his hair, pulling his head up. "Think you can run away?" I burst out into laughter. "Oh, wait … can't run when your bones are crushed, can you?"

I stomp on his broken ankle, and he cries out in pain.

"Hurts, doesn't it? You know what else hurts? Breaking shit in my damn church!" I smack his face down against the floor, hoping he bleeds.

Then I turn my attention toward his buddy, who's attempting to flee by running past the left side of the pews. "Yeah, you run to whoever sent you. Tell him I'll be waiting right here. And I expect payment for the destruction of property!"

"Don't leave me!" Batboy yells at his buddy, but he ignores him.

"Aww ... there goes your boyfriend," I muse. "Must be tough seeing him give no fucks about your life."

"Shut up!" he yells. He turns around to face me while still crawling away on his two hands like that will work.

I grab his throat with both hands, and he claws at my wrists to try to breathe properly. "Listen, you little shit, who are you and your buddy and what are you doing here?"

"Can't breathe ..." he chokes out.

"Then try harder!" I growl, getting up close with him as I sit down on top of him.

"We're no one ..."

"Of course, you're no one, but *someone* sent you," I say, squeezing harder.

He whispers, "Julio ..."

The mere mention of his name makes the hairs on the back of my neck stand.

Julio. 'El Campeón.' The brawler. Rumor had it he killed a thousand men with his bare hands, hundreds of those with just two fingers. Of course, those are rumors ... but terrifying nonetheless.

He's also the man who killed my wife.

"Why?" I hiss back. "After everything he took from me, he's still not done?"

He still struggles under my grasp. "Because he wants you gone."

"Why? He would've done it sooner if he just wanted me gone!" I smack him harder to the floor. "Didn't he want me to suffer? Huh? Tell me!"

He softly hisses, "You're hanging out with his daughter."

My eyes widen, and my gaze instantly darts to Laura, who comes out of her hiding spot behind the chapel wall. Her eyes bore into me. If only she could hear his words.

Or maybe it's better that she doesn't.

Laura Espino … Julio Espino's daughter.

I can barely believe it, yet it all makes sense.

She said she was on the run. Maybe he's tracking her. It would explain why she doesn't want to discuss her family. And then his lackeys saw me with her, and now, he wants me dead.

Of course … because I could use her against him.

As the realization dawns, I loosen my grip on my victim, and he immediately pushes me off him, scrambling away on one foot. But I don't care anymore. I know he won't show up here again. He's learned his lesson the hard way. Working for Julio and fighting me will give you broken bones, that's what.

He scrambles while my attention focuses on Laura.

I've been staring at a ghost of my past this entire time, dancing with fate itself.

She's his daughter. A girl he loves most dearly.

And it would be the world's worst pain to him if she

died.

If...

Would I ever be able to?

Am I that person? The one who wants vengeance so badly he'd even kill the only girl who gave him his spirit back?

Slowly, but surely, Laura comes walking toward me, but I'm not sure I'm prepared. The choice between good and evil is currently dividing me into pieces. I don't want to lose her ... but to see that motherfucker's tears is my dying wish.

How do I look at her the same way without feeling that pain?

"Those guys ... What did they want? Why did they trash this place?" she inquires.

Grinding my teeth, I hiss, "Please don't ..."

"Don't what?"

"Don't come closer."

She frowns in confusion. "Why?"

"They were after me," I say.

"So?" She still tries to come closer, but I take a step back. "Why are you acting this way? Just because you hurt them? I don't care about any of that."

"It's not that," I growl, taking a deep breath.

She stares at me, the flame in her eyes growing weaker. "Those guys ... I knew I recognized them from somewhere." She grabs herself like she wants to hug herself instead of me. "They work for him ... but you already know that, don't you? That's why they were after you."

She's so smart. Too smart for her own good.

"My father wants you."

"It's complicated," I say, swallowing away the lump in

my throat.

"He must've found out about us." She rubs her lips together. "He always hated seeing me with a man. And I hated his controlling urges." She sighs. "But that doesn't have to come between us. He can't decide who I'm with. That's not up to him."

I don't reply. I don't know how or what I should say. She doesn't even know the full story. The real reason for our mutual hatred.

"Can't we—"

"Please … just leave," I say, looking away.

"Frank …"

"I can't," I say. "You don't know what you're asking of me."

"I know my father is an asshole, but that doesn't mean you have to let him win and—"

"That's not why I'm asking you to leave," I interject, staring straight at her. Her teary eyes make me weak. Malleable. And it crushes me.

If anything could break me, she could.

"Tell me why?" she asks. "At least give me a reason."

"You're better off not knowing some things," I mutter. "But right now, I really wanna be left alone."

She grimaces. "If that's what you want."

It pains me to see her turn her back to me and walk out.

Not soon after, Mother approaches me from behind and places a hand on my shoulder. "She'll be back."

"I don't know if I want her to come back."

"Yes, you do. I know what you feel. I've seen the way you look at her."

I glance at her over my shoulder. "She's *his* daughter."

Her lips quirk up into a soft smile. "Love knows no bounds."

And just like that, she's managed to completely unhinge me.

Her wise words always manage to dig deep into my skin and make me rethink my resolve.

Even if I wanted to, just to see the look on his face, I could never kill her.

Even if it means he and his men will kill me first.

But if she only knew the truth ... she'd kill me herself.

CHAPTER SIXTEEN

Nine years ago

I'm the bad guy.

I knew that when I began dealing, and I know it now.

I know full well what I chose when I signed up for it. When I decided to shake people down and beat them up just for a bit of money. When I began to kill.

I knew every step of the way that I was as bad as could be, but I didn't care. Never do.

All I wanted was recognition. Someone to tell me that I finally made it. That I was the guy who they all wanted.

Except it's never enough.

Nothing I do will ever make this gang happy.

They'll always want more, more, more. To the point of making me do the impossible. Something unspeakable.

Something that creates a point of no return.

That one night ... when I broke my own rules ... that was when I turned my back on the gang.

The moment a woman crossed my path. A woman who didn't know any better. A woman who wasn't supposed to be there.

Yet she was.

And the moment I pulled the trigger, I already knew I made the biggest mistake of my life.

I didn't want her to die. It was never part of the plan.

But I was always taught to protect myself at all cost. To shoot before you look. To eliminate the threat before it even exists.

But she was never a threat.

She was simply ... there.

An unlucky chance of fate.

It was her house I was robbing, but I was told no one would be home. And when I found out I wasn't, I fired a shot without even looking to see who it was.

A fatal mistake.

It was a woman.

And she was pregnant.

In my shame, I ran to her body and began to pump her chest in the hopes of bringing her back to life, but it was to no avail. She never even breathed. Not a single whimper. Except the one coming from me.

I tucked my gun back into its holster and grabbed her arms, dragging her out of the room. I hauled her all the way back to my car and shoved her inside. In the dead of night, I drove with tears streaming down my face.

There were two golden rules. Never kill a woman and

never hurt a child. And I did both.

My mistake will haunt me for the rest of my life.

Ten minutes.

That's how much time has passed between then and now as I park my car in an alley and pull the body out. A trail of blood flows on the ground as I haul her body across the road. I don't know what to do. Where to go.

I can't go back to the gang. It's done. It's over.

I've hurt enough people and caused enough pain.

This is where I crossed the line, and I refuse to go back.

But I have no friends. No family. No one to go to for help.

Except for one place.

The church where I grew up. The same place I'm hauling a dead body to right now.

But the closer I get, the more my guilt weighs down on my soul, and dragging her feels more difficult with every step I take. How can I ever make this right?

In these past few years, I've lost touch with myself. With the church and Margaret. And with God.

How can I ever face Him now?

And still, somehow, for some reason, I find the will to persist as I haul the dead pregnant woman up the slippery stairs of the church.

Rain falls down on my face as I fight to get her to the top, but I don't give up. Not until I'm right in front of the door where I collapse in agony over what I've done. My breathing is ragged and my muscles hurt, but it's nothing compared to my heart.

At least I can be sure the rain will wash away any trail of the blood.

I bang on the wooden door as hard as I can, like a final cry for help, and within minutes, my prayer is answered.

As the door opens and light pours out, inviting me in like the end of a tunnel leading to heaven, I stare up into the face of judgment.

"Help me ... please ..." I mutter, tears and rain streaming down my face.

At first, Margaret's silent as she eyeballs the woman in my arms.

But then she closes her eyes, sighs, and holds out her hand.

I gratefully take it, and she helps me up from the ground. Together, we drag the body into the church, and she slams the doors shut. When she turns, she takes a deep breath and asks, "What did you do?"

I shake my head and whisper, "I'm so sorry, Mother. I didn't know where else to go."

"Is she alive?" she asks, approaching me and the body.

"No."

She sighs again, looking back and forth between me and the body.

"It must be kept a secret. Someone will come looking for her."

"I know," she says, and she passes me. "Come."

I quickly grasp the body by the arms and drag it all the way with me as I follow her to the back of the church and then outside. I place the body on the frigid ground and let out a few breaths.

Suddenly, Carl appears in the doorway, staring at us and the body.

A moment of silence passes, and I wonder if he's going

to run and call the cops.

"Help us …" I mutter.

He licks his lips, glances over his shoulder, and then rushes toward me.

I breathe a sigh of relief as Mother grabs two shovels from a shed in the far end of the yard and hands one to each of us.

"Dig." Her voice stern, as I remember it to be.

Without question, I take it and start digging a hole together with Carl.

I don't complain.

I ignore the pain.

I refuse to cry or get mad.

After all, I did this. I should be the one to carry the burden.

Under Mother's watch, we dig a hole deep enough to bury the body and cover it with earth. The same place where I'll bury my sins and keep them hidden forever.

Right before her hand disappears into the ground, I quickly grasp the ring that was on her finger, and I put it on my own finger. I need to wear this as a reminder of what I've done. So I'll never forget this body lying here in the ground.

When it's done, I place the shovel in the dirt and stare at the soil in front of us. The woman is gone, but this night will always remain.

I gaze at Mother and then at Carl.

"This will be our secret," I say. "You know that, right?"

Carl nods.

"If you go to the police now, you're an accomplice. You helped me bury her."

"I know," he says. "But I'll always help you."

I nod. Even after all these years, he's still fiercely loyal. The little boy who grew up to be quite the reliable kid. Surprising, to say the least. And now we're bound to each other.

"You will *never* go back to those people," Margaret suddenly snaps, her arms folded. "Understood?"

I nod, looking her straight in the eyes. I don't want to insult her by looking away even though I fear her judgment more than anything in this entire world.

"You belong to this church. Agreed?"

"Yes, Mother."

"Good. Because this is one debt you won't easily fulfill. But you can begin by cleaning up the blood." She points at the trail behind me, leading all the way back into the church.

I lick my lips and nod again. I'm not going to go against her wishes. I fucked up, and she saved me yet again.

After all this time, all these fuck-ups, the betrayal … and she still helped me.

There's no way I can ever repay her for that.

But I will try.

I will try with every last breath in my lungs and beating of my heart.

I will work toward gaining her trust.

I will learn to love this church and God once more.

After forsaking this church for so long only for a bit of recognition, I owe that to her. To myself. To God.

I will repent.

***

Now

My eyes open and I'm instantly awake. God, what an awful nightmare.

Sighing, I look at the clock. No use in going back to sleep because it will be time to wake up soon. Besides, I hate to bring up more memories, and they always come when I go to sleep sober.

I stare at the ceiling, wondering what the hell I'm doing with my life. I can't help but think about Laura and everything that happened. After I had found out she was *his* daughter, I felt the rage flowing through my veins.

Was I wrong to send her away?

It was ruthless, yes, but I did it for the right reasons.

At least, that's what I keep telling myself.

A knock on my door pulls me from my thoughts, and I sit up straight to see who it is. Mother peeks around the corner and asks, "Can I come in?"

I nod, and she pushes the door open further.

"I just wanted to … talk." She seems hesitant as she approaches me, and I wonder what's bothering her.

"Is it the mess in the hall? I'll clean it up."

"No, it's not that." She frowns.

"The broken benches? I'll ask Carl to buy new ones."

"No, it's not about the mess those two boys made," she says, and she sits down on the edge of my bed.

I sigh. "This isn't about Laura, right?"

"Are you sure you want her gone?"

"No, but it's for the best." With furrowed brows, I look away, not feeling up to this conversation. "Please don't try to change my mind."

"If I showed you something, would you be willing to fight?"

"Why? Does it matter?" I bark.

"Yes. Because, despite those filthy things you did on the altar, I still care about you. I care about your well-being. Don't you know that? I want you to be happy."

I chew on my lip. "Of course, I do …"

"Then you know I only want what's best for you. And that girl clearly makes you happy. You've been drinking much less since you met her, and you've finally started smiling again." She grabs my chin and makes me look at her. "Frank, this is important."

I don't know what to say, but then she opens her mouth again. "I wasn't sure if I should show this to you, but I decided your heart was more important than the hope you might be at peace again."

She rummages in her pocket and pulls out something that looks like a card. "One of the guys who came in and ruined the church dropped this on the floor."

She holds it up. It's a photograph.

Showing the image of my little boy way back when.

And my world feels like it's come to a stop.

I snatch it from her hand and gawk at his picture. I haven't seen this in ages. Actually, the last time was in my old home, which I haven't been to since I left it all those years ago. I couldn't stomach going back to that place with my whole family gone.

But how the fuck did those assholes get their hands on this?

Mother places her hand on top of mine and says, "If you want to go, I won't stop you."

I nod. "I need to find out more …"

"I know," she says, smiling softly.

I smile back. "Thank you. You don't know what this means to me." I stare at the picture in my hand, and I can feel the anger flowing through my body.

This isn't just an old picture of my son.

It's a call to action, and it ignites a fire in me that I'm not willing to put out.

It makes me wanna go after those fuckers and finally get my revenge.

"This is what you need," she says. "I tried to ignore it for so long, but now I finally understand," she says, still holding my hand. "But you have to promise me you'll come back."

"I will," I reply.

She leans in and presses a kiss to my cheeks. "Good luck."

Then she turns and leaves again. When the door closes, I jump out of bed and grab some clothes I haven't worn in ages and put them on. I straighten my cuffs, position the collar and tie exactly right, and put the cross around my neck. Along the very bottom of the wall, I pull out a loose brick and remove the knife I'd hidden there long ago, tucking it into my pocket.

From the corner of my eye, I spot the bottles of liquor right below my bed. A nuisance, and not what I want to remember. I'm a different person now. I can feel it in my veins.

So I grab the bottles and pour them out in the sink then discard the empty bottles. It feels good to finally get rid of it. A new start with a clean slate is exactly what I needed. And now that I've finally got a goal in life again, I'm not going to let anything get in my way.

Right before I go out, I take one last look at myself in the mirror while holding up the picture of my son. I pick up the Bible on my nightstand and open the pages until I find the verse I'm looking for.

2 Samuel 22:38 – "I pursued my enemies and destroyed them, And I did not turn back until they were consumed."

Dear God, give me strength in this time of need. Because now, more than ever, I'll need you by my side.

CHAPTER SEVENTEEN

Chewing on a piece of straw, I've been sitting on this bench a few feet away from Chuck's Bar for a few good hours now. It's not without reason. I'm waiting for a particularly stinky guy by the name of Gunboy or Pimpled Little Shit. I've beaten his ass twice now, and I think it's time for a third.

Maybe this time, he'll learn his lesson.

With a smug grin on my face, I keep a watchful eye, waiting for the little turd to arrive. I know it's the middle of the day, but that never stopped the assholes from showing up uninvited. They did it before; they'll certainly try again.

I just hope Chuck will let me have them.

I mean they've fucked up his place and scared away his

customers, so I doubt he'll be happy to see them. Not that it'll stop them from messing shit up again, which is where I come in to play.

And the moment I see a familiar car roll up and a certain Pizzaface come out, I murmur, "Gotcha."

Whistling, I get up from the bench and stroll to the bar, precisely the place he's heading. I'm only five minutes behind, which is the perfect amount of time for an ambush that'll make the pimples drop from his face. Maybe he'll be a prettier boy when I'm done with him. I'll smack those pimples right off.

Spitting out the straw, I look at the picture of my son one last time before I cross the street.

Once again, a preacher and a criminal walk into a bar. My life is just one giant joke.

Especially when I see Gunboy turn his head toward me and watch as his eyes almost pop out at the sight of me standing in the doorway.

Chuck frowns as he glares at both of us and growls, "Nuh-uh, no sir, not today." He snatches away the glass he just put down for Pimpleface and barks, "Get out."

"Fuck," the shithead says.

"Yeah, fuck's about right." I cross my arms. "If you don't come with me now, I'm gonna fuck your life up so badly that you won't be able to shit for weeks."

He jumps off his seat and scrambles away, trying to hide in a corner, but that ain't going to save his ass. No way. He's mine.

"Frank!" Chuck yells as I approach the boy. "Not again."

"Sorry, Chuck, but I got a bit of a thing going on with

this one."

Right as I grab his collar, Chuck roars, "Take it outside, for crying out loud."

I roll my eyes and sigh, still holding Gunboy who's whimpering with his eyes closed. "C'mon, fuckwad," I growl, dragging him with me. "See ya, Chuck," I say, as I walk past him.

"Rather not," he muses, making me chuckle as I haul the boy outside.

"Let me go!" he cries out as I pull him along to an alley not far ahead.

"Shut your trap," I bark, glancing over my shoulder. "You and I have business."

"I didn't do fuck nothing," he says.

"Who are you trying to fool? The Queen of England?" I spit, as I throw him into the dead-end alley. "Do I look like an old turd to you?"

He scowls. "I should've killed you when I had the chance."

I raise a brow. "Oh, please, like you *ever* had a chance."

When he tries to run, I shove him right back into his corner and growl, "Sit." Because he's a fucking dog, and he needs to listen.

"You think you could get away with firing a gun in my fucking church?"

"Look, I'm sorry, okay? It was just a job."

"A job? To scare the living shit out of my mother?"

"Your mother?" He frowns. "That old hag?"

I pick up a rock and throw it at his face, making him yowl in pain. It leaves a big red mark, and a bloody streak across his forehead. "Learn some fucking manners, will ya?"

"Jesus Christ! What is wrong with you?" he screams.

"What's wrong with *me*?" I point at myself and snort. "I wasn't the one pointing a gun at a preacher."

"I already told you it was a job!"

I come closer and corner him. "Who gave it to you?"

He crawls back against the wall. "Some dude in the gang. I don't know his name."

"Lie." I pick him up by his collar and hold out my fist. "See this pretty here?" I glance at my knuckles. "They're eager to say hi to your face."

"No, no, please."

"Then talk," I growl, and I pull the picture of my son from my pocket. "You asshats dropped this in my church. How did you get this?"

He looks at it in confusion. "I don't know."

I shake him. "I'm not playing games. Tell me. Now!"

"All right, all right, I got it from the same guy who gave me the job. Told me to go find you and give you a good scare."

"You mean beat the shit out of me."

He shrugs. "Whatever."

"What about the picture?"

"I dunno; they just wanted me to drop it so you'd see it. They didn't tell me why."

"Who? Give me a name."

"Sergio from the butcher's shop in the next town. You know."

Yeah, I know the place.

Grinding my teeth, I mull it over for a second. "Is he there right now?"

"I dunno; I'm only a gang member. I don't know

nothing," he says.

His innocent act gets me so worked up that I shove him back against the wall. "Listen up, fuckface. You're going to stop doing work for those gangs right now."

"What?" His jaw drops. "What the fuck? You've gotta be joking, right?"

"I'm not messing around. I'm done with you and your pal shitting on my neighborhood. You want money? Go find some honest work like the rest of us."

"Fuck you," he spits. "I need this."

"No. You need the money, but you're just not willing to work for it," I snarl. "What a lazy piece of shit you are."

"Lazy? Fuck you; I'm not lazy," he growls, pushing me away. "Who are you anyway? Some goddamn preacher doesn't know shit about the street."

I grasp his collar and shove him right back against the wall. "I've been in your position. I *was* a gang member before you could even piss straight. Don't think you know everything, you little shithead. Have some respect for your elders."

He laughs. "Elders. Right."

"Shut up," I growl. "You don't get to laugh. I'm sick of your shit. You'd better not show your face in Chuck's bar *or* my church ever again."

"Or what?" He raises a brow, challenging me.

Since he's asking for it, I might as well show him.

So I make a fist and pummel him right in the balls.

He squeals like a girl, grabbing his nuts. When I move away, he falls to his knees, rolling onto his side as he grimaces.

"Or that," I reply, enjoying the sight of seeing him roll

around in the dirt. "That's only the warning shot. I've got plenty more up my sleeve. Wanna try me?"

"No ..." he hisses. His throat's still clamped shut, probably from the pain surging through his body.

"You sure?" I smile. "I'm never opposed to a bit of kinky fisticuffs when the occasion arises. Maybe you could invite your buddy too; that way we can see if you actually have any balls underneath all that bullshit."

"Fuck you!" he curses as I turn around.

I wave and laugh as I walk away. "Yeah, good luck with that!"

Time to go to my next victim.

However, right as I pass by Chuck's Bar, I hear a familiar voice call out for me.

"Frank?"

I stop and turn to see Laura standing in Chuck's doorway. It looks like she came running out after she saw me.

"What are you doing?" she asks.

"I could ask you the same," I reply, pointing at the building behind her. "Drinking in the middle of the day? That's unlike you."

She puts her hand on her side. "I wasn't. I work here now. My shift starts in a couple of minutes."

"Oh ..." Well, that's a new one. Never expected Chuck to hire girls. Then again ... it sounds just like something that old dirtbag would love.

I shrug. "Well, good luck." I turn and start walking again, but she follows me and grabs my arm, making me stop again.

"Wait. Tell me what you're doing."

"Why?"

She makes a face. "I know you're doing something stupid."

"Stupid? Who, me?" I raise a brow.

"Stop joking." She playfully slaps my arm. "You've been acting weird since those two dudes showed up at the church."

I swallow, being reminded of what they said in church … and that she's Julio's daughter.

"It's not something that concerns you." I try to shake her off, but she won't let go.

"Yes, it does. I'm worried about you."

"Don't be," I reply. "I'll be fine."

"So you admit it …"

"Admit what?"

She narrows her eyes. "You're up to something."

I snort. "It's nothing good, so don't ask."

"Are you going to hurt people?"

I nod.

"You can't just … kill people, Frank," she says under her breath.

"No?" I retort. "Watch me."

"There must be another way," she says.

"They had a picture of my son," I say through gritted teeth. "It's personal now."

Again, I try to leave, and she clings to me, making me turn around and sigh. "You can't stop me from doing this, Laura. No one can."

"I don't want you to get hurt." I stand still as she wraps her arms around me and impulsively hugs me. I'm overwhelmed by her warmth even after the cold shoulder I gave her. How can I not feel guilty?

"This is crazy ..." she murmurs.

I agree. I don't want to walk away. I don't want her to stop. But I know I have to do this. "Maybe crazy is the only way I can function right."

"I don't believe that."

I don't know how to respond, so I don't. Anything I say is wrong, and we both know it. Besides, I don't want to get into it right now. I've got other things on my mind, and I think she can tell.

She pulls away and says, "Give me your phone."

I frown. "Why?"

"Just do it."

Reluctantly, I hand it over, wondering what she wants with it. She pushes a few buttons and then hands it back to me. "You've got my number now, so call me if you get into trouble."

"Okay." Well, that was surprising.

She hugs me again, almost squeezing the air out of me. As she lets go, she rubs her lips and says, "I'll drop by the church later. See if you're okay."

It's not a question, so I guess I have no choice in the matter.

When I turn around and start walking again, she yells, "Will you get hurt?"

"I'll try not to," I say.

"Be careful."

Her comment makes me smile, and I don't fucking know why. I shouldn't feel this way about his fucking daughter ... yet I do. Goddamn this fucking heart of mine.

CHAPTER EIGHTEEN

I kick open the door to the butcher's shop, not giving a shit that customers are inside. "Everybody get out!" I yell.

People seem confused at first, but when I rummage in my pocket, they scramble for the door. I'm not carrying a gun, but the mere idea that I might makes people run, which is exactly what I want. Chaos.

With furrowed brows, the shop owner barges past the cash register and toward me. "What the fuck do you think you're doing?" he growls.

I don't move one inch as he stands right in my face, towering above me. "I'm looking for Sergio."

"Don't know him," the man growls, folding his arm.

"Of course, you don't, but I know he's here."

He sneers, "What the fuck do you want?"

"I need to have a little chat with him," I reply, narrowing my eyes.

"About what?" He squints too now.

I really don't want to have more casualties than necessary, so I decide to take it down another route. With a wicked grin on my face, I say, "Oh, you know ... boy talk."

"Boy talk?" He raises a brow.

"Yeah ... he left his dildo at my place."

His jaw drops, but nothing comes out except for a little gasp. He seems flabbergasted, so I grasp the opportunity to peer over his shoulder at the door in the back where I see a guy flash by.

"I also wanted to ask him if he could bring condoms next time," I add, grinning as I watch him freeze.

"Uh ..."

"You wanna hear more?" I ask.

"No, no, he's right up there," the guy says, pointing at the door I was looking at.

I place a hand on his shoulder, and he quickly steps aside. I pass him and say, "Thanks."

He wipes his shirt precisely where I touched him, which makes me snort, but I have to keep my composure. Using the gay card is such a fun thing to do around homophobes.

I enter through the door and carefully look around before closing it behind me, twisting the lock to keep everyone out. I don't want anyone to interrupt.

I knock on the door to see if he hears me, but he doesn't. Instead, the guy actually leaves his store and walks away, just like that. Crazy, but it's true. Guess he doesn't wanna get involved in the dirty game he knows is about to go down. Although it's gonna be a different kind of dirty than he probably thought.

I shrug. Not my monkeys, not my circus.

I look around and take in my surroundings. From the look of this room, I'm almost certain it's soundproof. Probably because my business isn't the only dirty business going down here.

It's cool in here too, which isn't surprising, considering meat is hanging from the hooks and lying on the racks. Shivering, I wait until I hear a sound coming from the back. In a small office up ahead, a man's standing in the doorway with a cup of coffee in his hand. Rummaging in my pocket, I take out the knife and hold it tightly as I approach. He turns to look at the television hanging from the wall, and it makes me stop in my tracks.

Why?

Because I recognize his face.

He's the same man I saw six years ago … the day they took my wife.

He hauled her away from my house.

I could crush the knife in my hand right now.

Instead, I tiptoe toward him, trying not to make a sound as I approach him from behind. The closer I get, the more rage spills into my body and makes this freezer feel like a goddamn volcano. But I'm keeping it together … until I'm right behind him and put my knife against his throat.

"Don't. Move," I hiss in his ear.

The man is utterly quiet, his lips almost sewn together as he trembles in place.

"Put the cup down," I say.

He does what I ask, placing it on a table just inches away.

"Please don't," he pleads.

"Give me one good reason …" I hiss.

"I'll do whatever you want," he says.

"I don't want you to do anything." My blood feels like it's boiling right now.

"You want money?" he asks.

"Shut up," I say, pushing the blade further into his skin until I can feel drops of warm blood spill over my hand.

"You know why I'm here."

"No, I don't," he says.

"Listen to my voice … recognize it?" I murmur into his ear. "You've heard it before … roaring out loud the moment you took her … six years ago."

Out of nowhere, he reaches for the knife and smashes my hand away from his throat, causing it to drop to the floor. He immediately turns and smacks me in the face, making me tumble backward.

"You should've stayed a fucking drunk," Sergio growls, coming closer.

I adjust my jaw and wipe the blood from my lips then I retaliate with a fist to his stomach. However, he takes it like a pro, even laughing as my hand is still against his belly. "Think that'll hurt me? I've felt much, much worse."

Grunting, I swiftly elbow him in the chin, making him stumble backward.

"You took my fucking wife!" I scream, and I punch him in the nose. "You killed her!"

He laughs again as he takes a repeated beating to the face. "You think that's all we did to her?"

"Shut up!" I scream.

We're fighting like crazy dogs in a freezer filled with meat, and I'm a hundred percent sure one of us will end up on those racks.

Why?

Because I'm not walking away from here until he's dead.

He punches me in the gut so hard I stumble backward.

"You should've heard her. 'Frank, Frank, please help me.'" He imitates my wife's voice in such a degrading way that I lose my shit.

I ram into him with my head and shove him all the way into the back of his office, slamming both of us into the wall. He coughs as he tumbles to the floor with me on top of him. My hands twist around his neck, and I squeeze as hard as I can.

"You took my family away from me!" I spit in his face.

When he's almost blue, I release him and slap him hard. "Tell me where he is!"

"Who? Your son?" He laughs again, so I grab the knife lying on the floor and jam it into his cheek, piercing his mouth.

He screams as blood pours onto his tongue, and I pull out the knife and hold it to his throat again. "Tell me where Julio is," I say. "I know he moved, so don't give me that bullshit old address."

He spits out the blood and smiles like an idiot. "Why did you come here, preacher?"

I pull the picture out of my pocket and show it to him. "One of your minions dropped this in my church. It wasn't an accident."

Sergio chuckles like a lunatic. "You should've stayed

away from her, Jesus Boy!"

"Stayed away from Laura? No, that's not why you and your pussy gang threatened me." I shake my head. "This picture has nothing to do with it, and you still wanted me to see it. Why?"

"Yeah ... to fuck with your head!" He spits blood in my face.

So I cut his arm and make him bleed as retribution.

"Motherfucker!" he squeals.

He tries to fight me off, but I push him down by sitting on top of him. "This is your last chance, asshole. Tell me exactly where Julio is or I'll cut you again and again and again until you bleed to death."

At first, his eyes glance toward a few papers on his desk, which makes me think he's got the address hidden here somewhere.

But then he turns his head back to me and shows me his bloody teeth. "Fuck you!"

I shrug and sigh. "Suit yourself."

I cut into his arms, his chest, and his legs, and then punch him in the gut so hard he gulps for air. More blood pours out from his skin, and he groans in pain. I let him loose and get up, and he vomits over the floor. Guess my punch was nauseating enough.

"Disgusting," I murmur as I focus on the papers and search for the address.

I throw aside everything that doesn't matter until I find what I'm looking for ... Julio's new home.

"He'll kill you, you know," he mutters, still coughing up blood.

I cock my head at his comment. "Not if I kill him first."

His frown makes me smile.

But then more shit pours from his mouth. "Your kid cried so much … I wanted to strangle him in the car."

"Keep your mouth shut, or I'll cut out your tongue too," I snarl, pointing the knife at him.

He laughs. "You think I'm scared of you? I live under Julio's rule; there is *nothing* you can do to me that'll make me fear you more than I do him."

"Maybe you should've chosen a different path then," I say. "Just like I did when you took my family away from me."

"God won't save us," he spits. "You think He cares about any of us?"

"He cares enough to give me my spirit to fight you and your pussy gang," I reply.

"Ha … he should've given you the spirit to run faster when your lady and your kid were being dragged away."

"What did you say?" My eye begins to twitch, and my grip on the knife grows stronger again.

"You heard me." He coughs. "You could've saved them if only you were faster. But you didn't. And now they're dead because of you."

I rush to him and grab him by the collar while pointing the knife at him. "Say that again; I dare you."

He smiles as he slyly whispers, "Did you know we made your boy listen to her scream as we took her, one by one?"

That's it.

I roar as I shove the knife into his hand.

He squeals out loud, the sound only interrupted by choking noises as I drag him along his collar back into the freezer. While he squirms on the floor, I lift him up and push him ... straight into a hook hanging from the wall.

More blood comes from his mouth, and he yowls in pain as I pull the chains so his body rises from the ground. Then I take my knife from his hand and jam it into his chest, sliding it down toward his belly, so he bleeds out completely.

It won't kill him right away, though.

No, his death will be slow and agonizing; he'll slowly bleed out in a cold frozen void between the pigs where no one will ever hear him scream.

CHAPTER NINETEEN

Covered in blood, I step out of my car in the middle of the night and stumble into the church. My limbs feel heavy, and my heart is burdened with yet another murder. But I don't regret a thing.

That motherfucker had it coming for him.

I push the doors open and slide inside. Luckily, no one's inside. At least, not from what I can see.

Rubbing my forehead, I make my way to the altar, wiping away the blood from my face when I see the statue in front of me. There, I fall to my knees and make the sign of the cross on my chest.

"God … please forgive me for my sins," I murmur, and I grab the cross hanging from my neck and press a kiss to it.

Blood drips down to the floor as I let out a sigh and

stare up at His image, welcoming His judgment. I know full well what I did ... that I committed a heinous crime. But if God will not punish those responsible for my misery, then I will hand out the pain.

Suddenly, I feel something on my shoulder. In a moment of fear, I pull my knife and almost lash out.

I barely manage to stop myself from slicing Laura.

I stare into her eyes as the knife drops to the floor.

Oh, God. Oh, fuck.

I almost hurt her.

"I'm sorry," I mutter.

She smashes her lips together and shakes her head. I wonder if she'll run. If she's afraid of me. She should be.

I'm covered in the blood of my enemies.

I still feel like an animal after killing the gang member working for her dad.

She knows he and I have business now ... and she's in the middle of it all.

Still, she stays, unmoving, the look on her face as certain as it's always been.

But I can't look her in the eyes the same way I could before. My gaze falls to her feet as the thought crosses my mind that I could use her as leverage. But I could never risk her life.

I couldn't even touch her like that.

The moment the knife almost cut her ... I haven't experienced terror like that in ages. A feeling I haven't felt in years. The last time was when ...

I shake my head and rub my lips together. The metallic taste of blood enters my mouth, reminding me of my sins.

"I killed someone," I mutter as my eyes slowly rise until

they meet hers, which shine with endless compassion, and the guilt rushes through my veins.

She swallows, visibly constrained. "I can tell."

I look at my arms and hands. I look like I've bathed in blood.

She drops to her knees right in front of me and tilts my chin up. "You don't have to tell me anything. God is the only one who can judge us."

I nod, and she puts her shoulder under my arm, helping me up.

I groan as pain shoots through my stomach, probably from my fight with Sergio.

"Are you hurt?" she asks, wrapping her hand around my waist.

"No, I'm okay," I say. "It's only a few bruises. No big deal."

She helps me to my room, but when I glance over my shoulder and see the trail of blood behind me, I say, "I'll have to clean that up."

"Don't worry about it," she says, guiding me inside. "I'll do it."

She turns on the faucet and wets two cloths, handing one to me. "Clean yourself up a little. I'll be right back." She leaves with the other wet cloth, probably to clean up the mess I made.

While she's gone, I take off the ring around my finger and place it by the sink. Then I look at myself in the mirror, disgusted with what I see. I wipe away what I can, but the cloth is quickly drenched in blood, and adding water doesn't help one bit.

When she comes back, I glance over my shoulder right

when she turns on the light.

She stops in her tracks, clearing her throat as she focuses her gaze on me. Then she closes the door. The way the left side of her lip quirks up makes me suddenly aware of the fact that we're alone. As she approaches me, I grasp the sink, worried that I might hurt her. I'm still tormented by my own need to inflict pain on those who did me wrong, and for some reason, it's hard to distinguish friend from foe.

She carefully peels my bloody fingers loose and pulls me along with her into the shower. She turns it on, and warm water pours down on my clothes and skin. Blood mixes with the water, creating an eerie color, but she doesn't seem fazed.

Instead, she only comes closer, running her fingers through my dirty hair, cupping my face. Testosterone is still raging through my body, and my hormones go on full tilt the moment she rips open my shirt and pushes it off my arms.

I love feeling her hands on my muscles. What can I say? Underneath this rugged beast is still a man made of flesh ... and his flesh is getting stiff as a board.

With a firm hand, she tugs on my belt, pulling me closer as she pulls it out of the loops. I watch her, meticulously licking my lips as she throws the belt away and unbuttons my pants. In one go, she pulls down both my pants and boxer shorts, leaving me naked and with a rock-hard dick.

One quick glance and she's grinning.

Of course, she is.

I smile, shaking my head, which is still covered in blood. This is really fucked up.

"Why are you doing this?" I ask, unsure how to respond

to her warmth.

"I've seen men like you before," she says.

"What … covered in blood?" I reply. "Or with a raging hard-on?"

She smiles. "Both."

I raise a brow. "At the same time?"

Her smile broadens. "That's a first."

Laughing, I close my eyes and let the water pour onto my face, washing away the blood with my hands. Her hands wrap around my neck, and her head leans on my shoulder, her tits pushing against my chest.

"I'm glad you came back," she whispers in my ear.

Goose bumps scatter on my skin as I look down into her pristine eyes, and at that moment, I realize I'm starting to fall in love with the daughter of my enemy.

God, I'm so fucking screwed.

She leans away and grabs my hand, placing it on her soaked blouse. She guides my hand across her tit, and my cock responds with a bounce. As she bites her lip, she pushes my hand further down until it's between her legs, where she squeezes tight.

That's it.

I've tried to fight temptation, but with her standing here in my shower and her clothes completely soaked, it's impossible.

And as I'm overtaken by lust, I grab her waist and push her against the wall, smothering her mouth with mine.

I don't care what anyone thinks or what I should think.

She's mine, and nobody will take her away from me.

Not even my own need for revenge.

My tongue flicks along her lips, eager to take her right

here and now. Arousal courses through my veins, a remnant of the power I felt mere minutes ago when I murdered one of my most hated enemies. And now, I'm taking it all out on her.

When she raises her hand, I grab her wrist and pin it to the wall. I nudge her legs apart and make her feel the hard-on she caused. She doesn't seem to mind as she grins against my lips.

I use the opportunity to take her mouth with my tongue, swiveling around hers. I want her so badly; I can't control my urges anymore. She tastes so damn good; it's like a drug to me.

My hands travel down to her tits, and I pinch her nipples, rolling them around between my fingers. She moans into my mouth, and my dick pulses against her pussy with greed.

I swiftly spin her around and shove my hand between her legs, lifting her skirt and claiming her.

"You're mine and no one else's ..." I growl, pulling her panties aside and rubbing her clit.

"I don't want anyone else," she murmurs, parting her legs for me.

I slide my fingers up and down her slit to enjoy the wetness, and I press a kiss to the nape of her neck. "I'm so glad we're on the same page."

She snorts and tilts her head back, allowing me to nibble on her earlobe. "I'm still mad at you, you know ..."

"I know. I chased you away. So let me make it up to you," I whisper, sucking on her skin.

She bites her lip as I bury my finger into her pussy.

"Fuck ..." she mutters.

"Oh, I'll fuck you all right," I groan. "I wanna feel you come like the good little sinful girl you are."

"Are you calling me a little girl?" she retorts.

"Would you prefer good little whore?" I muse. "Because, either way, you're fucking mine."

She grins as I circle her clit. "I'll take either … just keep doing that."

"Oh, I will …" I groan, licking my lips as her clit engorges from my touch. "I'll make this pussy come so hard that you'll beg this preacher to impale you."

"Who's being the whore now?" she quips.

I shove her against the wall, and she gasps from the coldness against her nipples. Then I push my hand between her thighs and prop my dick between her ass cheeks.

"You ready for me, babe?"

"Fuck, yes …" she moans at the same time I push the tip in.

In one go, I push in completely, burying my cock deep inside her. She holds her breath as I pull out, and when I thrust in again, another loud moan comes from her mouth. I cup her pussy with one hand while fucking her, and with my other hand, I form a knot in her hair and twist, pulling her head back.

"Fuck," she hisses, almost like she can't handle me.

"Shouldn't have come into the shower with me," I growl. "Now you'll feel my rage."

"Rage?"

"You think I come off killing people easily?" I mutter, banging her hard. "Fuck no."

I ram into her again, this time putting every inch of myself inside her until I hear her squeal. "Come," I growl.

"Milk me."

I spank her ass and use her waist as handles as I thrust into her. As I flick her clit, her legs wobble, and she can barely stay upright. I hold her in place as she tiptoes around my large cock, barely able to keep up.

She lets out a big moan, and her muscles clamp around my length, wetness pouring out of her. Fuck, it feels so good that I come too.

Howling like a fucking animal, I go in balls deep and pump my seed into her, again and again. When I pull out, my dick is still hard, even though her pussy is creamed. As my jizz drips out of her, she leans her face against the wall and takes large gulps of air.

"Fuck ... you're so damn dirty," she murmurs out of breath.

Damn right I am, and I'll prove it to her right now.

I twist her around and put my hands on her shoulder, pushing her down to her knees. "Open your mouth," I growl as I grab a fistful of her hair.

When her lips part, I shove my cock inside and start pumping again. She looks a little dazed, shocked even that I'm fucking her mouth, but I don't care. I want this. I *need* this. So I'm going to take it like the greedy motherfucker I am.

With fervor, I thrust deep into her throat, making her gag. I love the sounds she makes and the way she looks up at me with those pristine blue eyes, begging me to come again. I can tell she likes it because her hand is between her legs.

Her tongue rolls around my dick as I push inside, and I tilt my head and close my eyes to enjoy the feeling. God, how I fucking love what she does with her filthy mouth, and for now, that's enough for me.

I groan and grasp her hair tighter, using it as reins so I can fuck her even harder.

She doesn't seem to mind.

In fact, I think she's starting to like it, judging by her needy gaze.

"You're so pretty when you let me fuck you," I murmur, holding her head with both hands. "But you're even prettier with my cum inside your mouth."

She eagerly licks my cock, and it bounces up and down against her throat, making her gag again.

I push harder to hear that sound again, and I pinch her nose with my fingers just to feel her muscles tighten. "Take it," I growl. "Show me how filthy you are."

When I let go, she gasps for air, and I pull out to let her breathe.

"Fuck …" she mutters. "You weren't kidding."

"This is the one time I'm not," I reply, grabbing her chin and pulling her mouth open. "And I mean it when I say I'm going to coat your tongue with my cum."

She smiles and bites her lip at the same time, making me even hornier.

Goddamn, this woman. She'll be the death of me.

I push my cock back inside and go hard and fast, not giving a shit about how wrong it is. She spits on my length, and I use it as lube to slip in and out easier. When I'm in deep again, I pinch her nose again, forcing her to feel my length down her throat.

Three more thrusts and I'm done for.

"Make yourself come," I groan as my cock explodes in

her mouth.

Her pleading eyes almost roll into the back of her head as she brings herself to what looks like a delicious orgasm.

My seed jets into the back of her throat, and I hold her jaw as she struggles to keep it inside. "Swallow it all ..." I mutter as she breathes raggedly through her nose.

She nods, and when her tongue rolls, I push in and out again to make sure she licks it all up. When I'm sated, I swipe my thumb along her lips. She grabs my finger and tugs it into her mouth, licking it until every bit of evidence is gone.

She's still on her knees in front of me, and with the hot water pouring down on my skin, I finally realize what kind of a dirty angel she is.

She's *my* dirty angel, and no amount of anger can ever replace that wantonness I feel when I'm around her.

I smile and cup her face. "Thank you," I say.

Because she's all I needed to have right now, and I'm so damn grateful that she came.

Literally and figuratively.

CHAPTER TWENTY

We lie down in my bed, and I pull the blanket over us both. I wrap my arm around her and turn off the light. I asked her to stay tonight. Not because I'm weak, but because I think we both need each other's comfort right now.

Her fingers gently play with the necklace cradled between her tits. It's a cross ... and the moment I touch her hand, she flinches.

"Sorry," she mumbles.

"Don't be. You keep touching that. I was just curious."

"Oh ... yeah, it's special. To me, anyway."

"How come?" I ask.

She blows out a short breath. "My mother gave it to me

when I was young. Said that I could always find her there, tucked away between the silver."

I smile and plant a kiss between her shoulder blades. "That's a nice gesture."

"Hmm."

I stare at the sink where our clothes are drying off. She crawls closer to me, her warmth filling me with momentary happiness. Is it okay to feel this way? Am I allowed to let go of the past and enjoy what I have?

"Tell me what you're thinking," she asks.

"Nothing," I say, smelling her hair to calm myself down.

"Don't lie. You're tense, and you won't stop sighing."

I sigh again, smiling. She can read me so well it's almost scary.

"You're worried about those men," she fills in for me. "If they'll keep coming after us."

"I'm worried about how many more I have to kill to be safe."

She swallows. "Those men you were after ... they were my father's men, weren't they?"

I nod against her skin, pressing a kiss between her shoulder blades.

"Do you think he wants you *dead*?"

"He gave them a picture of my son just to make me mad. I think he means business," I reply.

"But you don't have to let him get to you." She glances over her shoulder. "You could run."

"I've already run too many times."

"What then? Are you going to kill all of them?" she asks, turning around in my arms.

"If I have to."

"What about this church? And Margaret?" She leans on her elbow. "Will you just abandon them?"

"I can always come back …"

"How do you know?"

"Because I came back before … back when I was still in a gang myself."

She sighs and lies back down on her pillow, her eyes boring into mine. "Tell me more about your past."

"You don't want to know more, trust me."

"Yes, I do. If we're going to be … *something* … I have the right to know more."

Something.

I wonder if that means what I think it means.

"Like I said, I wasn't just a dealer. I was a murderer too. Whatever the gang asked, it was never too much for me. I did some shit I'm not proud of, and I'd rather forget it all."

"And this gang … were they enemies of my dad's?"

I nod.

She blows out another breath. "So this isn't just about us."

I don't say a word. I don't know what to tell her. And I think she already knows where this is going.

"You can't do it."

"He won't leave us alone," I say.

"But he's my dad."

With furrowed brows, I say, "I know that, but you hated him too, right?"

"Yes, I hate what he's done, but …" Her face darkens. "He's still my dad."

"How can you call a man like that a dad?"

"His blood runs through my veins." She raises her

hands, gazing at them like they're not hers. "I am him as much as he is me."

I grab her wrists and lower them. "That's not true. You are compassionate. Loving. Good." I entwine my fingers through hers, trying to persuade her my way. "Everything he wishes he could be. That's who you are."

"How do you know?"

"I just do." I shrug.

"Hmm." She gazes off into the distance. "Guess I'm more like my mom in that way."

My throat clamps up, and I suddenly find it hard to breathe.

"Still," she continues. "He is my dad. I don't want to ... lose him." She swallows like she's afraid I'm going to kill him.

And that feeling is correct.

"He's everything that's wrong with this world, Laura."

"I know." She rubs her forehead with her hand. "I wish I could pull my dad out of that monster. Like sometimes, I want to separate them, but I can't. He's one and the same. A kind daddy ... and a vicious mobster."

I rub my lips together and say, "Exactly. Someone has to stop him ... and if it's me, then so be it."

She nods a few times and then turns around again, curling up into a ball. I wrap my arm around her and pull her closer to smell her scent again.

"Good night," she whispers.

I'm not sure whether we're on good terms or if she's upset.

But what I do know is that we both need our sleep ... to prepare for what's to come.

***

When morning arrives, she's gone.

Not a single hug or kiss given and not a trace left. Even her clothes are gone, and the room is exactly like it always was. As if she vanished into thin air.

Swallowing, I sit up straight and look around, sighing.

I guess she really was mad about our conversation.

I can't blame her. I would be too if someone said they were going after my father. But she also knows he deserves it, which is why it's such a difficult thing.

I don't want her to be mad at me, though. We should talk this out first before I do anything stupid. So I get dressed and make myself some breakfast. After I've finished eating some good old cereal, I straighten my jacket in the mirror and reach for my ring, but it's gone. Frowning, I stare at the sink for a while as if that's going to help. Must've fallen into some nook or cranny after we put our clothes here.

I shrug and put on my necklace, kissing the cross for good luck before I go out. I'm going to need it because I plan to do something terribly stupid. To make it up to her, I've decided I'm going to cook her dinner. You know like manly men do. With bare hands and bear love.

In my good outfit, I go to the supermarket and put some fresh veggies, cream, cheese, fettuccine, and chicken in my basket. Why? Chicken fucking alfredo, that's why. I've never met a person who doesn't like it. And if they don't … well, then they're not human.

With my basket full of shit, I go to the cash register and

stand in line when I recognize the dude standing in front of me. I cock my head and grin then tap him on the shoulder.

At first, he glances at me with a gangster look in his eyes, like he wants to straight up murder me or something, but then a relaxed smile follows.

"Ricardo," I say, "what a coincidence."

"Hey, dude," he says, giving me a bro-fist.

"How's Sofia doing?" I ask.

He scratches the back of his head. "Who?"

When I make a face, he laughs and punches my arm. "Relax, dude; I'm kidding."

"Sounds about right," I reply. "She dead yet?"

"Nah, bro, 'course not. I'm not that kind of a shitty dad."

I shrug, and now, it's his turn to make a face.

"Dude, look at my basket," he says, holding it up to show me how much he's stuffed it with food. "Does this look like something a shitty dad would do?"

"I dunno. Have you learned how to cook yet?" I raise a brow. "Or do you have some side chick cooking for you now?"

"Tsk," he retorts. "Like I got time for a bird with a baby in my home."

"Right …"

"Hey, see this?" He points at one of the pots in his basket. "That's asparagus, yeah. High-class shit. They don't serve this to babies, do they?" He cocks his head. "Except this badass daddy."

I snort. "I've eaten those; they're not just for rich people."

"What'd you get then?" He peeks in my basket.

"Chicken, huh?"

I pull my basket behind my back, annoyed by his snootiness. "You can do a lot of fancy shit with chicken."

"Oh, yeah? Like what?" he says.

"Chicken alfredo." I purse my lips. "Do you even know what that is?"

"Fuck you, course I do. I grew up eating chicken for breakfast."

I burst out into laughter. "That your momma made for you."

"What? You think I can't cook my own shit?"

I'm still laughing my ass off. "Dude, I've seen you give a baby Cheerios with milk. No way you can cook this shit."

"Bitch, please. I can cook your ass into next week. I don't care what the recipe is."

"Really?" I snort. "I'd love to see you try."

He moves closer. "Oh, you're done for now. It's on …"

"Excuse me?" The lady behind the cash register clears her throat.

He gives me the side-eye then walks ahead and puts his items on the counter while I trail behind him. I watch him lay it all out, giving him stupid looks in between just to annoy him.

It's only then that I notice he's got a brand new tattoo.

It's a barcode … Right below his nape.

I don't know how I missed that. I must be really blind.

"So you got a new tattoo?" I ask.

Ricardo glances at me again, giving me the stink eye, but then he opens his mouth. "Got it last week. Showed a picture of a barcode to my tattoo artist, and he put it right below my hairline. Hurt like a motherfucker, but it's totally worth it."

"How so?"

He raises his brows. "So I can do this."

He slams his head down on the counter, grabs the scanner from the lady's hands, and lets it bleep near his neck. It actually registers.

"Twelve fifty," Ricardo says as he stands up straight, gazing at me with big eyes. Then he bursts out into laughter. "That's what I'm worth."

I don't know why—maybe it's the way he's laughing—but for some reason, I'm laughing too, and I can't stop either. Meanwhile, the cashier looks at us like we've lost our damn minds. I don't blame her. This is one fucked-up dude.

"Sorry, can't help it," he jests, packing up his stuff while I place mine on the counter.

I pat his back. "You always give me a good laugh when I need it."

"Well, that'll be twelve fifty then."

We both burst out into laughter again.

I can barely contain myself as I pay for my stuff and Ricardo walks off with his groceries. "See ya."

Right before he's gone, he turns around and calls out my name. "Hey, Frank! Next week, yeah? Cookout. Me and you." He points at me like he's already made up his mind. No use in arguing with that. Besides, I'm too damn curious to see if he can pull it off. With his twelve fifty tattoo.

Shaking my head, I laugh it off, grab my stuff, thank the cashier, and leave the store.

***

A few minutes later, I knock on her door and wait. It takes a while for someone to come to the door, but it's not Laura.

"What do you want?" It's Bruno.

I smile. "Hey squirt, it's me. Frank."

"Oh, hi!" He opens the door, wearing hippo pajamas. "Sorry, Laura tells me not to open the door to strangers."

"But I'm not a stranger anymore, now am I?" I wink.

"No," he says, grinning. "But Laura isn't home right now."

"Oh … well, that's a shame," I reply, peering over his shoulder to see if he's lying or not, but I don't see anyone. "When do you think she'll be home?"

He shrugs. "She didn't say. I'm watching the house with my brother."

"Can I … come inside real quick?" I ask. "It's just that I was thinking of making you all dinner, and I brought all these delicious things." I lower the bag to show him the goods, and his eyes glimmer with curiosity.

"That looks yummy," he says, and he opens the door a bit more so I can step inside.

"Thanks, bro." I rub his head, messing up his hair.

He grins and says, "Bro? No one ever calls me bro." He seems genuinely excited as if calling him bro makes him feel older or something.

I smile back. "Well, you're my bro now."

"Ah, yes!" He makes a fist pump in the air, making me laugh.

"Dude, why'd you let him in?" Diego scowls at me as he switches the channel on the TV.

"Because he's our friend," Bruno declares.

"Says who?"

"Me."

I grin and high-five Bruno. "Thanks, bro."

Diego rolls his eyes. "Whatever."

"I promise you; I won't be an annoying shithead today," I muse.

"Yeah, right."

"Hey ... I'm trying to do my best here, okay?" I say.

"No, you're trying to get in my sister's pants," he retorts, raising a brow.

"So? Haven't you ever liked a chick?"

"She's my sister," he sneers. "And ew."

"What, don't like girls?"

"Of course, I do," he says. "But not in this house."

"Well ... I do, in this house. And your sister and I are *very* close."

He blinks a couple of times and makes a face. "Please stop, I don't wanna hear it."

"Hear what?" Bruno asks.

"Don't," Diego murmurs, making me laugh.

Bruno sits down beside him, and they watch the game show together while I place the groceries on the kitchen counter and start unpacking everything. That's when my eyes slide across the kitchen and into the living room to a picture sitting on a small table. While putting the chicken in the fridge, my eyes are still completely transfixed on the image. My body moves toward it instinctively, and the closer I get, the less I can breathe.

My fingers tremble as I pick up the picture and stare.

It feels like my heart is beating out of my chest.

Like I'm frozen to the floor.

Because the image under my thumb is of the woman I killed ... and on this same table is her ring.

"What's wrong?" Bruno asks, pulling me from my thoughts.

A cold shiver runs up and down my spine as I put the picture down. Completely frazzled, I reply, "Nothing," as I make my way to the door. "I have to go."

"Why?" Bruno asks, staring at me as I open it.

But I can't answer his question.

Only Laura can.

Clutching the wood, I sigh and look out at the street, wishing I didn't see what I just saw. Wishing I could take everything back. Then I close the door behind me and run.

She knows.

I killed her mother.

CHAPTER TWENTY-ONE

I close the back door and sit down on a bench behind the church. Just finished another sermon and I really tried my best this time, but it didn't feel right. Laura wasn't there, of course. Although I had hoped she might be there.

I grab a cigarette and light it, blowing out the smoke as I stare at the ground. Right there, two feet away, is where her mother's body is hidden. I shiver, not wanting to think about that night even though it instantly crosses my mind.

The worst part is that she knows.

She knows I killed her mother.

She recognized the ring, took it, and now she's gone. After all, who would want to stay with their mother's killer?

I take another drag and think about calling her. I have to

explain it to her. It's the only way to see if she'll forgive me. I don't wanna lose her. Not even if she's *his* daughter.

I swallow at the thought of him, wanting to crush his skull with my thumbs.

Fuck.

Another drag.

Damn, I need this cigarette more than I needed that damn sermon. I was too distracted anyway.

The only thing that'll calm me down right now is finding out how she feels about me ... and hopefully talking it out. So I take my phone from my pocket and call her number. It rings, but no one picks up, and soon, it goes to voicemail.

Sighing, I lower my phone again. Of course, she won't pick up when she knows I'm calling.

Suddenly, a loud bang and screams have me jumping up from the bench and running back into the church. It's Carl ... and he's lying on the floor in the middle of the hall with blood all over his shirt. I immediately look around and find a guy I recognize running away with a gun in his hand.

It's one of the men who dragged my wife away.

Making a fist, I contemplate going after him, but when I hear Carl cry out in pain, I ignore the urge and go to him.

"Shit," Carl mutters. "I've been shot."

I look down at his stomach and watch as the blood soaks through his shirt. Margaret rushes out from her room in the back, yelling, "What happened?"

"It's Carl. Call an ambulance," I say.

She nods and goes back into her office to immediately dial 911.

"I'm sorry, Frank," Carl mumbles, tears welling up in his eyes. "I failed you before but not this time."

"Don't say that," I say. "You didn't fail me. Ever."

"No, I did," he says. "When they got me last time, I couldn't keep my mouth shut ... At least now I could ... but look at me, I'm still shot. Still dying on the floor."

"You're not dying, Carl. Not on my watch," I growl. I rip off a piece of my shirt, wrapping it around his wound. He groans, so I growl, "Lie still. Otherwise, you'll bleed out."

"Why aren't you mad at me?" he asks, his speech slurring from the pain and the tears.

"I'm not so get that out of your head."

"But ... all those years ago ..."

I hold his hand, and he squeezes tight. "The past is the past."

He nods and lowers his head to the floor again. "Fuck ... it hurts."

"Don't move," I tell him. "Help is on the way."

"The guy who shot me, he was looking for you. I didn't tell him. And then ..."

I nod and squeeze his hand tighter. "It's okay, Carl. You did good."

He smiles, and another tear rolls down his cheek.

It's painful to see him hurt because of me.

That bullet was meant for me, not for him. And still, he took it like a champ.

Mother comes walking out again with a first-aid kit. "How is he?"

"Not good," I say, and I look at Carl, whose eyes are barely staying open. "Don't die on me, okay? Carl, promise me."

He doesn't respond.

"Say something, ass-face!" I yell, almost wanting to shake him, but Mother stops me. "I retract what I said. I don't forgive you. Now stay alive and make things up to me."

Mother wraps more bandages around him and says, "We have to wait until the ambulance arrives, but they said they're on their way."

"Good," I say. "Hear that, Carl? They're coming, so don't you go anywhere."

He briefly smiles again, whispering, "Not planning to …"

I laugh a little, relieved he's not kicking the bucket this soon.

"How many more times will this happen?" Mother asks.

I look up at her and frown. "None."

Fear crosses her face. "Don't you understand? They'll just keep coming here until you make it stop."

"I will," I say, balling my fist again. "After I kill the son of a bitch who's behind it."

When the ambulance arrives and the paramedics wheel Carl into the ambulance, I swallow away the lump in my throat and wave at him. The doors close, and it drives off, leaving Mother and me standing outside with a dark, hollow feeling.

I wrap my arm around her and pull her close, hugging her from the side.

"Will he be okay?" she asks.

"We have to trust the paramedics to do their best. His family will probably be there to look after him, so it's best we don't get in the way."

She nods, and it's quiet for a few seconds before she

opens her mouth again. "Frank …"

"Yeah?"

"Punish them."

And with that, she turns around and walks right back into the church without saying another word.

***

With Julio's address in my pocket and a gun in the other, I make my way to the alley beside the walled complex and scout the area. No guards are here, but some mill around the fence, so it's better to remain unseen.

I check whether anyone notices me before I jump and grasp the ledge, pulling myself up. I quickly look around and hoist myself over, landing on my feet. Someone patrols the area a few feet away, but he's wearing earplugs, probably listening to some music too. He's completely oblivious as I approach him from behind. I quickly pull out the knife I carry in my inner pocket, hold it up to his throat, and put my hand over his mouth.

"Julio."

He nods, and his eyes hone in on the door to the left of the complex, which isn't the front entrance.

"Is he there?"

The man nods again. "Please don't kill me," he mumbles through my fingers. "I have kids."

"Oh, I won't … but you need to keep quiet," I whisper.

"I will, I will," he repeats.

I smack him on the back of the head, and he falls to the ground unconscious. "Good."

I never said I wouldn't hurt him. Besides, if you work

for Julio, you'd better expect some violence. The man lives in it.

I rush to the side entrance and stand beside it, jerking on the door handle to create some ruckus. Someone immediately bursts out, looking for the culprit, but I'm behind him. Right as he turns around, I shoot him in the neck.

"Nothing personal," I mumble as I step over his body.

With my gun aimed at whoever comes close, I check my surroundings. It's a home and a luxurious one at that. If there's one bodyguard, there must be another. And I'm goddamn sure one of them is the same dude who took my wife.

In fact … I think I see him right now. Standing in the hallway, he's adjusting his collar.

"Don't move," I growl.

The image shifts, and it suddenly dawns on me it was a mirror's reflection I saw, not him. Right then, someone shoots and a bullet ricochets off the wall behind me. I duck. Another bullet shoots straight at me, scraping my leg. I hiss from the pain but remain calm as I get up and point my gun at wherever it's coming from.

He's in the kitchen.

I don't go inside. I roll past the door and shoot. Straight in the legs.

He howls in pain and falls to the floor. However, he grabs a knife from the counter and throws it at me. It jams into my shoulder, making me drop the gun, which slides across the hall.

But I don't give up.

I pull the knife out and rush at him. We struggle for

power, fighting man to man over the knife in my hand and his life.

"You ... you killed my wife!" I scream at him.

"I thought you were fucking dead!" he growls, rolling on top of me.

"Think you'd get away with doing that to her? To me?" His hands are around mine as we fight for control over the knife, which moves between both our throats.

"You shouldn't have killed *his* wife to begin with!" he yells back, pushing so hard the knife is against my throat. Blood drops roll down my skin, and I swallow.

"Fuck you!" I yell. "You have no idea what I've been through, and it's all because of *you*!" Somehow, I find the strength to push him off me. I kick him in the balls, and he tumbles backward, creating enough room for me to jump on him and ram the knife straight into his chest.

He howls again. "No, fuck you! We will *never* go down."

"Remember Sergio, your buddy? He already did," I say with a smile, pulling the knife from his flesh. "And guess what? He didn't die a glorious death. He died alone, afraid ... and it was motherfucking painful."

I jam the knife back into his abdomen, turning and twisting it until his blood comes pouring out. "And this is for Carl ..." I growl.

He chokes on his own blood. It looks magnificent, and it fills me with unmeasurable euphoria.

I want him to feel what my wife felt when he took her life, so I pull out the knife again and shove it right there ... below the belt.

He groans, grimacing with more blood as I grin like a motherfucker.

"Now you know what she went through when you took her and used her," I growl. "And like your buddy, you'll die a painful and useless death like the useless piece of shit you are." I spit on his face and pull out the knife again.

God, that felt good.

Making the sign of the cross on my chest, I say a prayer in my head. Then I get up, leaving his half-dead body on the kitchen floor as I make my way back to the hall.

I pick up the gun and make sure to hold on tight, despite the pain in my shoulder, as I check the entire house. No one's found on the first floor, so I move upstairs, trying not to make a sound. Each of the doors I kick open leads to an empty room, so I go up another flight of stairs. There's only one room left in the house, so I take a deep breath before I go inside.

I let the door fall open as I swallow away the lump in my throat and clench the gun.

There he is … the man who has haunted my dreams for ages.

Julio. 'El Campeón.'

He's behind his laptop, and his eyes barely move away from the screen.

"Hello, Frank … how lovely to see you here."

"Don't move," I hiss.

"How did you get past the gates?"

"I didn't." I move in, closing the door behind us.

"Oh … so you jumped over," he muses, licking his lips. "Guess I should hire more guards."

"Won't help, I'll kill them all," I reply, closing in on him.

"How many?"

"Just two, I spared another."

"How nice of you." He gives me a wretched smile.

"Save it, fuckface," I spit. "Like you ever gave a shit about any of your men."

He puts his hands in the air. "I do hope you realize you won't get away with this."

"I didn't plan on it," I say, circling his desk.

"Oh, so this was a suicide mission?" He raises his brow. "Just because I tried to have you killed? You should know, hanging out with my daughter wasn't a good idea."

His admission is proof he's been keeping tabs on her … or me. "I don't give a shit about that. Your daughter isn't why I'm here, and you know that."

"For a man who wanted revenge so badly, you sure don't have your priorities."

"I don't care if I die as long as you die with me." I put the gun to his head.

"You don't wanna do that, Frank," he warns, still staring at me.

"Give me one good reason," I say through gritted teeth.

His lips part faintly, and a brief smile appears on his face. His eyes dance with fire … a flame so bright they burn the oxygen in my lungs.

"Your son is alive …"

CHAPTER TWENTY-TWO

My heart comes to a momentary stop as I freeze up completely.

My body feels numb.

My senses dull.

His words ruin me.

"What?" I mutter, barely able to pronounce the word. My fingers tremble around the trigger as I fight to keep it together. Is it true? Or is he lying to save his ass?

A sudden flurry of rage overtakes me. "Don't lie to me!" I scream.

"It's not a lie," he snorts. "I wish it was."

"How? Where?" I'm frantic now, and my heart races in my throat.

"You could see him ... right now," he rambles. "But you won't if you kill me."

Of course, he's trading this for his life. Playing with my feelings to get what he wants. The ultimate failure of revenge in exchange for the life of my son.

How cruel. How vicious. And something I should've seen coming.

My throat feels so dry I can barely speak. "Where is he?"

"I can give you the address and send a picture to your phone if you leave the premises."

"No, I don't believe you," I hiss. "If I leave here, you'll have your guards kill me."

"No, I won't. Where's the fun in that?"

I mull it over for a few seconds. "What then? A standoff?"

He shrugs. "Well, it's only fair."

"Fuck fair," I growl, pushing the gun back to his forehead. "You don't deserve anything after what you did to my wife!"

"And what do you deserve, huh, Frank?" He grinds his teeth. "You killed my wife and my unborn son."

The mere mention of her death forces me to feel the pain again, and it hurts.

"It was an accident ..." I mutter.

"Accident or not, she died, and you paid the price. An eye for an eye." The way he says it makes me wanna throw up in my mouth.

"You bastard ... I should pull the trigger."

"You could ... but then you'd never get to know your son."

I want to.

I want to *so* damn badly.

I want Julio to suffer. I want him gone. Erased from this planet.

Yet … I can't … because my son might still be alive.

I have to know if it's true. I *have* to see him.

"Tell you what; I'll give you the address now … and when you leave the property, I'll send you the picture. Deal?" Julio says, holding out his hand.

I make a face, thinking about it for a second. I don't wanna make a deal with him. He's the fucking devil. But if it means I'll have the slightest chance of seeing my son … whom I thought was long dead … then it's worth every bit of misery I'll feel.

Just that one moment with him. I'd give my life for it.

I lower the gun and say, "Deal."

I shake his filthy hand. The devious smile on his face makes me wanna rethink my decision. He grabs a notepad and writes down an address and a telephone number, ripping off the paper to hand it to me. "There. He's at school now, so you'll probably find him in the yard outside. My number's also on there, so text me when you're outside, and I'll send you the picture."

I tuck it into my pocket, still pointing the gun at him as I slowly back away. "If you don't send that picture, I will kill each one of your guards, and then I'll come back for you."

"I know how you work, Frank. Do you think I'm that stupid?" He raises a brow and taps his fingers together. "Besides, I'm a man of my word. A deal is a deal."

He's right on that part. Julio's always had a reputation for being trustworthy. Whatever that means in this underground business. Of course, once he's sent the picture

… there's no telling what he'll do now that I killed his men.

"Go on then … What's stopping you?" Julio muses as he leans back in his chair, staring at me as I slowly inch backward, keeping my gun pointed at him.

"This isn't over," I say through gritted teeth, and then I storm out of his room.

I run down the stairs and go outside as quickly as I can, jumping up to the wall again. My shoulder stings from the painful jab, but I ignore it as I pull myself up and crawl over, jumping down in the alley below.

Rummaging in my pocket, I take out my phone and the note, typing in the number he gave me. I start walking as I text.

Frank: Give me the picture.

Julio: Here you go.

It takes a while to load, and the more time passes, the greater my excitement.

However, nothing can prepare me for the face appearing on my screen.

My jaw drops, and I almost walk into traffic. A loud horn makes me step back, my feet only just on the sidewalk as I stare at the phone in my shaking hand.

The boy … *my* boy …

It's Bruno.

CHAPTER TWENTY-THREE

From the moment I first met him, I knew he was a special kid.

I don't know why, but I could feel it in my bones. Some sort of exceptional connection. Characteristics we shared. A certain look in his eyes. The smirk.

It was all there, yet I never saw the truth.

Not once did it dawn on me because it seemed impossible.

Because I hadn't seen my boy since he was a baby.

Who knew boys could change so much in just a few years?

I sigh and stare ahead at the schoolyard, wondering when the appropriate time arrives. I guess it never does.

When do you ever tell a boy you're his father? It's not an easy thing to do, and that's why I'm so scared.

In fact, I'm terrified.

Terrified of rejection. Terrified he might not even believe it. Terrified he won't want me.

How has he lived all these years without me? And why did they let him live?

Is it because of Laura?

Is that why she ran away from her dad?

The pieces of the puzzle are falling into place, but the more I think about it, the angrier I get.

I pick up some grass and gaze at it. Nothing makes sense. Laura knew he wasn't her family ... and she still took him in. Did she know he was mine?

I look up and observe the kids running around the schoolyard. He's out there, playing with them.

My son.

Those two words alone make me wanna take in a big gulp of air.

God, I still can't believe it.

Is it even true? It must be ... Why else would Julio give it up as a final card? He'd never tell me willingly unless his life was on the line. After all, he wanted me to suffer, and this isn't it. This is the exact opposite because finding out my son was still alive was like picking a piece of fruit from a tree in heaven.

He'd never want me to feel this hopeful.

So it must be true. I have to believe it.

I breathe in and out again, drawing strength from up above. "God ... please be with me. I need you," I whisper into the wind. Then I grab the photo in my pocket and stare at it. When I think about it, he does have the same physical traits as Bruno. Like … a perfect match.

I can't believe I didn't see it before. It's like I was blinded by my own ignorance.

Wiping away a tear, I pull a pen from my pocket and scribble down something on the back then tuck both back into my pocket.

Then I get up and start walking, squashing the pieces of grass I had in my hand and letting them fly away with the wind.

The closer I get, the heavier my feet feel, but I don't give up. Not until I'm near the fence, gawking at the boy running around the schoolyard with a bucket on his head and using a tiny shovel as a scepter. I smile and laugh, feeling the tears well up again as I watch him play.

Then he looks at me … and I'm frozen in place.

"Hey, Father Frank!"

His voice cuts deep into the coils around my heart. Deeper than it ever has. And for the first time in years, I feel like I can finally see clearly.

He runs toward the fence and clutches it with his little hands, and I smile at the sight of those fingers that I've missed for so many years. If I'd only known it was him … I would've held him from the start and never let go.

"Hey, Bruno …" I mutter, struggling to keep the tears at bay. "How are you doing?"

"Oh, I'm great! I'm the king of all the kids right now. Look!" He points at his bucket hat.

"I see that," I say, winking. "You're the greatest king alive."

"Do you think so?"

I sink to my knees so I can speak to him on his level.

"Of course, and you know what else? I think you're also one of the smartest."

"Well, I'm not the best in class right now ... especially not with math ..."

I chuckle at his comment and at his attempt to calculate something on his fingers.

I grab his hand and squeeze tight. "A king doesn't need to count. He's got his people to do that for him."

"Oh ... right!" He smiles so brightly it makes me wanna cry.

"Hey, Bruno ... do you think you could step outside the fence for just a moment?"

"I dunno. The teacher might get mad."

"Tell her I'm Laura's boyfriend."

He immediately turns his head around and screams at the teacher as only a kid can. I almost have to plug my ears, so I don't go deaf.

Grinning, he says, "Okay!" and he runs to the gate.

I stand again and look at him run on those two little legs of his, wondering how I could've missed all these years. God ... I've got so much to catch up on.

I hold out my arms and wait ... and when he's finally here, in my arms, I hug him tightly. The warmest smile finds its way to my face as I hold him closely, wishing I could stay this way forever. I can't believe he's really here in the flesh. My son. It's like a gift from God.

When I release him again, I have to wipe a tear away.

"Are you crying?" he asks.

I was hoping he didn't see it, but I guess I was too late.

"Oh, no, I ... had something in my eye," I lie.

"If you're not happy, you have to tell me, you know?"

I raise a brow. "And why's that?"

He beckons me with his little hand, and I bend over so he can whisper in my ear, "Because Laura said we have to take care of you."

I snort, shaking my head. "Did she now?"

He nods a few times, grinning again. "But I won't tell her if you're sad. I promise."

I run my fingers through his hair and rub his little head. "Thanks, squirt."

A car drives up to the school parking lot, and when a window is rolled down, I can clearly make out Laura's face even though she's wearing sunglasses to hide.

I know she can see me. I don't care.

"I think that's her," I say.

"Oh?" He turns and puts his hand above his eyes to shield them from the sunlight as he looks out at the parking lot. "That's her car, yeah."

"She's probably here to pick you up," I say. "But before you go ... can you do something for me?"

He turns back to face me. "What is it?" he asks, with one finger in his nose.

I pull out the picture from my pocket and hold it out to Bruno. "This is a very important secret between Laura and me. Can you promise you'll give it to her without looking at it?"

He slams his lips together and nods vehemently.

"Promise?"

"Promise," he says.

I hold up my pinky, and we pinky swear on it. Then I pat his back and say, "Go on. She's waiting for you."

As he runs off with the picture in his hand, I think of the words written on it, and how she might react when she reads them.

'I know Bruno is my son.'

She'll either have the shock of her life ... or the biggest laugh. Either way, this isn't going to go away, and I hope she knows that too.

And as I stare at the car driving off, with Bruno waving at me from the back seat, I can't help wonder what could have been ... and what will be.

Because now that I know he's mine, there's no way in hell I'm going to let him go.

CHAPTER TWENTY-FOUR

With deliberation, I stand in front of her home, and I pull the door handle.

Surprisingly, it opens.

I thought she'd have locked it, or at least pretended not to be home, but apparently, she was waiting for me.

I let the door fall open slowly as I gaze around the house.

There she is.

In the middle of the kitchen, preparing some tomatoes for a dish.

She doesn't even look up. Not until she's completely finished slicing them and putting them into a bowl. She places her knife on the cutting board and lifts her head. Her penetrating gaze makes me narrow my eyes.

"Diego ... take your brother outside."

"Why?" Diego's sitting on the couch and gives her a grumpy look as he turns off the television.

"Don't ask questions. Just do it."

He rolls his eyes but gets up anyway, after giving her a big-ass sigh. "Fine."

Bruno walks out of his room and asks, "What's going on?"

Nobody answers, but seeing him makes my stomach feel like twisted knots.

Diego grabs his hand. "Let's go."

"Where are we going?" Bruno asks.

"Out. To play." Diego seems annoyed. However, Bruno grins uncontrollably.

They both pass me, and I wait until they're out of sight before I turn my attention back to Laura.

I swallow away the lump in my throat as I think about my first words. "Did you get the photo?"

She nods. Not even one word slips from her mouth. Damn her.

Grinding my teeth, I grip the doorjamb and say, "He's my son … You knew, didn't you?" Fury grows inside me. "Of course, you knew he wasn't your family, and you still ran off with him and hid him. Did you ever even tell him Julio wasn't his dad? That his dad was still out there, looking for him?" I tear up. "I told you everything … and you never even thought that *he* might be my son?"

Her face contorts. "Don't you talk to me about lies." She picks up the knife on the board and points it at me. "You … No wonder my dad came after you. He didn't just want you far away from me. He wanted you dead because you killed his wife!" Her voice increases in volume as she struggles to keep it together. "All this time, I thought my dad was the bad guy, but you killed my mom!" she spits, tearing up.

She clutches the knife firmly and inches closer. "That's why he went after your wife and son, too, didn't he? You knew this. You always knew. And you never told me. How could you?"

I close the door behind me and stand tall, refusing to give in. She knew her father did something horrible, and she never said a word.

"You killed my mother and her baby!" she screams, charging at me with the knife. "How dare you!"

I barely deflect her attack, but I grab her wrist and twist it to make her drop the knife.

"Fuck you!" she hisses, slapping me in the face. "You don't get to come in here and claim your son when *you* did that to us. To *me*!"

She punches me in the chest again and again, and I let her. "Like you're any better. You knew he wasn't your family, and you still kept him. All these years ... did you ever stop to think? Did you ever think for a single second that he could be mine?"

"Of course, I did!" she squeals, her face covered in tears. "But I love him like my own blood, and don't you dare claim that I don't." She slaps my face again. "Shame on you for killing an innocent woman."

I grab her wrists and hold them tight. "I didn't do that on purpose. It was an accident."

She spits in my face. "Liar!"

I wipe it off with a scowl. "It's the honest goddamn truth," I growl. "I knew I made a mistake the moment she died."

"You knew it was my mother!" she yells. "It was in the

church, right? When those two fuckers came in and decided to trash the place. That's when you knew, didn't you?"

I nod.

"I knew it. That's why you wanted me out of there."

"I was contemplating whether or not I should use you to get to your father," I hiss. "Be glad I didn't do it."

"Oh, I'm so damn glad!" she scoffs. "Why did you do it, huh? Why her?"

"There was no reason. She was just there at the wrong time. Trying to protect your father's assets or something. I don't know. I was only there to steal his money."

She jerks free and kicks me in the nuts, making me heave. Then she picks up the knife again, but before she can push it into my throat, I grab her arm and push her all the way through the room. Eventually, we end up against the back wall, and the hard shove makes her lose control. I snatch the knife and throw it away.

"Do you think I don't feel guilty? Of course, I fucking do. I've lived with regret ever since that day."

"Regret doesn't bring back my mother!" she hisses.

"And it didn't bring back my son either," I hiss back. "But you knew he was alive."

"I didn't know he was your son until you told me with that photograph."

"It didn't even cross your mind?" I narrow my eyes at her. "Of course, it did. You just didn't want to think about it because you might lose him."

She makes a face and refuses to answer, which proves my point.

"Why? Why did you do it?" I growl. "Answer me!"

"I *saved* him," she says through gritted teeth. "My father

brought him home. I didn't know who he was or where he came from, only that he would kill him. Of course, I took him! As if I could let him do that to a child."

I swallow again as the emotions coil up in my throat. "That's why you fled his home and came here …"

"Yes, but what I did wasn't malicious. I took him to keep him *safe*. But you?" She taps my chest vigorously. "You killed my mother. That was vicious and unforgivable."

"What do you want me to say? Nothing will bring her back. I know I'm bad."

"You could've told me! All along, you knew she was *my* mother, and you never thought to tell me." She's trembling in place. "God, I can't believe I actually fucking wanted you so badly." She rolls her eyes. "I'm such an idiot, always falling for the bad guys."

"Hey, I'm not a bad guy. I'm trying to right my wrongs," I say.

"By killing people? Yeah, right," she sneers. "No, you know what? Fuck you. Fuck you for coming into my house like you own it. Fuck you for abusing my trust. Fuck you for screwing with my life, and fuck you for ruining my family."

I place my hands on the walls behind her, trapping her. "No … fuck you for seducing me. Fuck you for making me think I was ever worthy of love again. And fuck you for making me see the good things in life again and for giving me hope."

She swallows too now, and the intense, smoldering stare in her eyes doesn't help my cause.

Goddamn, this fucking woman.

Messing with my head.

Making me confront my own demons and hers.

And making it so hard for me to let go.

"Dammit!" I ram my fist on the wall. "Why did we have to do this?"

"Ask yourself that question," she hisses, leaning back against the wall. "If you hadn't killed *my* mother, none of this would've happened. My dad wouldn't have killed *your* wife, and I wouldn't have had to take care of *your* son." She taps my chest again to emphasize her words.

"I did what I had to do to survive!" I say. "And I would never have shot her if I'd known it was her."

"But you'd have shot any other random person? Great," she scoffs.

"I was reckless. I was young. What else do you want me to say? Sorry won't bring her back."

She frowns. "But it's a start."

I shake my head with frustration. "I can't believe this is happening. Sometimes, you make it really hard for me; you know that?"

"Fuck you; this is all your doing," she curses, slapping me again.

"You're right about that," I say.

She slaps me again. "You killed my mother. I fucking hate you!"

"I accept that."

Another slap. "Good!"

This goes on until she gets worn out and sighs, saying, "Why aren't you doing something?"

I shrug. "I am. I'm letting you hit me."

"Why don't you fight back?" Her expression hardens.

"Because you need this. And I need it too."

She punches my chest and then hisses, "No, fuck you;

you don't get to move on so quickly."

"Move on? I'm not moving one inch," I reply. "I'm staying, and there's no way in hell you can ever take me away from my kid. Let that be clear. He is mine, and I will do whatever it takes to keep him."

She folds her arms and looks away, blowing out some air.

I mull it over for a few seconds, thinking about all the ways this could've gone. But it went much better than I thought it would. And to be honest, now that I've got it off my chest, I feel much better. The more I think about it, the less I'm starting to resent her for what she did.

I do fucking hate to feel this way, though. Ripped apart by my need for justice, and at the same time wanting her so badly. It's driving me insane.

Mad … To the point of grabbing her face with both hands and claiming her mouth. Right now.

I kiss her as hard as I can, trying to push away all the raging thoughts and focus on one thing … healing. I refuse to lose any more people I love. I refuse to give her up.

But fuck, she fights me on every turn, biting my lip when I try to keep kissing her. And goddamn, her hatred tastes delicious.

"Frank!" she hisses, slapping me.

I grin and lick up the blood on my lips. "Sorry … old habits."

"What the fuck," she mutters, her eyes like a burning fire, so explosive.

But then she does the most peculiar thing.

She wraps her arms around my neck and kisses me back even harder than before.

CHAPTER TWENTY-FIVE

What the fuck?
She's kissing me?

No matter how fucking weird this is, I can't stop kissing her either. Her mouth tastes divine, and I want ... no, I *won't* take anything less.

But when her lips momentarily unlatch from mine, she slaps me again.

And proceeds to kiss me again.

Her kisses aren't sweet or nice.

They're frantic. Harsh. Frenzied. Like a girl addicted to my love, desperately trying to fight withdrawal while also trying to kick the habit.

"Fuck ..." she murmurs, and she bites my lip, drawing

more blood. "I fucking hate you so much right now."

"Hmm ... I can tell," I muse, licking the top of her lips and pulling her closer. "And I fucking hate that too."

"Fuck you; you're the cause of all this," she whispers as I let my tongue roam free across her neck.

"You were the one who seduced me. This is what you get," I tease, licking her skin.

She leans back and tries to smack me again, but this time I grasp both her wrists and pin them to the wall. "You wanna do this the hard way? You got it," I growl, and I nudge her legs apart with my knee. "But I'm not going anywhere, and you know it."

"Damn you," she hisses, so I cover her mouth with mine to stop the complaining.

She wants this.

She clearly does, or she wouldn't have kissed me.

She's just mad that she does, and that's okay. I'm pissed off too.

But that doesn't mean we can't fix this shit.

And what better way to make up than with a bit of hard, rough fucking? Nothing.

So I curl my fingers under her shirt and rip it off, not giving a shit that it's tearing at the seams. And lucky me ... she's not even wearing a bra.

"Hey!" she calls out, but I smother her with more kisses and lick the seam of her mouth until she parts her lips and lets me in. My tongue always shuts her up.

Her tits are a handful and feel so nice as I rub my thumb across her nipples, hardening them.

"You know you like this," I murmur against her lips, grinning like a motherfucker as I twist her nipple.

"Shut up," she growls, and she rakes her fingers through my hair as she kisses me.

"We'll see about that," I mutter. "After I take your ass." Her comeback is to rip off my shirt and buttons fly everywhere.

I love it when she gets feisty.

I spin her around so she's facing the wall. "Mine."

"*Mine*? You wish," she says, so I push my hard-on against her thighs.

"Oh yes, you're mine, all right. Feel this? *That's* what you do to me. *That's* how crazy you make me, even when we hate each other's guts."

"Just fuck me. I'm done talking," she hisses, eyeing me from over her shoulder as my hand slithers down her belly.

I rip down her zipper and pull the button loose, taking down her pants and underwear in one go.

She squeals again, but I cover her mouth with my hand and whisper, "Don't want the kids to hear you moan ..."

She still looks furious as my hand dives between her legs. I grin when I feel her slickness, even when she tries to keep her legs together.

"See?" I muse.

"I so wanna smack that grin off your face," she growls.

"You can try ... but nothing can beat *this*." I rub my fingers up and down her slit, slowly easing her into it until her legs part and I can swivel across her clit. "As much as I hate to say it ... you're mine now, and I don't let go of what's mine."

I wrap my arm around her waist as I finger fuck her with my other hand, making sure she feels how serious I am. When she bites her lip, I tear down my own zipper and pull out my rock-hard cock. I spread her cheeks and ram it into her pussy, fully burying myself inside her.

"God … that feels good," I groan, thrusting in again.

I grab her wrists and pin them to her back as I slam into her hard and fast, not giving a shit whether this is right or wrong.

My eyes travel across her body and then end up finding a wooden cross with round edges on the wall. And I get this crazy idea. I rip it off the wall and spit on the end then I push the top into her ass.

"What the fuck—"

"You know how I like to fuck …" I muse, pushing it in farther while I spit on it some more for easy lube. In and out the tip of the round cross goes, giving her double the pleasure… and me double the fun.

I know it's wrong. I know it's sacrilegious.

And I know that I don't give a shit because I want this more than anything right now.

The more I fuck her, the easier the round cross goes inside, until it's buried deep inside her. I twist it around until I hear her moan, and then I slap her ass for good measure. I know she can feel that, which is exactly why I do it again, only this time on the other cheek.

"You like it when I fuck you like an animal," I growl.

"Fuck you," she murmurs again.

"Exactly," I muse, smiling as I thrust harder.

I wrap my arm around her waist and let my hand slide down between her legs. I grip her pussy and fondle her clit, circling it with fervor. God, I fucking love this—just getting wild after a big fight.

I speed up the pace as I bang her against the wall,

making sure her senses are on overload. Her moans turn me on so much that I can barely contain myself. But first ... I wanna feel her fall apart so I know we're still good.

After all ... I don't think any man can give her what she needs as well as I do.

She wants me just as much as I want her. She can deny that all she wants, but she and I both know that's a lie.

So I pump harder and give her everything I have until her knees grow weak and her body begins to buck against my hand. Her engorged nub thumps under my finger, and her muscles contract around me, sending delicious shockwaves down my length.

"Fuck ..." I hiss, pulling out before I come too. I'm not done with her yet.

As she's panting, I swiftly grab her off the floor and throw her over my shoulder with the round cross still plugging her ass.

"What are you doing?" she squeals as I walk her to the table and put her down on her back, making sure her butt sticks out. When she parts her lips again, I place a finger in her mouth and push the cross further in, making her groan.

"Enough talking ... now, it's my turn," I say.

I quickly pull out the cross and flip it around to the clean side. Then I stuff it into her pussy.

With a firm grip, I lift her legs and prop them against my pecs. Spitting on my dick, I push it into her tiny hole, burying myself deep in her ass until I find that sweet spot again.

She licks her lips, saying, "You're an ass man, aren't you?"

I grin and bite my lip. "Isn't that obvious?"

Groaning with excitement, I thrust in and out, enjoying the feel of her tightness, while I move the cross around too. She seems to like it, despite the fact I'm tainting the holy cross.

However, her hand slips out from behind her back … holding a knife.

Shit. She must've gotten it off the counter when I flipped her on my back. Sneaky fuck.

She puts it against my throat, but I don't stop fucking her. If I'm going to die, this is the happiest place I could be.

"Do it," I say, inching closer.

She grinds her teeth, the blade almost piercing my skin. "You deserve it …"

A few seconds pass by, and I stare at her, wondering if she's going to make the decision.

"What are you waiting for?" I ask.

She rubs her lips together, breathing loudly through her nose as she gazes me in the eyes. "Nothing."

I move closer, allowing a drop of blood to roll down my neck. "I'll help."

But she doesn't push. Instead, she pulls away each time I get a little closer. And the longer this moment lasts, the more agitated she seems to get. "Fuck!"

Growling, she throws the knife away and grabs my collar, kissing me so hard I swear my cock got even stiffer. I return her frenzied kisses with passionate ones, giving her all the licks and warmth she needs right now while also claiming her as mine.

She tastes so delicious; I could kiss her all day, every day. That's how addicted I am.

When our lips unlatch, she murmurs, "God, I hate you

so much."

I smile. "You already said that, but you can't get enough either, can you?"

"No, so fuck me. Hard. Fast. I don't care; just do it dirty and do it good."

I lick my lips and wink as she drops back to the table. "My specialty."

My pants drop to my feet, but I don't give a shit. I'm too focused on giving her everything she needs. I push the cross in deeper and bury myself inside her too, making her feel the fullness. I don't stop until I see her mouth make an O shape, at which point I pull out and thrust back in completely again.

Her muscles clench, and I know she's coming again. Grabbing her tits, I pump her like a madman, the sound of her moans keeping me going.

"You ready for me, babe?"

"Fuck, yes," she moans, her nails digging into the wood. "Come all over me."

Her filthiness pushes me over the edge, so I pull my dick out and jerk off until I come, spurting my cum all over her tits. It even reaches as far as her mouth, and she licks up the drops like a druggie. Goddamn ... I think I'm in love with this woman.

When I'm spent and gasping for air, I lower her legs and the cross drops to the floor. She sits up straight, still leaning back on the palms of her hand as I stand between her naked thighs, wondering how we go from here.

With pursed lips, she glares at me, and I do the same. But I also grab her hand and pull it up to my mouth, kissing the top to show her it's not just about the sex.

However, there's no time for more because one second later, someone's jerking on the door handle.

"Shit!" she whispers, and she shoves me aside and jumps off the table to quickly grab her clothes and run into her bedroom.

"Fuck, where are you going?" I hiss, trying to find my shirt and all the buttons, but I'm running out of time. The door is almost open, and I'm still butt-naked, hopping around while I desperately try to pull up my pants. And right as two boys waltz inside, I manage to jump into her room and slam the door shut.

I'm pretty sure they saw my ass.

CHAPTER TWENTY-SIX

I place my ear against the door and a finger on Laura's mouth when she opens it. "Shh…"

"I saw you!" Diego yells.

Laura almost bursts out into laughter. Only my hand stops the sound from coming out.

"Fuck …" I mutter, stepping away from the door. "Guess we're screwed."

"It's not like he hasn't seen ass before," she muses.

"Really? How many?" I raise a brow.

She shoves her elbow in my waist. "Stop being an asshole."

"What? If I'm going to be your boyfriend, I'd like to know how far in line I come. It's only fair."

She grabs a Bible lying on her bedside stand and slaps me on the head with it. "Frank …"

"You too?" I say, laughing a little at the fact that she punishes me exactly the same way as Margaret does.

"Like you're so innocent. Your dick's hanging out all the time." She folds her arms.

"Only for you." I smirk, and she gives me another slap with the Bible, this time on my arm.

She throws it on her bed and cleans up her tits and face before she goes to her closet to grab some clothes.

"Get dressed," she says, as she puts on her panties and a blouse, covering her up naked skin again. Goddamn, I already miss it.

I walk up to her, wrapping my hands around her waist and propping my chin on her shoulder. "I'm sorry," I whisper in her ear.

She pauses, her hand slowly drifting up to mine. "Thank you."

"I really am. I wish I could undo everything I did, but I can't. I can't turn back time."

"I know." A pause follows. "Your wife died because of it … That must be horrible."

"It is, but I've come to accept that now. I had my revenge."

"And now you have your son too …" she murmurs, glancing over her shoulder.

I softly spin her on her heels and place my hand on the wardrobe. "I want things to be okay between us. Tell me what I have to do."

She sighs, looking down at her feet while she fumbles with the pants in her hands. "I honestly don't know. You took my mother away from me. And my little brother ... I'll never get to meet him." She sniffs, tears welling up in her eyes. "And I hate it."

I lift her chin up so I can look at the pain I've caused. I want to face it. I'm not running away from it anymore. "I promise I will never hurt you like that ever again."

She nods softly, but of course, nothing I can say will help, so I pull her into my embrace and hold her tight.

"God ... Laura ... your mother ... I can't even tell you how messed up it is. I mean, I was sent to steal stuff from your father. But then she was there." I sigh. "I wish I could take it back. I've wished it every single day of my life."

"But you can't," she mutters.

"No, and because of that, I lost my wife ... and years of my son's life."

"Guess there's a silver lining there."

"What do you mean?" I ask.

She looks up and smiles briefly. "You can spend the time you lost with him now."

"Hmm ... but I don't wanna do it if it means losing you," I reply, cocking my head. "And I don't blame you if you say you don't want me anymore. I just ... can't get over you that easily."

She shakes her head, snorting. "I get what you're saying ... Heck, I even felt it."

I lean in closer, tipping up her chin again. "Is there ever a chance you'll forgive me?"

"I don't ... I don't ..." she mutters, and I see the agony on her face.

It's so hard for her.

Not just to forgive me.

But to forgive herself for wanting me ... despite the fact I'm her mother's killer.

I want to make it easier for her, so I press my lips to hers, kissing her gently. I don't want to overstep her boundaries, so I take it slow and easy. However, she doesn't push me away. In fact, she's kissing me back.

"It's wrong," she murmurs between our kisses.

"It doesn't matter," I say.

"It should." Her grip on my body tightens.

"If we both want it, there's no shame in it."

"I can't stop ..." Her voice sounds heady, and her lips are tantalizing, warm, and needy. Exactly the way I like them.

"Then don't stop," I say. "I need you so badly." My fingers run through her hair in a desperate attempt to get closer to her, but nothing's ever enough.

"But my mother ..." she mutters as our mouths unlatch.

I brush my thumb across her lips. "She'd want you to be happy."

She closes her eyes and nods. "You're right."

"And I prayed to her ... every day ..." I grab her hand and squeeze. "To forgive me for my sins. I never wanted her dead; you gotta believe me."

Laura places a finger on my lips and smiles softly. "I understand now."

I frown. "You do?"

"Yes and no. I understand why it happened the way it did. But ..." She taps her index finger against my chest. "Don't you think you'll get away with what you did. I won't forgive you that easily. It'll take a lot of groveling and begging."

I smirk at her comment.

"And maybe some cooking and cleaning and ass kissing," I add.

She smiles too now. "Yeah, that *might* do the trick."

Elated, I grab her by the waist and twirl her around in my arms, kissing her so hard I feel like I'm on cloud nine. I know it's wrong for me to want her so badly after the history we have, but the past is the past, and I wanna move forward.

"I promise I'll do whatever I can to make you happy," I say, putting her down again. "And if after all that, you still wanna kill me ... I'll hand you the knife myself."

She snorts. "You're making this way too easy for me."

I shrug. "I don't care if I die. I deserve it."

Her brows draw together. "I do."

"Hmm ..." I narrow my eyes. "I seem to recall you wanting to murder me just minutes ago."

She makes a face. "Like you don't know how anger feels, Mr. I-Kill-Everyone-For-Revenge."

I wink. "Got me there."

"Are you guys coming out yet, or do I need to call the fire department?" Diego yells. "Because that mushy shit smells."

I laugh and so does Laura, and it's the first time in a long time that I can genuinely say I'm happy, right where I am right now.

But then I realize ... Bruno's in there too. Right behind that door. And I can't help but stare.

"You wanna talk to him?" Laura asks.

I nod. "I ..." I turn my head to her. "What do I say?"

She shrugs. "Whatever you want. He's *your* son."

I lick my lips and think it over for a few seconds. Laura places her hand on my shoulder and squeezes. "You'll do fine. You've already talked to him before. Nothing's changed."

"*Everything* … has changed."

She nods, finally understanding what I mean. "But …" She swallows, staring me straight in the eye. "You can't take him away from here."

I frown in confusion.

"I mean … you can't take him away from his family," she adds. "Diego and Bruno are the only family I've got. My father hates me."

"Why?" I ask.

"Because I saved your son. He wanted to kill him, but I took him and ran, and he never forgave me. Especially because I took Diego with me too. That, and I've always been against all the illegal shit he's in."

"I see." I rub the back of my head. I understand what she means, but I can't stay away either. "But you have to understand … I *want* to see my son. Even if you don't want me here."

"I know," she replies. "I don't mind."

"Really?" I raise a brow. "Your mother's killer in your house?"

She squints and rubs her lips together. "Stop … saying those words."

"Already in denial?" I muse.

"Just don't mention it. Like, at all."

"Right. As long as I grovel and suck up to you, right?"

She sniggers. "Exactly."

"Well, I guess that means I'll be hanging out here even

more," I say with a grin.

"You done yet?" Diego yells. "Bruno's hungry."

"Coming!" Laura replies, and I let go of her so we can put on our clothes properly.

I quickly check my hair in the mirror before she opens the door and peeks out. "How do I look?" I whisper.

She muffles a laugh. "Stop being so self-conscious; you'll do fine. C'mon."

She walks out the door and goes to the kitchen. The boys are already sitting on the couch, watching the television. And me? I'm stuck in the doorway, unable to move an inch the moment I see him.

"What were you doing in there?" Bruno asks.

I lick my lips, but I can't come up with an answer. Or maybe I'm too fucking paralyzed by the thought of having to tell him I'm his dad.

"Grown-up stuff," Laura answers, taking the pressure off for me.

"Yeah ... next time, you might wanna grab the buttons scattered on the floor," Diego says, pointing at them.

Laura cringes, visibly disturbed by the fact that Diego seems to know exactly what went down here. "Yeah, well, sometimes things just get a little rough." She casually washes her hands and grabs a few tomatoes, dicing them up again as if nothing ever happened.

"Eww ..." Diego winces. "I seriously don't wanna know that."

"What? Don't you have girlfriends or something?" Laura muses.

"Of course, I do. I get pussy every day."

Now, she gives him the look.

The same one she gave me minutes ago before we fucked like animals on the kitchen table.

"Language," she hisses.

"Yeah, yeah." He rolls his eyes. "What's for dinner?"

"You if you don't watch it."

"What?" He makes a face and so does she.

"Lasagna."

"I love lasagna!" Bruno suddenly shouts, almost jumping up from the couch.

"You do, huh?" She winks. Of course, she already knew. That's why she's making it.

I smile when I realize he's been here all along under her perfect care … I can see the love, and it only makes me feel more grateful than I already am.

I clutch the doorjamb and wistfully gawk at her and the boy, but then he looks me directly in the eye, grasping my full attention.

"Father Frank, do you like lasagna?"

Me? He's talking to me.

But calling me Father suddenly sounds so different … so earthshattering.

Lasagna. Do I like it?

"Yes …" I clear my throat, still smiling. "I love it. Anything Laura makes must taste good, right?" I look at her. "I mean … have you seen her cook?"

She grins. "Already starting with the groveling, I see?"

I shrug. "Better start early if I wanna pay my debts."

"What debt?" Bruno asks, leaning up on the couch like it's a monkey bar he can climb.

"Grown-up stuff," Laura murmurs.

"Aww … Why is everything grown-up stuff? I won't get

to know anything!" He gives me the cutest pout I've ever seen, and I'm almost tempted to tell him everything, but I suppose that wouldn't be the smart thing to do with a young kid. He'd be scarred for life.

"You'll know when you're old enough," she says.

"You don't wanna know, trust me," Diego interjects, pulling him down to the cushions before he falls off the couch. "Sit down."

I go and pick up the buttons from my shirt off the floor, tucking them into my pocket.

"So is he staying for dinner?" Bruno asks.

"Well ..." I look at Laura who gives me this weird look, so I guess it's fine.

"Can he? Please?" Bruno begs her, making her laugh.

"All right, all right. But only because you've been doing so well in school."

"Yay!" he cheers, and I can't stop smiling or ogling.

Jesus, I'm so fucking weird.

"It'll take a while before the lasagna is finished, so you two go watch some cartoons, okay? And no buts." Laura points at Diego.

"Fine." Diego sighs. "But I'm picking the channel tonight."

Laura smirks. "Grab a cloth and clean the table, would you? It looks filthy."

I grin as I walk over to her. "I think I know why."

When I'm near the faucet, she whispers, "Are you afraid of him?"

As I grab a cloth and hold it under the water, I glance over my shoulder and whisper back, "It's kind of weird, you know? Telling a kid you're his father. It's not something you just do."

"Why not? What are you waiting for? Some kind of sign from God?"

I shrug. "Maybe. It would be welcome right about now."

She shakes her head and laughs as she continues to dice mushrooms and onions.

I go to the table and wash it with the warm cloth, making sure to go over it with a disinfectant too. Then I set the table and make sure everything's perfect. I'm not doing it because I want to avoid talking to the kid.

Of course not.

I mean … he's just a kid. What's there to be nervous about?

But when I'm done with all the chores I could possibly do, I'm stuck twiddling my thumbs, waiting for this moment. This one moment when I'll know exactly what to do and what to say.

However, a sudden idea isn't what distracts me, but my phone buzzing in my pants.

I take it from my pocket and open the app. My heart comes to a stop when I see the message on the screen.

Coming out to play?

It's from Julio … and he just sent me a picture of Margaret.

CHAPTER TWENTY-SEVEN

"Fuck," I hiss, and I immediately rush to the door.

"What's wrong?" Laura asks, running after me.

"They've got Mother!"

I don't even take the time to properly say goodbye to Laura or the boys. I have to get to Mother in time before … fuck!

If he hurts her, I'm going to fucking murder him.

I'll give him the slow, painful death he's deserved all along.

Fuck!

I knew I should've killed him when I had the chance.

In my car, I speed through the streets to get to the church as fast as I can, not giving a shit about the fact that

I'm running stop signs. I have to get there before he does something irreversible. Before I lose another person I love so deeply.

It'd kill me too.

My wheels screech as I jump corners and skid to a stop right in front of the church.

I jump out and run through the doors ... only to find Mother standing there in front of the cross, gazing at me with a confused look on her face.

With a pounding heart, I gape, completely fazed. "What ..."

"What's wrong?" she asks.

"You're alone ..." I approach her.

"Of course, I am," she replies. "Who were you expecting?"

"No one came here?" I ask.

She places a hand on my arm. "No ... Are you okay? You're sweating."

I wipe my forehead with my sleeve and say, "No. Absolutely not."

"Tell me what's happening."

"Julio had a picture of you ..." Now that I think about it, she looked way too relaxed in the picture. It's like it was taken from afar. So that means ...

"Shit!"

I should've known it was a distraction.

I turn around and start running.

"What's happening?"

"Lock the church down!" I yell over my shoulder. "Julio's going after Laura and the kids."

She puts her hand in front of her mouth in shock as I

rush out the doors and jump back into my car.

I don't think I've ever hit the gas this hard in my life—that's how fast I'm going. Rage fills me up inside, and when I'm stuck behind another car, I swear out loud and smash the horn.

"Fuck. Goddammit. FUCK!"

It doesn't release the pressure building inside.

The innate fear that I'm not just about to lose the one girl I love ... but my long-lost son as well.

I can't let it happen. I won't. I'll do anything to prevent them from dying. If I have to, I'll sacrifice myself for them. If that's what it takes to keep them safe, I'll do it.

"Faster, faster, faster," I mutter to myself as I race through the streets, trying to get back to her house in time.

However ... the moment I get there, I already know I'm too late.

What I see is like a vision from a nightmare.

The same scene unfolding as that day I vowed never to forget.

Laura, Diego, and my son being dragged to a car by a few of Julio's men.

And *he* is sitting in the front seat ...

Right before I get there, I can still hear Bruno's cries as he calls out my name, his eyes solely focused on me as the car drives off.

Fuck.

I can't let them get away.

I *won't* let it happen ... not again.

So I hit the gas as hard as I can.

***

I've been following them for fifteen minutes now, and we're driving all the way into the middle of fucking nowhere. It's not looking good. When they finally stop, I'm still a long ways behind. Too far because the three are kicked out of the car, and Laura scrambles to protect both Diego and Bruno.

"C'mon, c'mon, c'mon!" I shout at my car, trying to push it to its limits.

Julio steps out too now, and he's wearing a rotten smile I wanna wipe off his face. He pulls a gun from his pocket while the two sons of bitches point theirs at them too. Bruno begins to cry, and Diego's screaming for help while Laura is trying to negotiate with her dad. I can't hear what they're saying; all I can see is a bit of their movement, and it scares the shit out of me.

"I'm coming," I growl, trying to get there before he pulls the trigger.

The closer I get, the more the frightened looks on their faces burn into my brain. I have to get them outta there, no matter the cost.

So when I'm finally there, I park my car right next to theirs, drawing their attention away from Laura and the boys.

I tuck my phone far into my pocket and grab my gun before I step out.

Three guns are now pointed at my face as I point mine at Julio.

"You son of a bitch …" I mutter.

He laughs. "Frank, how nice of you to join us."

"You couldn't just go after me, could you?"

"I'm surprised you actually took the bait," he muses, cocking his head. "How is Margaret? It must be hard on her to see her boy losing his mind."

"Shut up!" I spit.

The two men raise their guns at me, but Julio waves them off. "Wait."

I look at him and then at the scared little face of Bruno. Then at Laura, who immediately grabs Bruno and pulls him toward her, hugging him tightly. I know what she's thinking. If they wanna kill them ... she'll die protecting them.

With a foul taste in my mouth, I glare at Julio and hiss, "Let them go."

"No." He laughs again. "Why the fuck would I do that?"

"They're innocent."

"No, they're not."

"They're your kids, for fuck's sake," I spit, still keeping my gun aimed at him.

"Dad? Why are you doing this," Diego mutters, but Laura slaps her hand in front of his mouth to shush him.

"Shut your mouth," Julio spits at him. "You shouldn't have run away with your sister, Diego. You know, I thought I was a good dad. Apparently not good enough, it seems." He glares at Laura now. "When you all ran, you thought I didn't know where you were? Wrong. But I gave you your space; I let you live on your own. And then you go around and betray me like that? With that bastard?" He points at me.

"It's none of your business," Laura replies.

"Yes, it is. You were my daughter," he growls. "But not anymore. None of you are my children, you fucking pussies."

Diego's eyes tear up too now as he's coming face to face with the fact that his dad literally abandoned him after his sister took him in.

"How dare you? They're your goddamn kids," I hiss.

"So? They should've stayed by my side. This is the lesson they learn."

Julio walks to Laura and snatches Bruno away from her.

"NO!" Laura screams. The men have to physically hold her back, and the altercation causes her necklace to break and scatter.

Bruno's shrieks go through bone and marrow as I struggle not to pull the trigger on Julio right there and then.

"Do it," Julio barks, looking me straight in the eye. "I dare you."

"If you don't let them go, I will," I say.

"I'll kill your son before it happens," he growls, pointing the gun straight at Bruno's temple.

"And then you're next," I reply. "I won't let you get away with it. Not a chance."

"If you shoot me, you die next," he says. "My boys won't let you run."

"I don't fucking care."

He smirks and then bursts out into laughter. "You know, I admire your tenacity. It's not every day that I find a man willing to sacrifice himself for his family, even though it's futile."

The barrel is pressed harder against Bruno's head.

I hold up my hand. "Wait!"

He narrows his eyes. "Why should I? You know how it works. The death of this kid for the death of my men. An eye for an eye."

"No," I say. "You'll hurt your daughter too."

"I don't care about that little bitch, just as I don't care about that other little bitch. The moment they ran away from me was the moment they stopped having the right to call me father."

"Kill *me*, Dad," Laura begs. "Kill me but leave Diego and Bruno alone." She gets up from the ground and begs. "Please."

"As far as I see it, we'll both be dead when this ends," I interject, and Julio sets his sight on me instead.

"What did you say?"

"You heard me. If you touch any of them, I'll kill you personally."

"And then what?"

"Nothing, but at least you'll be dead."

He frowns, but then he starts laughing again. "You're serious."

"Dead serious."

"You want to die?"

"If that means stopping you, then yes."

My determination makes him lash out as he tightens his grip on Bruno's arm, who cries even louder.

Laura goes to her knees and begins to pray to God. Grinding my teeth, I contemplate my options and even ponder whether I should throw myself in front of Bruno to serve as his shield. But I know that's futile. Sacrificing myself won't save them.

I have to give him something he wants most of all.

Something he can't say no to.

"Take me instead."

He frowns, and a pause follows, but then he parts his

lips. "Go on."

"You can do whatever you want. I'll give you my gun, and I won't fight back."

"No, don't do this," Laura begs.

I ignore her plea.

Not because I don't wanna hear it or because it pains me, but because it's the only right thing to do. For once in my life, I have to pick the good instead of the evil.

Julio scratches his stubble. "If?"

I take a deep breath.

"If you let them take my car and spare their lives."

"Frank, no!" Laura yells.

"It's the only way," I say.

"No, that's not a solution," she says. "It's suicide."

"But at least you and the boys will be safe." We stare at each other for a moment as she finally comes to the realization there is no other way out of this mess.

"So … this is what you choose?" Julio sniggers. "You know, I never pegged you to be the hero type."

"You don't know me at all," I retort. "So we got a deal?"

He gives me an arrogant smirk and nods a few times. "All right, preacher … we've got a deal." He steps closer, releasing Bruno from his grip, who immediately runs back into Laura's arms. Julio extends his hand, and after careful deliberation, I take it with my left hand.

Laura closes her eyes, a tear rolling down her cheek as she grips the boys tight.

"You will leave them alone and let them live. Got it?" I say, still pointing my gun at him with my right hand to make sure I get my end of the deal.

"Of course ... I never go back on an agreement." Another rotten smile. God, how I wish I could rip it off.

I pull my hand away and turn toward Laura. "Go. Take my car. Take them home safely and stay there."

She nods with tears in her eyes. "Thank you," she mutters softly.

Then she quickly grabs the boys and rushes to my car. She locks the doors and, after a thoughtful look, drives off. The last thing I see is Bruno's sad face as he waves goodbye a final time.

God, I'll miss that boy.

But I can live with it now that I know he's alive.

Or rather ... I can die in peace.

He'll be okay without me; I'm sure he will.

Julio whistles at the two men still standing there, and they come to snatch my gun and frisk me, taking my cell phone too. I knew it was coming. I just didn't know they'd grab my arms too and hold me down like some prisoner.

One fast punch to the gut and I'm bucked over, heaving.

"That's for fucking with my daughter."

Julio kicks me in the chin, causing one of my teeth to lodge itself into my lip, making me groan in pain. "And that's for breaking into my home and killing my men."

He spits on the ground in front of me then directs his attention toward one of his men. "Grab the shovels and the rope." The guy walks off and returns moments later.

The two men pull my wrists to my back and tie me up until the rope burns into my skin. Julio walks off, beckoning the guys to follow him. They drag me along like a rag doll, but I don't know where we're going, and I can't see. I'm way too fucking dizzy from the pain and just struggling not to fall. We stop somewhere farther up ahead, where Julio points at a spot on the ground and flicks his fingers.

The guys begin to dig.

Long and deep.

Like … coffin deep.

And all I can do is stare and wait until they deliver my fate.

"So you thought it was a smart idea coming here, did you?" Julio jests. "Wrong." He bursts out into laughter again as he circles me like a vulture. "And then you made a deal with the devil. Oh, oh, oh … preacher. Do you know what I'm going to do to you after all the shit you pulled?"

I shrug. "I don't care."

He stops in his tracks and frowns at me, cocking his head. "Are you sure about that?"

I glare ahead, not even giving a shit whether he's looking at me or not. It's a lost cause. I can't change anything about my fate anymore. He can't do anything more to me to hurt me. He made the deal. Gave me my dying wish. And now I've surrendered to God.

I'm untouchable.

"Aren't you even a little bit scared?"

"No."

At first, he seems confused, but then he laughs again. "You motherfucker." He spits on my face, but I keep on staring ahead. I will not lose my dignity to this man. I will go down like a soldier. Like I should've done all along. All those years wasted on liquor and sorrow. No more.

"Can you believe this shithead?" Julio jests, looking at his men.

They gaze up and momentarily stop digging. "No," one of them replies. "He's crazy."

A pause, followed by Julio frowning and yelling, "What the fuck are you doing? Get back to work!"

"Uh, yes, boss," the other one says, sweating like crazy as they both continue to dig without speaking another word.

"Now, where were we? Oh ... that's right. I was going to tell you how you're going to die." He grabs a cigar from his pocket, taking his sweet time to put it in his mouth and light it. "At first, I thought maybe I should just shoot the motherfucker and get over it. But then I realized that's too easy. It's too nice. And the man who killed my wife and took my daughter doesn't deserve nice. So now you know ... I'm not going to shoot you. No, your death will be much, much worse."

He takes a drag and blows the smoke in my face. "You know what's going to happen to you?"

A drop of rain falls on my face, and I look up at the sky to see a string of ducks fly by. Julio looks up too, and at this moment, I find my peace with whatever may come next.

"Ducks ... hmm ..." he murmurs, taking another drag as he lowers his head to look at me again. "Strange animals, they are. Have you ever seen a duck being chased by a dog?"

I don't respond. I don't even nod or shake my head. I've stopped caring.

"Well, since you're so interested, I'll tell you anyway. You'd think the duck would fly away, right? But because of its panic, it will run across the street like an idiot." He makes flapping motions with his hand, pretending to be the duck. "Until ... the dog comes close enough, at which point ..." Julio stiffens like a board. "The duck falls and plays dead in the hopes of being left as spoiled meat. A last ditch effort." He smiles. "And you know what happens next?"

Again, I don't reply. I just stare at the men who seem to be done digging their hole as they stick their shovels in the dirt, panting out loud.

"The duck still gets eaten," Julio continues.

I cock my head, giving him an annoyed look while he takes another drag and blows more smoke into my face. "The duck could've flown away, but it didn't. Instead, it fluttered and crashed, running from its predator, until it died anyway. A futile death if you ask me," he muses, sniggering like a crazy son of a bitch again.

"It's done," one of the guys says, and Julio turns around to look at the hole.

"Perfect. Put him in."

They grab my arms and drag me closer then shove me forward, so I land in the hole. I only manage to twist myself around before they start throwing dirt on my body.

"Spare his face for last. I wanna hear his dying words. Maybe I can savor them like I did with his wife."

That familiar fire burns inside me again, but it's too late to do anything right now.

As he walks off, I yell, "You'll meet your end, Julio." He glances over his shoulder, waiting until I open my mouth again, which I do. "One way or another ... you will die a lonely, horrible death, and no one will mourn over your corpse."

He narrows his eyes and his brows furrows, after which he laughs like a lunatic again. "Good joke." He waves it off. "Go on, boys. Cover him up."

***

When the grave is filled with dirt all the way up to my neck, the guys stop shoveling and signal Julio. He waltzes back from his car with a brand new cigar stuffed in his mouth. He grins as he sees my uncovered face, blurting, "You almost look decapitated."

"Hmm ... a talking head," I murmur, spitting out some dirt that got into my mouth.

"Now that would've been a sight to see," he says, laughing, but then it grows eerily quiet. "Well, got any last words?"

"I currently lack the ability to give a shit," I reply, trying to move, but my body feels stuck as a rock. "But please have my imaginary finger."

He shakes his head, blowing out more smoke. "Such a shame. If only you'd been more remorseful, maybe I would've been more kind." He takes his cigar from his mouth and signals his boys to throw more dirt on my face.

"Too bad, preacher. See you in the next life. But first ... I've got a certain old lady to take care of."

My eyes widen, and I shout, "What? No, you fucking wouldn't. You took the deal. You swore you wouldn't touch my family!"

He shrugs and holds up his hands with a disgusting smile as he walks off. "I never said anything about *her*. Better say some prayers for your church, preacher," he muses.

"You can't do this! She's innocent!" I sputter as they throw more dirt on my head, but he doesn't even turn around. "Don't you fucking touch my mother! I swear to God, I'll haunt you for the rest of your short, shitty life!" I roar.

But no matter how hard I scream, he doesn't come back.

And the more steps he takes, the further my face is covered in dirt until I'm no longer able to speak.

Fuck.

Within a few seconds, the earth has covered me to the nose. I hold my breath.

Three more shovels of dirt and I'm under.

I hear their laughter as they walk away, and I'm praying to God to give me the strength to outlast my fear. I thought I was prepared. All these years I begged for the end. But now that the moment has finally arrived, I know for sure … I am not ready to die.

CHAPTER TWENTY-EIGHT

Ezekiel 37:13 – And you shall know that I am the Lord, when I open your graves, and raise you from your graves, O my people.

One. Two. Three. Four.
Breathe out.
One. Two. Three. Four.
One more breath leaves my mouth.

I have little more to give, and the urge to gasp is almost taking over.

But I refuse to swallow dirt. I'd rather suffocate than feel sand going down my throat.

In silence, I pray to God to help me get through this.

And for some reason, I can feel him with me. Right here, underneath the ground, close to me.

One. Two. Three. Four.

I count down the seconds, but each time, it's getting worse.

God, the pressure is so high.

When I'm finally out of breath, I squeeze my lungs together, refusing to give in. A bright light shines through a tiny hole, and for a second there, I believe I've actually died and gone to heaven. God is coming to pick me up in true God-like style. I could almost hear the trumpets blare in my ear.

Except when I open my eyes, it's just a pair of lips screaming at me.

That doesn't look like God at all.

That looks like …

"Frank! Fuck, Frank." Hands pull my head up from the dirt, and the moment my lips meet sweet air, I take a gulp and let the oxygen flow into my lungs.

"Ric-card-do," I stutter, sucking in air like an addict.

"Fuck, dude, are you okay?" he asks, pulling my head out further.

"Do I look like I'm okay?" I sneer. "Jesus, dude."

"Sorry, man, I'm just … not used to this type of shit." He swallows.

"Yeah, well, that's what happens when you mess with the wrong people," I say. "Help me out, will ya?"

"What the fuck did you do to this guy to get him so pissed off?" he asks.

"I killed his wife."

"Jesus, Frank! You could've told me," Rick says. "What

if he was still here? He could've killed me too!"

"He's gone. Stop complaining and get me out of here." I look down at my nonexistent body, which gives me the creeps.

"Yeah, yeah, leave it to Rick to get your ass outta trouble. But you have to agree that my debt is paid then. Yes?"

I roll my eyes. "Yes, fine, I already told you. Just get me out."

"All right," he says, and he starts digging with his hand. "When you sent me that voicemail, I sure as hell thought you were playing a prank on me. You're lucky my girl was there and told me you weren't."

"Your girl?" I raise a brow.

"Yeah, we're kinda doing it you know ... but we're not back together or anything."

"Right ..." I nod, frowning.

"Hey, a man has needs. Like you don't know that," he retorts.

"Rick, what you do in your own time is none of my damn business," I reply.

"Exactly," he says.

"But I am curious, though ... you didn't believe me, but she did?"

"Yeah ..." He shrugs. "Women, they can feel things, you know? Got this ... fifth sense or something."

I chuckle. "Sixth sense."

"The movie?"

"No." I roll my eyes again. "Just keep digging."

"Yeah, but this ain't getting me anywhere. Be right back. I think I got a shovel in the back of my car." He gets up and starts running.

"You're saying that now?" I yell, but he doesn't hear it.

Goddamn, how I wish I had a megaphone right now.

Being buried neck-deep in dirt is really shitty if you wanna talk to people and they keep running away from you. But I can't complain. I'm already dead-happy he came for me.

It was a crapshoot to leave him a voicemail from my car on the way here, but I knew it was the only thing I could do to make sure I'd come outta this alive. Call it a fail-safe.

After I helped him take care of his child, Rick still owed me, so I told him the location and to bring a few guns as well as some water. I didn't know what to expect. Julio's known for his outlandish punishments to crime, so I had to be prepared. And phoning while driving ain't easy or smart, I'll tell you that. Almost hit a tree.

Still, made it here … and I'm alive.

Whether I'm also 'well' has yet to be seen, though. If this fucker can finally dig me up from the ground so I can save my mother before Julio kills her.

When Ricardo's back with the shovel, I tell him to do my feet first so he can drag my body out. It's much quicker that way, and there's no time to waste. He digs as fast as he can, sweat drops falling down his face as he toils. I know it's hard in the burning sun, but we've got to be fast.

"Put your whole body into it," I bark, watching him struggle.

"I know how to dig a damn hole, Frank," he replies, still shoveling away.

"He's going to hurt Margaret," I say. "We have to be fast."

"I'm going as fast as I can!" he shouts between digging.

When my shoes finally emerge, I say, "There! Grab my feet and drag me out."

"But won't that pull your head under?"

"Yes, but if you pull hard enough, it'll do the trick. I can hold my breath."

"But—"

"Just do it," I spit.

He nods and grabs my feet. "One, two ..."

On three, I take in a load of air and slam my lips shut. He pulls me under, dragging me through the dirt. It's agonizingly slow, and for a few seconds there, I worry he might not be able to pull it off. I can hear him groan as he puts all his weight into it, pulling as hard as he can, and slowly but surely, my head comes up again.

I take a big gasp as he tugs me all the way out and rolls me onto my belly. "Untie my hands," I say.

He takes a knife from his pocket and slices through the rope, setting me free.

I get off the ground and pat down my clothes then rub my wrists. "Goddamn, that feels good," I say. "Thanks."

"You're welcome," he replies, tucking the knife back into his pocket. "So what now?"

"Take me to the church," I say, running toward his car.

He grabs the shovel and runs after me.

Ricardo throws the shovel in the trunk, and we hop into the car, chasing off.

With haste, we make our way back to town. In the rearview mirror, I look at myself and brush the dirt out of my hair and straighten my jacket too. I look like a walking zombie, but at least I'm a zombie with flair.

Still, as more minutes pass, the more anxious I get. We should've been there already. Every second wasted is another one I can't afford. So I look at Rick, and ask, "Can I borrow your phone for a sec?"

"Why?" He frowns.

"They took mine," I say. "I have to warn them."

"Oh … right." He rummages in his pocket and throws it at me. "Here."

"Thanks." I quickly type in Margaret's cell phone number and call, but she doesn't pick up. Damn. She always hated that damn phone. I resort to texting her, saying that she needs to get outta there, hoping she might read it in time. Then I text Laura and tell her I'm still alive and on my way, and that she needs to stay put.

Right as we're nearing the church, I throw Rick's phone back at him and say, "Drop me off here. You go to Laura's house and make sure she's safe. I put her address in your phone."

"Why? You don't want me going with you? What if that dude's in there with a bunch of his guys? He'll kill you for real this time."

"I'll handle myself," I say, jumping out. "Take care of Laura and the kids. They're more important than I am."

"All right … if you say so."

"Thanks, dude." I slam the door shut, and he drives off.

When my feet hit the steps, I rethink my plan of attack. They'll be expecting people to come through the front door, but I doubt they know about the back door. So I stop and turn back, running around the back while holding my head down. Don't want any of those fuckers to see me coming. I climb up the steel fence and jump over into the garden, and when I softly pull the door handle, it opens. Lucky for me, Mother forgot to lock it this time.

I slip inside as quietly as possible and look around. Three men, including Julio, are sitting in the back with Mother between them. The other two motherfuckers are the same ones who buried me in the ground. They're talking to her ... or rather, laughing at her, while they make stupid jokes and scare her. Having fun with my fucking mother. My fist balls. I'm going to fucking kill them.

But first, a weapon.

I sneak along the back part of the church, using the statues and pillars to hide when they glance my way. Luckily, they're facing away from the altar, so that gives me the opportunity to slide alongside it. I carefully make my way back to my room and quickly lock the door from the inside in case they did notice me.

I swiftly open the closet and push back a board, pulling out a miniature gun that I hid there just in case shit went down. Well, shit's definitely going down right about now. This beauty doesn't hold a lot of bullets, but it's fast and does the trick.

I also grab a knife from my drawer and tuck it under my belt before I open the door again.

Slowly but steadily, I walk out, aiming my gun at the men sitting in the back of the church. Mother's terrified eyes are the first that look my way, her tears setting a fire ablaze inside me.

And as the guy to the left notices the startled look on her face and turns his head, I shoot.

The bullet hits him right between the eyes.

"What the—" Julio's voice rumbles.

One down, two more to go. However, Julio jumps up now, grabbing Mother. Meanwhile, as the other dude searches for his gun, I quickly shoot at him. One goes in his shoulder. He attempts to shoot. A bullet ricochets off the wall near me. I shoot again. This time, I hit him in the chest. He falls down to the bench.

I move away from the pillar and find Julio dragging Mother along with him, grasping her tight. He's using her as a shield as he moves closer to me and then he reaches into his pocket and takes out a gun, putting it to her temple.

"Don't you fucking do it," he hisses. "I'll kill her."

"Let her go, fuckhead," I growl, aiming for his head.

But I don't pull the trigger. I'm terrified I'll hit Mother instead.

"How the fuck did you get out of that fucking hole?" he hisses.

I narrow my eyes, making sure to keep them on him as he approaches me. "Magic."

"Don't take me for a goddamn fool," he spits, pushing the gun even harder against her temple.

She whimpers and quivers with fear as he uses his filthy hands to pull her near the altar. I don't stop him because I want him to get closer … it's the only way I can get her out of his grasp safely.

However, it also means he could shoot me easier. But I won't let that happen.

"You'll never get rid of me, Julio," I hiss.

"No, you're like a fucking disease," he replies.

We're dangerously close to each other now. "Just so you know, I take offense to that."

"You should've died in the ground," he spits. "Now,

you'll get to witness me murdering your little old granny, and after that, I'll nail you to the fucking cross."

"Over my dead body," I snarl, trying to take better aim to see if I can take the shot. He's keeping her so damn close to his body, constantly swaying around to make it harder. Goddammit.

Suddenly, the front doors to the church open and the people running in distract us both.

It's Laura, Diego ... and Bruno.

CHAPTER TWENTY-NINE

Laura, Diego, and Bruno appear right in the middle of a fight.

What are they doing here?
The should be safe at home.
Why?

"Fuck!" I hiss as Julio's seen them too.

But instead of shooting at them, he fires at me.

I duck, hiding behind the altar as he shoots again.

He pushes Mother aside so hard she falls to the ground, but he doesn't even care. All he's focused on is shooting at me and everything surrounding me.

When he momentarily stops, I shoot back, hitting the wall.

I duck again before he has the chance to blow my brains out. From the corner of my eye, I watch the kids huddle close behind a bench while Laura's holding her phone against her ear, probably to call the police.

She must've been worried about me or Mother, and that's why she came here. But I wish they hadn't. They're a liability. I *have* to keep them safe.

After Julio fires another shot, I take aim at his gun and shoot. It bounces away from his hand, and he growls from both pain and shock as it tumbles to the floor.

His eyes widen when I crawl out and get up, pointing my gun straight at him. Not once do I think before I pull the trigger.

And then I realize I'm shooting blanks.

The look on his face changes from raw fear to rage as he charges at me in full force, ramming me like a bull.

He slams me to the ground, and a fist lands on my face. My vision gets blurry, but Laura's scream keeps me wide awake. I hit back, punching him in the gut, but it doesn't get him off me. He lands another punch on my shoulder, and I howl in pain.

"I'll show you why they call me El Campeón," he growls, hitting me again.

Each fist hits like a truck, forcing the air out of my lungs. I can barely breathe.

Another fist to the mouth and blood flies around.

But the fearful faces of Bruno and Diego give me strength, and I fight back, kicking him in the balls. If I have to play dirty to win, so be it, but I'm not going to lose to this son of a bitch. No fucking way.

"Stop!" Laura yells, her voice sounding more like a cry

than anger.

We roll around the floor, punching each other, kicking and throwing fists wherever we can. However, when his hands wrap around my neck, I know I'm done for.

"Dad, don't!" Diego yells. Even he's on my side now. But it's no point if I'm choked to death.

Then I remember the knife I had in my pocket, and I swiftly pull it out to try to stab him. He pushes me back and gets up from the floor. I do too, and I swing at him with the knife, making him walk backward. He slips on the carpet and falls. Perfect.

I jump on him and try to shove the knife down his throat, but his hands are in the way. He props himself up and punches me so hard in the gut, I heave and feel the bile rise. He grabs my wrist and twists. The knife falls from my hand as I groan in pain. Then he kicks me so hard I literally fly across the hall.

Fuck.

Landing against a wall with your back is painful. So painful, I can barely breathe.

God, everything hurts, and it's so damn hard to focus. I feel around the floor to get a grip of where I am, at which point my hands reach for something odd.

Something metallic.

Julio's gun.

But then, from the corner of my eye, I spot Bruno pushing Laura away, freeing himself from her grasp.

"Bruno, no!" she calls out to him, but it's too late.

He's running … to me.

"No, stay away," I mutter, but I can barely pronounce the words. My throat is clamped, and he can't hear me from afar.

Too late. Everything's going so quick. It's like time has sped up and now he's already at my side. "You gotta get up and fight," he pleads, hugging me tightly. "I believe in you." He pushes me with his little hands like a child trying to wake his parents.

It unravels me.

Until I see Julio appear behind him with my goddamn knife ... and he grabs him.

"No!" I scream, immediately crawling up.

But it's too late ... Julio has Bruno in a tight grasp, holding the knife dangerously close to his neck.

"Let him go; he's innocent!" I yell.

Laura approaches us with Diego, but Julio's roar stops them in their tracks. "Don't come closer!"

"Dad, no! Don't do it!" Laura screams with tears running down her cheeks. "Why? He's just a little kid."

"This is it, Frank," he murmurs, looking directly at me. "Say goodbye to your goddamn son."

"No," I hiss, and I grab the gun from the floor, aiming it at him. "You can kill me for all I care, but you *will* let him live."

Bruno's eyes grow big as he struggles in Julio's arms, muttering, "Son ...?"

I swallow away the lump in my throat.

Never in a million years did I imagine he'd find out this way.

If it were up to me, it'd be different, but I was too careless. Too distracted from what really mattered. And now I'll pay the price.

"I'll kill him faster than you can shoot, Frank," Julio

barks, pushing the knife even further into the boy's skin. "Don't even think about it."

"No ... Please ..." Laura falls to her knees in front of us, tears streaming down her face. "Please, don't do this."

I don't know whether she's talking to him or me, but I respond anyway. "I have to shoot him," I say. "It's the only way to save Bruno."

"Don't let him make you a killer again, Frank," Laura says through gritted teeth. "It's not worth it. There's gotta be a way out."

"There isn't," Julio hisses. "He has to die."

"No!" she yells.

"I have to take the shot," I hiss.

"You can't! You'll hit Bruno," she shouts, angrier than I've ever seen her.

Still, I try to perfect my aim. "It's the only way ..."

"Stop! Just fucking stop!" Laura screams.

Suddenly, Julio's eyes roll into the back of his head, and he falls down to the ground, releasing Bruno with it, who runs off to Laura's arms.

Only when Julio's body hits the ground do I realize what happened.

Mother smacked the back of his head with a giant cross she pulled off the wall.

"I thought he'd never shut up." She spits on his body. "Shame on you! No one will forgive you for your sins, not even God himself," she growls.

I gape with my jaw unhinged, wondering if what I'm seeing is a figment of my imagination, but it doesn't appear to be.

Not when I see Diego's wide-open mouth and Laura's

wide-eyed glare.

We're all stunned.

Completely and utterly stunned by this old woman beating the crap out of Julio, the brawler. El Campeón.

Who'd have thought Margaret would save the day?

No one.

CHAPTER THIRTY

A few minutes later, the cops have arrived.

I put some rope around Julio's hands and tied him to one of the pillars, so he wouldn't try to escape. I'm still not sure whether I should be glad I didn't kill him, but at least Laura's content. It'd be hard on her to watch her daddy die. I just couldn't do it to her, and luckily, Mother took the choice away from me.

I'm still a bit mad over it.

Hell, I would've loved to shoot him instead.

But this … this is better.

This doesn't make me a monster again.

We tell the cops exactly what happened: Three armed men tried to rob the church, one of whom was Laura's father, which is the reason she came. She knew he would do it, so she tried to warn the people inside the church. And I tried to stop it, using any weapon I legally had in my possession, and they were eventually overpowered.

The cops actually believe us.

Of course, it's a bit skewed from the full truth, but they *did* come in uninvited and threaten to kill an old lady in a church. No one, and I mean no one, likes that. It's like some unwritten rule that you never attack a granny.

Who does that anyway?

Julio motherfucking Espino, that's who.

And I'm so damn happy they're dragging him away in cuffs.

"When I get out, you're gonna pay!" he yells at me.

"By the time you get out, we'll both be dead." I snort as they pull him through the church doors and shove him into their car.

More men come in to assess the remaining bodies and bag them up while medics come in to tend to our wounds. I'm poked with needles and stuffed with medicine, which I fucking hate, but at least it numbs the pain a bit.

"Thanks," I say with a gritty voice as they tend to me.

"I'm sorry, but we're going to have to take you to the hospital."

"Aw, c'mon …" I sigh, looking at Laura and the kids. "Really?"

"Yes, we need to check for internal damage."

"Right." I nod. "But can I at least say bye to them first?"

"Sure. Why not," the medic says, and he and his buddy go check on Mother first.

I look at Laura and the kids who all go down on their

knees beside me so they can get on my level. I'm still lying against one of the pillars for support, too fatigued to get up. Besides, the medics don't want me to move. Probably afraid I have a fracture or something, but if that was the case, I'd probably feel it, and I don't.

Still, to say I feel like shit is to put it lightly.

"How are you feeling?" Laura asks, grabbing my hand.

I chuckle. "I've been better." I squeeze her hand and look her in the eyes. "But at least you're all alive."

She immediately wraps her arms around me and hugs me tightly, unable to keep her emotions at bay. "Fuck, I was so worried, Frank. I thought you died. I really thought you … and then Ricardo showed up at our doorstep, telling us you sent him to take care of us. Of course, I asked him if you were still alive, and when he told us where you were, so I immediately came here."

"Of course, you did." I snort. "You left him there, didn't you?"

"Well, I told him to watch our fish," she muses, making me laugh.

"Since when do you have a fish?"

She shrugs. "I don't, but at least it'll keep him busy looking for it. Sorry."

I roll my eyes. "I should've expected as much."

"What? Of course, I came here as soon as I heard." She smacks me. "You terrified the shit out of me, Frank! God, I almost thought you died."

"So you admit you don't want me dead?" I muse, raising a brow.

She gives me another smack on the leg. "You asshole! Of course, I don't want you dead! Who gave you that idea?"

"Maybe that knife you tried to pry out my guts with?" I say, hinting at our furiously sexy battle in her kitchen.

"I was upset, and you know damn well why." She puts her hands on her side like it makes her murder story more understandable. "And by the way, you could've at least let us know you were alive. Or, you know, that you were planning to escape." She scrunches up her face. "You kept us out of the loop on purpose."

"What else was I supposed to do? Tell you all my secret plans right in front of Julio so he could sabotage them?"

She raises a brow. "No, but you could've called."

"I was a little busy if you hadn't noticed." I look around us at the mess the three men caused.

"Yeah ... well ... you're lucky you survived." She playfully punches me again, right on that painful spot.

I cringe, and she immediately softens her look and her touch. "Oh, shit, I'm sorry."

"It's okay," I mutter, smiling. "I'm just glad we're all alive." I reach for her face and caress her cheeks softly. "I don't know what I would've done if you'd ... if you'd ..."

"Jesus Christ, can you *please* stop the lovebird act? It's driving me insane," Diego grumbles as he gets up from the floor.

We both laugh about it. "I'm happy you're alive too, Diego," I say.

"Thanks." He shrugs. "For saving us, I suppose."

"It's the only thing I could do after causing all this trouble."

"Damn right." Laura puts her hands against her waist. "I should scold you some more, but I'm too happy that we're all still in one piece."

"Hey, your dad's the asshole here, okay? He tried to murder Bruno, and he even kidnapped his own children. If that isn't the next *American Psycho*, I don't know what is."

She sighs and shakes her head. "Oh, Frank … when will you ever learn that nothing will ever come between family?"

"Does that mean you still care about your father? After everything he did?" I ask.

"Well … he is my father …" She looks away, tentatively biting her lip before glancing at me. "But I'm glad he's in jail. He should pay for all the things he's done."

"Good."

"What about you?"

"How I feel about it?" I point at myself, and she nods. "Well … I suppose I'm happy. I mean he can't hurt anyone where he's going, so that's good."

"Still looking for revenge? Even when your son is alive?" She looks at Bruno, and when I follow her gaze and find his sheepish eyes gawking at me, I melt into a puddle.

"No." I reach for him, grabbing his tiny hand to hold him tight. "I'm okay now. It's over. It's done now."

Tears well up in my eyes, but I push them away, smiling brightly.

I'm done crying. I've shed enough tears. It's about time I let them go.

"Hey, buddy."

"Hey," he says, a little awkward.

"Thank you," I mutter.

"For what?" he asks.

"For being here." I don't mean literally here … more like … alive. But I don't want to scare him, so I don't say it out loud.

My finger brushes along his cheek as I try to memorize what he feels like. If it's the same as I remember ... back when I first held him as a baby. And as I stare into those beautiful eyes, I finally see him for who he really is.

Mine.

"Sorry." The paramedic coughs. "I don't mean to interrupt, but we really have to go now."

I look up to see they're wheeling Mother out on a stretcher, and the medics place one beside me too.

"Oh, right ..." I clear my throat as I look up at Laura and Bruno. "I'm sorry."

"It's okay." She smiles. "Let them fix you. You're no use to anyone if you can't even walk," she jokes, making me laugh but even that hurts.

The medics push the stretcher underneath me and roll me over it, strapping me to it and putting a nice warm blanket on top.

"Well ... see you all later then, I guess," I say, as they lift it up.

"We'll come visit you in the hospital." Laura picks Bruno up. "Say bye," she tells him.

I grab his hand and squeeze tight. "Will I see you later, bud?"

He nods, probably still shy about the whole situation. I don't blame him. I mean coming face to face with the fact you have a completely different father can be quite the shock ... if he even remembers. He's such a young kid. Gosh, we'll have to explain that all to him.

But now is not the time.

Now is the time for mending and for making peace with our mistakes.

And as I'm rolled out on the stretcher and placed in the ambulance, all I can do is smile. Not because it's painless because it's not. But because I'm finally free of the burden I carried all this time. Free from the coils entangled around my heart.

CHAPTER THIRTY-ONE

Hospitals are so damn boring.

Really, you just sit around and do nothing all day while you stare at a television and drink some juice. If I was still drinking alcohol, this would be amazing, but unfortunately, doing literally nothing is not that big of a deal when you're sober.

Shame.

Lucky for me, they put me in the same room as Carl. He looks a lot better now that he isn't lying in a pool of his own blood. He already showed me his scar from where they took out the bullet. Like he's proud of it or something. Oh well, you know what they say about scars … wear them like a war medal.

He can't seem to shut up about my epic battle with Julio, though. I regretted telling him the whole story the moment I finished. This dude is like the ultimate fan. Well, except for the fact that I'm not a fucking celebrity, and I don't wanna be. But I get it. He needs a role model, and I'm pretty much the best he can find.

That either says a lot about his life … or about me.

Take your pick.

Either way, he seems pretty impressed with my escape stunt.

"I can't believe you actually held your breath for that long. Two minutes? Man, I can't even keep my head underwater for more than a minute."

"Well, it's not like I had a choice now, did I?" I say.

"Yeah, but that's so cool!" He gives me this huge smile, which inflates my ego, big time.

"Learned from the best," I muse, taking a sip of my drink.

"Who?"

"Myself." I grin, and he laughs at my reply.

"So you told Ricardo where to dig you up?"

"Well, I didn't know what they were going to do to me, but I had an idea. So I gave him a list of things, including finding a mound that had fresh digging marks."

"Wow …" He nods like he's trying to picture it.

"Yep." A pause follows, and I take another loud sip of my juice, which goes through a straw, by the way. I specifically requested one.

"Jesus, Frank … why do you keep doing that?" Carl asks, hinting at my straw.

I take another sip and say, "I love it when everyone can

hear the annoying sounds I make. It's another battle strategy. Did I mention I want to get out of here as soon as possible?"

He laughs, shaking his head. "You're one weird motherfucker." He holds up his hands. "I mean that in a good way."

"Thanks."

"Besides. Who wouldn't want to get out of a hospital as quickly as they can?" He twines his hands behind his head as he relaxes on his pillow.

"Exactly. Especially when all you've got is a few bruised ribs, a slash in your lip, and a black eye." The hospital staff wanted to keep me for a night, just to make sure my organs weren't damaged from the hits I received.

"Pfft ... that's easy," Carl huffs, showing me his scar again. "See this? This is a battle scar."

I roll my eyes. "Yeah, yeah, we get it. You fought off the baddies at church."

"Hey, at least I kept Margaret safe. Can't say the same for you." That smug bastard actually raises a brow at me.

"How many people have you actually killed?" I ask, but when he doesn't respond and just opens his mouth without a sound coming out, I say, "Exactly."

"Hey, that's not fair. I'm not a criminal."

"Yet."

"I don't plan to become one."

"Oh, really?" I narrow my eyes. "Last time I checked, you asked me for my contacts."

He sighs, looking away. "That was before ... you know."

I nod. I understand. He's changed his mind, and that's

nothing to make fun of. It's a decision he should be proud of, and I am.

"I'm proud of you," I say.

His face lights up. "You mean that?"

"Of course. As long as you keep taking the good jobs. Not the bad ones." I eye him down. "Got it?"

"Got it." He smiles.

Suddenly, there's a knock on the door, and we both look up to see who it is.

My face lights up when I realize it's Laura, Diego, and Bruno. "Hi!" She waves while walking in with the boys.

"Oh, you've got visitors ... lucky you," Carl muses, winking at me. "And a beautiful lady too, might I add."

"Thanks." Laura shakes her head as she turns a bit red.

"He's right, though. You do look beautiful." I smirk like a motherfucker when her face turns even more red.

"Stop," she murmurs, grinning.

"Never."

"Oh, please," Diego grumbles, rolling his eyes. "Not this again."

"Great to see you too, Diego," I say. "Been taking good care of your brother and sister?"

"Of course." He folds his arms.

Laura pokes him with her elbow. "Didn't you have something you wanted to say?" she whispers in his ear, but I can hear loud and clear.

He looks a bit uncomfortable as he rubs his lips together and stumbles through his sentences. "I wanted to ... say thank you. For you know ... rescuing us and shit."

"And shit," I repeat, chuckling a bit.

"Yeah, you know."

"Well, it was my pleasure." I grab his hand and give it a good shake. "You're a good guy, Diego."

"Thanks. And ... I'm sorry for being shitty to you."

"It's okay. Comes with the territory of being your sister's boyfriend." I wink, which makes Laura's eyes almost bulge out of her face.

Bruno giggles. "Boyfriend?"

"We'll explain it all later," Laura quickly says, clearing her throat.

"Okay ... I'll give you four some space." Carl grabs his crutches to get off the bed. "Don't break down the whole place while I'm gone."

"I promise I won't touch your stack of magazines, I mean porn," I yell as he goes through the door, and he sticks up his middle finger at me, making me laugh.

Laura sits down on my bed and grabs my hand. "It's so good to see you well."

"Yeah, I just have a couple of bruises and tiny slash in my lip. No big deal."

"You could've died, Frank. It was a big deal."

"So? I'm alive, and you are too. That's all that matters," I say with a smile, and I let my hand roam free across her face, caressing her cheeks and lips. I don't know why. I just have this tendency whenever I'm close to her ... I wanna touch her ... memorize every inch of her skin.

"So ... what about me?" Bruno suddenly says with a high-pitched voice.

We all look at him, and Laura says, "Oh, right ... I promised you something, didn't I?"

She lifts him up from the ground and sets him on the bed beside me. "Frank ... I think you want to tell him something, don't you?"

"Right …" I nod, licking my lip. I grab his arms and rub his back. "Bruno … I just wanted to say—"

"You're my dad," he interrupts.

Confused, I frown and smile at the same time. "Did you …?"

"I heard it with my own ears," he states. "Is it true?"

I nod.

And then the most unexpected thing happens.

He just falls into my arms and hugs me.

Like a real, genuine, soul-crushing hug.

I wrap my arm around him and hold him tight, finally feeling his heartbeat against mine.

"My son," I mutter, tears welling up in my eyes.

Bruno looks up and asks, "But if you're my daddy … does that mean I have two daddies?"

"No." I chuckle. "Julio is Laura and Diego's daddy. But I'm the only daddy you've got."

"Oh." He shrugs. "Well, I like you a lot, so this is better." He returns to hugging me, making me wanna cry and laugh at the same time.

"Aww … I like you a lot too, Bruno," I say.

Laura also seems to be unable to hold back the tears as she puts her hand in front of her mouth and struts around uneasily. Meanwhile, Diego's looking out the window, clearing his throat and pretending he doesn't care, but I still notice the glistening in his eyes.

Bruno pushes himself up from me and looks me dead in the eyes. "If you're my daddy … then who's my mommy?" he asks with furrowed brows.

"Well, it's not Laura and Diego's mom," I answer,

brushing his tiny cheeks. "Your mommy ... isn't here anymore. But she loved you so very much."

"Why did she go? And where?"

"To heaven, Bruno," Laura answers. "We already talked about that, remember?"

"Oh ... so she died?"

I nod, feeling bittersweet.

"But it's okay ... Mommy is where she's supposed to be, looking down on us and watching over you." I poke his chest with my index finger. "And she knows you're finally where you're supposed to be."

"Where's that?"

"With me." I grin, grabbing him to tickle him hard.

His giggles fill the room with laughter and smiles, and I can't stop ... I don't wanna stop feeling this way.

Happy.

For the first time in years, I feel happy.

"Stop, stop!" Bruno says, giggling like crazy.

"All right ... but only if you promise to always listen to Laura, understand?"

"But if you're my daddy and her mommy isn't my mommy ... then she's not my sister either, right?"

"She is ..." I raise a brow at his smart comment. God, how do I explain this? "Your sister... is still your sister in here." I point at his heart. "You don't have to be related to be family."

"Oh ..." he hums and then smiles. Guess it's that easy with kids.

"So you're part of my family too now," he says.

"Yup," I reply.

"Does that mean you're staying with us now?"

"Oh, well … we'll have to see about that. Have to ask your sister what she thinks." I look at Laura, whose jaw is wide open, and her cheeks have the same color as a strawberry.

"Well …" She folds her arms. "Your dad and I will have to discuss that. In private."

"Aw …" Bruno scrunches up his face, so I kiss him on the forehead.

"It's okay, kid; it'll only take a while. Besides … you'll see me again in no time."

His face brightens up. "Really? When?"

"When I get outta here … First thing." I wink.

Diego approaches us and helps Bruno off the bed. "C'mon. Let's find a vending machine. Maybe we can get you some Skittles."

"Skittles? Yes!" Suddenly, he's happy again. God, it's so easy with kids. They change moods in less than a second. I wish I could do that.

When the two are gone, Laura sits down on my bed again and puts her hand on my arm. "How are you really feeling?"

"Better, now that I'm alone with you."

Oh … so smooth.

I can't help but grin from my own comment, but she rolls her eyes.

"I'm glad you're feeling like your old self again."

"Oh, no, I'm not going back to being a drunk-ass bitch again. No way."

She hides a laugh behind her hand. "Good. Your talents are wasted with all that alcohol."

"What talents? Or do you mean my tongue?" I dip it out

and roll it around my lips, making her groan and smack my arm.

"Frank!"

"Sorry, sorry," I joke.

"So ... are you okay with the fact that my dad's not dead? Despite everything he did to you?"

"To us, you mean," I say. "He hurt you too."

She nods, looking down at the sheets.

Maybe that was a bit insensitive of me. "I'm sorry about your dad," I say.

"Oh, no, you don't have to be sorry. He deserves to go to jail for the rest of his life. I mean I'm glad he's there. At least he won't be able to cause any more pain." She smiles softly. "I just wanted to say thank you for saving us."

"Like I had any other choice. I'd much rather die than see you, Bruno, or even Diego hurt by his hands."

She smiles again and bites her lip, looking at me with those dreamy eyes. Gosh, I wanna kiss her so badly. And then I figure ... why not?

So I grab her face and pull her close until our lips touch and our mouths lock. I can't help but smile as I kiss her because every second I taste her on my lips is another win.

She's everything I ever wanted, and I think I'm only just beginning to understand what this means for me. For us. For the future.

When our lips unlatch, her face still hovers so close to mine. I can feel her hot breath on my skin, and it makes me wanna do all the dirty stuff I promised the nurses I wouldn't. The question is: Would anyone notice if we did?

"I know what you're thinking, and the answer is no," she quips, putting up a finger.

"Aw … c'mon." I sigh.

"No! This is a hospital, for crying out loud." She snorts. "But I'm glad your dick still works perfectly fine."

"You can break my bones and shoot me down, but nothing will ever stop this monster dick from getting stiff as a rod, trust me."

She snorts, and I kiss her again for good measure, tasting the sweetness that is her mouth so I can remember it while I'm stuck in this stupid hospital bed and she's gone home.

"Ugh … I wish I could stay," she murmurs against my lips.

"Can't you?"

"I'm not a patient, remember?"

"You could be. There's an empty bed. I'll kick Carl out."

She sniggers from my comment. "You'll be out in no time."

"And what then?" I ask. "Are you coming to live with me in the church or …?"

"No, thanks. I don't wanna get killed by Margaret. Or worse … give her a heart attack."

"Heart attack?" I frown.

"She'd die of one if she caught us having sex one more time."

I laugh. "Well, she'll just have to deal with that then. I mean, c'mon, a man's got his needs, right? She knows that."

"Does she even like me?" she asks, toying with my hair.

"Of course, she does." I grab her hand and kiss the back. "You like me … so she likes you too. The two go hand in hand."

"Really?" She raises a brow. "Because I know what we

did last time we were there, and it wasn't pretty."

"We'll be more ... secretive from now on," I muse, biting my lip. "And I can't wait to defile the church all over again." I grunt and pull her onto the bed with me, smashing my lips to hers, fiercely taking her.

I can't help myself. It's just the way I am. A needy asshole who can't get enough of her.

"Stop," she murmurs, grinning. "We have to behave."

"For now. But wait until I'm outta here. Then we'll see how bad I can get."

"Who says I wanna?"

"Don't lie to yourself," I tease, poking her in the belly. "You and I both know you want me."

"Fine." She rolls her eyes. "I'll take you back, but ..." She pushes me back with a flat hand. "You still have some making up and groveling to do, Mister."

With a lopsided smile, I say, "Call me Father Frank ... and I'll make you confess all your sins."

She giggles and grins as I grab her and force my mouth on hers again, finally claiming what's always belonged to me.

She even kisses me back with the same amount of greediness, never taking her lips off mine. I literally have to grab her arms and push her away so I can ask the question that's been on my tongue since forever.

"So ... we good then?" I ask.

"Yeah, I guess," she says with furrowed brows. "What do you mean?"

"Well, Bruno asked if I was part of the family now, so I guess I had to ask." I shrug.

She playfully slaps me. "Of course, you are, silly."

"So does that mean I get to move in with you guys

then?"

She rolls her eyes, and her jaw drops. "You did not just ask that."

"Oh, yes, I did. I'm tired of living with old Granny Margaret. Got a spare room? No, no, wait. I can sleep in your bed ..." I wiggle my eyebrows, and she makes a funny face.

"You ... I'll make you regret the day you begged me to come stay at our house."

I smile and so does she, and I reply, "Oh, I'll definitely take you up on that challenge. Starting tomorrow."

CHAPTER THIRTY-TWO

We're finally going back home today, and as Ricardo had something to make up for, he came to pick us all up. His face immediately turns sour the moment we step out of the door and into the parking lot.

"Hey, Ricardo," I say, and both Carl and Margaret greet him too.

"Hey, guys ... look, I'm sorry," he immediately begins.

"Too late, bro," I muse, laughing. "It's already done and over."

He rubs the back of his head. "I hope it wasn't too painful. Fuck. This is all my fault."

"Why? Laura and the boys didn't do this to me," I say. "It was Julio."

"No, but if they'd stayed at the house, maybe they wouldn't have distracted you. I mean you could've died," he says.

"I'm alive," I reply. "That's all that matters."

I try to act cool because that's just how we roll. I'm done feeling guilty, and he should be too.

"How do you feel?" he asks.

I shrug. "As good as I look."

He rubs his lips together. "I'm really, really sorry. I really am. I just couldn't stop them from coming to the church."

"Dude, it's not your fault," I say. "She was determined to come rescue me or something. I dunno."

"She even stole my damn car," he growls, pushing Carl's wheelchair.

"She did?" I raise a brow, impressed with her skills. Ricardo isn't easy to bypass. He's a big guy.

"Yeah, well, after she locked me in the house, they all jumped into my car and raced off. Even left skid marks on the street. So damn lucky my car wasn't damaged. I would've been pissed."

Guess I was wrong about the fool part.

I look at him. "Fish, huh?"

He raises his brows. "What? She was very … convincing."

I narrow my eyes as I help Carl into the back of the car. "Just admit that you're thick."

With a straight face, he says, "Fuck you, Frank. You're just as thick. Who the fuck goes into a shootout without a gun? Like, who does that?"

I laugh. He's right; it was stupid, but he didn't know I had one hidden in my room. "I did get a gun, though."

"Where?"

"In my room." I shrug.

"You keep a gun in your room?" Margaret suddenly asks as she sits down in the passenger's seat.

"Well, I did. Not anymore, of course." I smile. "It was only to protect us."

"I guess it served its purpose well then," she answers, taking a deep breath.

"Exactly. I saved our asses. That's all that matters." I sit down beside Carl and close the door.

Meanwhile, Ricardo gets behind the wheel and glances at me over his shoulder. "You're one lucky son of a bitch; you know that, right?"

I grin, feeling even more lucky as we drive away from this damned hospital. "You betcha."

***

When we get to the church, I hop out of the car and help Mother out too. We dropped Carl off at his home where he'll be taken good care of by his family. Ricardo helps Mother back inside the church while I grab the bags from the trunk.

"Thanks, dude," I say as I walk in after him and drop them on the floor.

"Don't mention it." We give each other a bro-hug. "But … I consider the debt fully paid now," he adds with a wink. "More like overpaid."

I nod. "Got it."

He turns around, but before he leaves, he asks, "We still on for that cookout next week?"

I grin. "Oh, yeah … it's on."

He smiles and waves as he leaves.

I bring my bag to my room. Meanwhile, Mother's already waddled back to her room in the back. I bring her bag to her. "Here you go, Margaret."

"Margaret?" She looks up at me with big eyes. "You never call me that."

I frown as she approaches me and puts her hands on my shoulder. "You don't like it?" I ask.

She straightens my jacket for me like she always does when she's worried. "I like it when you call me Mother. It makes me feel useful."

The warm smile on her face makes me happy, and I place my hand on top of hers and squeeze. "You'll always be my mother."

"Are you sure? Because it looks like you gained another one on the way." She chuckles, and then eyes the door like I'm supposed to look. When I do, I notice Laura's peeking through it all the way from the hallway.

"She's quite the girl," Mother whispers. "Feisty to the bone and sassy as can be." She gently pats my cheeks. "Exactly my boy's type."

I snort. "She sure is … and quite the mother too."

"I think you two will do well with Bruno …"

"You do?" I do value her opinion. A lot, actually.

"He's just as spirited and courageous as you were when you were young," she muses.

"Really?" A lopsided grin appears on my face.

"Of course, and you know what? I think they're waiting for you."

"But …" I grab her hand. "I can't leave you alone in this

huge place."

She snorts. "Course you can. You did it before."

I scratch the back of my neck. "True ..."

"But those boys and that girl are actually a good reason." She pats me on my cheeks again, this time even harder, making it feel like she's trying to teach me a lesson.

"So you're okay with ...?"

"Course I am! Just go." She twists me around and pushes me. "Be where you're supposed to be."

"But I'll still come do the sermons ..." I mutter.

"Yes, yes. But not today." She gives me a surprising slap on the butt that stings a little. "Now go."

"All right, all right," I say, laughing a little.

Warmth fills my chest the moment I see Laura's glinting smile as she greets me. "Hey."

"Hi, yourself," I muse, rolling my eyebrows until she laughs. "One sec, I have to grab my bag."

"Okay," she replies as I quickly run into my room and back to her again with my bags in hand. "Ready when you are."

She playfully slaps my chest and says, "C'mon. They're waiting."

"They being 'the boys,' I assume?"

She folds her arms. "Who else? Besides, they asked why you weren't at home."

I put my arm around her shoulder as we turn and walk toward the exit. "You do realize you basically gave me the go-ahead to move in with you, right?"

She chuckles. "Like that was even up for debate."

I pull her closer. "Now you're getting it."

I can't stop grinning. The whole way we drive back to

her place, I'm just goddamn happy. And that says something.

When I jump out of the car, Bruno's peeking through the window with a big, fat smile on his face, shouting at his brother. He runs off and opens the door for us.

"Daddy!"

His face and the smile that follows as he runs out into the yard and into my arms are all I need.

I'm here.

I'm exactly where I belong.

EPILOGUE

Holding Bruno's hand, I walk into Chuck's Bar and sit down on a stool with him. He claps his hand with excitement, looking up as Chuck walks in from the back.

"Well, well, if it isn't Frank Romero." He puts down a few new boxes of liquor on the floor and shoves them under the bar. "I didn't expect to see you back here."

"Yeah. For a minute, I didn't either," I jest, snorting.

"What happened? Got in a bar fight again?"

"Eh, something like that," I answer, winking at Bruno who I know has many questions he can't wait to ask.

"And who's this young fella?" Chuck asks him.

"I'm Bruno." He holds out his little hand, and when Chuck grabs it, he dramatically shakes it.

"Well, it's nice to meet you, Bruno." Chuck's rumbling laugh fills the bar.

He puts down a glass in front of me. "The usual?"

"What's the usual?" Bruno asks, curiously looking at the

glass.

"It's something for grown-ups," I say. "You'll get to try it out too, one day. But …" I clear my throat. "Let's have a drink together."

"Oh, yes! Something fizzy." He grins. "Laura doesn't let me have fizzy drinks."

"Well, you can have them here," Chuck says.

"Coke," I say. "Two."

"Two?" Chuck raises a brow.

I shrug. "No more alcohol for me."

"Really?" He frowns, surprised.

"Yup." I feel kind of proud about it, if I do say so myself.

Just as proud as I am of my son.

I pat him on the back and ask, "You like that, kid?"

"I don't know. I've never had Coke, but I can't wait to try it!" he says, a little too over the top, like kids always do.

I smile. "But you gotta promise me you'll drink it fast. We have to be at the church soon."

He nods, but his eyes are immediately distracted by Chuck pouring Coke into the glasses. It's as if he can already imagine what it tastes like. His innocent excitement really makes it that much more fun.

Chuck dunks a decorated straw into Bruno's drink and pushes it toward him. "There you go, kiddo."

"Oh, look at all the bubbles!" Bruno squeals, leaning over to hear them burst in his ear.

I lean in and whisper, "If you blow into your Coke, you can make even more."

He forms an O shape with his mouth and then immediately puts the straw against his lips, blowing hard.

Half the Coke spills over his glass, but the giant bubbles that form make him giggle hard.

Chuck shakes his head and laughs as he gets a small towel and wipes off the bar. "You're teaching him all the wrong things. Guess no one could expect anything less from you."

"Damn right, he's gotta be just as bold and brass as his dad."

Chuck smacks down the bottle he was unpacking onto the counter, his jaw wide open. "Dad ... wait, what?" His eyes flash back and forth between me and Bruno, and the more he seems flabbergasted, the more I'm starting to grin.

"He's ... *your* son?"

I take a big gulp of my Coke before I answer. "Yep." I wrap my arm around Bruno's shoulder, who's happily slurping down his Coke.

"But I thought he was ..."

"Lost," I say, winking. "It's a long story."

"My God ..." Chuck shakes his head like he still can't believe it, and he leans over the counter. "Let me take a good look at you." He eyeballs Bruno like he can't believe what I'm saying, but the longer he stares, the more I see a smile. "He does look a little bit like you. Damn."

Bruno sticks his finger into the air and yells out, "Damn!" Making us both laugh.

"He's got your vocabulary all right."

With a smug face, I lean back on my stool. "Told you. My son."

"God ... I still can't believe it." He shakes his head in disbelief.

"Well, it was a surprise, to say the least. I guess God

really does care about me after all," I joke.

"Maybe he saw how much of an ass you were making of yourself and decided enough was enough," Chuck retorts, and I nod, smiling like an idiot.

"Damn straight, and we both deserved it, didn't we?" I hug Bruno and rub his head, messing up his hair.

"My previous daddy wasn't nice at all, but Frank is. He makes a lot of jokes and takes us out to the park and the zoo. Sometimes, he farts too, and they're just as smelly as mine are."

Chuck and I snigger.

"And he even cooks spaghetti!" Bruno adds cheerfully, sipping his Coke.

"Previous daddy?" Chuck raises his brow. "Do I even wanna know?"

"No chance." I chuckle. "Maybe another time, but not today. We've got somewhere to be." I drink the whole glass and put it down then climb off the stool. "Ready, Bruno?"

He makes a few last bubble sounds with his straw before finishing up.

"Done!" he boasts, handing the glass back to Chuck with flair.

"See you next time, kid." Chuck winks. "Pleasure to meet ya."

"It was nice to meet you too, sir!"

"Such a gentleman, hmm." Chuck nods, clearly impressed. "Must've gotten that from your mom because he sure as hell didn't get it from his dad."

I laugh as I help Bruno off the stool and grab his hand. "We'll see you soon, okay?"

"Sure," Chuck says as we turn around and walk for the

door. "Oh, and tell Laura to buy some lights for tonight before she comes to work. I need to get them fixed, but I keep forgetting."

I stick my hand in the air, yelling back, "Will do!"

***

An hour later, I've finished my sermon about hardships and how God will always help you find your way back to happiness.

For the first time in ages, people are smiling at me.

For the first time in forever, Mother didn't interrupt my speech halfway through and demand I stop.

It went so well that even Laura came up to kiss me, embarrassing the boys to the point of them blushing and telling us to go find a room.

I'm still reeling with excitement as the people leave the church, thanking me for my help. It seems like ages ago that I last acted like a total douche even though it was only a few weeks. So much has changed between then and now. Looking back, I can only say … I'm so damn glad I went through everything I did.

Why?

Because it meant meeting my son again.

Because it meant falling in love all over again.

It's not easy starting over.

But the people who love me definitely make it worth it.

Laura walks up to me and smacks me on the butt. "Well done, dude."

"Thanks." I grin. "You already said that."

"I know," she says with a mischievous grin. "But I want

you to remember that."

"Is that some kind of hint?" I muse, pulling her toward me and grabbing her butt.

"Maybe …"

"Eww," Diego mutters.

"Guys, why don't you go back home?" Laura tells the boys. "You can play the new game we bought …"

"Really?" Bruno's eyes light up like there's a fire behind us.

"Yes. But only if you and your brother behave." She holds up a finger. "No fighting."

"Yeah, yeah. I still need to write my résumé, so I don't have much time anyway," Diego says, grabbing Bruno's hand. "C'mon."

"Does that mean I go first?" Bruno asks as they walk to the door.

"Sure, why not," Diego says casually, waving at us as they walk out.

"Résumé?" I mutter.

"Yeah, Diego's looking for a job." Laura winks. "Finally."

"Good. I'm proud of him. He's come far," I say.

"Yeah …" she agrees.

Mother has already left to go get some groceries for the small refrigerator she has in her room, so now Laura and I are all alone in this big, empty church.

I wonder what will happen.

"So …" Laura fiddles with my shirt. "I've been thinking … It's been too long since I last did a confession."

"Oh, really now? Is there anything you need to tell me?" I ask, grabbing her fingers to kiss, one by one. "Anything …

filthy? Raunchy? Wrong?"

She bites her lip. "All of it ... and I think we should go discuss it in the confessional."

"Hmm ..." I nod, raising a brow while a devious smile appears on her face.

"One on one, you know ... to get down to the core." Her hands are all over my crotch, making my dick hard and my grin even bigger.

"I may have a little bit of time for that ... After all, you never know when Margaret will come back," I say, grabbing her ass and squeezing tight.

"It'll only take a few minutes ... Not a lot is going to come out of my mouth. Just in." She grins.

I grab her chin, and our lips graze before I give her soft kisses, which quickly turn into rabid ones. We slowly stumble backward until we hit the confessional, and she squeals when we fall inside.

I sit down on the bench and pull her on my lap, rubbing my hard-on against her underwear. She's only wearing a skirt, so I can easily slip my fingers underneath and touch her.

"Forgive me, God, for I'm about to sin like fuck," Laura murmurs as she kisses me and rubs her tits all over my chest.

"Oh, yes ..." I whisper, smiling as I brush my lips against hers. "Let's sin like fuck together."

EPILOGUE TWO

Hand in hand, we stroll to the back of the church. I take her outside to the private garden where her mother's body lies. Laura takes a big gulp of air and stares down at the ground.

"Point me to it," she says.

I told her a long time ago where her mother really was.

I didn't have the guts at first, but when she asked, I couldn't keep it hidden any longer.

She needed to see this to be able to say a proper goodbye. She deserves no less. So I point at the grave in the corner with the tiny tombstone resting in the earth. "There."

She saunters over to it, clutching herself as she gazes at the soil.

For a while, she just stands there. Then she goes to her knees. She puts her fingers to her lips and kisses them before placing her hand on the ground.

"I love you, Mom …" she murmurs.

Nothing I will say changes the fact she's dead. No sorry will bring her back, and I know that. I've accepted that burden.

But I think we're okay now. Laura and me. I know for sure when she turns her head and doesn't give me a scowl. Instead, it's a gaze of relief.

She shivers even though it's not cold, so I approach her and put my hand on her shoulder. "If you need time alone, I understand."

"No, I like it better this way," she says. "I prefer something to hold. To feel. To keep me here, you know? I can't explain it."

"I know the feeling," I say, nodding. "Take all the time you need. I'm here."

She briefly touches my hand before she lowers her head and begins to pray.

I take my cigarettes from my pocket and pull one out, putting it in my mouth. But right before I light it, I realize I don't even like this shit anymore. So I walk to the bin and throw them all into the trash. I'm done ruining my body.

When I turn around, Laura has already gotten up and is walking toward me.

"Hey, you okay?" I ask.

She nods. "Thanks. For bringing me here, I mean."

"Of course," I reply, clearing my throat because it's a little uncomfortable. Not because a dead body is buried behind a church or anything, but mostly because I was the one who killed her.

"Anything to make it up to you," I say.

"I know. I appreciate it," she says. "It must be hard on you."

"Not as hard as it is on you." I rub her back.

"Thanks." She leans in, and I hug her. "Is it okay … if she stays here?"

"Sure. I don't see why not."

"It's just that … she always wanted to be close to God, and I can't think of a better way to honor her than to keep her close to a church, you know?"

"Of course." I briefly smile and nod when she looks up at me. "You ready to go?"

She nods softly. "Let's go home."

***

Back at home, Ricardo's already fired up the grill. "Hey, Frank! Finally back, I see."

"Hi," Laura says with a big smile, instantly cheered up by the grins of the people around her. Especially when Bruno comes running into her arms, hugging her tight. His smile is so damn infectious, it gets me every time, and I take him from her to tickle him good.

"Ahh, let go!" he squeals, laughing.

"Can't run away from the tickle monster," I growl playfully, pulling him up by his ankles so he can fly upside down. I pull all sorts of crazy stunts with him, and he likes it so much that he begs me for more.

But I have other things to do too, so I put him down and say, "Hey, Laura needs some help setting the table. Think you can do that?"

He nods quietly, and when I say, "Go," he runs off like a good boy.

"So … you ready for this?" Ricardo asks, holding a

spatula as he looks back and forth between me and the grill.

"You betcha." I grin. "But I'm not cooking on a grill."

"What? Too manly for you?" He raises a brow.

I give him a side elbow. "Fuck you, Rick. I'll show you who's boss."

"Yeah, can't wait to see that."

I crack my knuckles. "I already prepared half the shit I need. It's sitting in the fridge as we speak."

He snorts. "Yeah, right. You're just saying that because you're not prepared."

"Pfft. For what? This here?" I point at his burger patties.

"Excuse me, but that's quality meat, yeah? Some fine ass cow died for this, so you'd better appreciate that." He chucks them onto their side. "Besides, no one can grill a burger patty like me. I'm the king of the burgers."

"More like the king of the Cheerios, you mean."

"Fuck you, dude," he says, and I smile deviously.

I just love messing with him.

Can't wait to show him who's boss of the kitchen, though.

I'm so damn glad I agreed to this cookout. Now I can show Laura what a great asset I can be. And maybe, just maybe, she'll reward me for the effort with a nice suck and swallow.

"You two seem to get along nicely," Carl interjects as he holds out a beer to us both. "Take this. It'll calm your tits."

"No, it won't," I say, grabbing it anyway. "But I'll take it."

Ricardo snatches the beer from Carl's hand and gulps it down in one go, burping out loud when he's done. "Ahhh …"

"Manners, Ricardo!" Mother yells.

"Sorry," he says, rolling his eyes.

"Thanks for the invite," Carl says. "I love it when I don't have to cook. But please don't start a fight over the food. I hate it when dinner is spoiled."

I grin. "Oh, we're fighting all right. But it's a manly match without fists. Only food and cutlery are involved."

"You just wait till I'm done," Ricardo says.

"Right back atcha," I say, walking into the house.

"If you run away, I swear I'll chase you with these motherfucking burgers until you eat them all!" he yells.

"Everyone will be full by the time they finish with *my* dish!" I yell back, chuckling.

I quickly go into the kitchen and take out the marinated beef along with some green onions, bell peppers, and mushrooms. I chop everything and prepare a pot of boiling water. I put the noodles in then throw all the veggies and meat in a pan with some soy sauce, ginger, pepper, honey, a splash of vinegar, and sesame seeds. When everything's done, I mix it up and bring it outside in a big bowl.

"Bon appetite," I say with a big grin as I place it on the table.

"Finally, dinnertime," Diego grumbles, immediately filling up his plate.

Bruno's face lights up, and Laura licks her lips. "Looks good, Frank!" she says.

"It's even better in your mouth." I wiggle with my eyebrows, and she smacks me with her spoon.

"Here comes the better food!" Ricardo yells, bringing in two plates of patties stuffed with sauce-coated meat and veggies.

Mother walks in and out of the house, bringing a salad bowl. "Here are some more greens."

"Yummy!" Bruno says, stomping his fork and knife on the table. "Let's eat!"

I smile and sit down too. "Go ahead!" Everyone digs in and fills their plates while Ricardo and I eye each other like gunmen in a Western showdown. He even picks up his fork and pretends to shoot at me then blows on it. I softly whistle the tune from *The Good, the Bad, and the Ugly*.

We both wait until everyone's started eating, watching without taking our eyes off each other.

"How's the meat?" I ask.

"Good!" Laura says.

"Delicious!" Bruno tops it up.

"Yes, it's quite nice," Mother says, slurping a noodle.

Diego mumbles with his mouth full, "It's okay."

"I'm tackling the burger first," Carl says, munching on the bun.

I take a bite of my own noodles and enjoy the rich flavors then I take a bite of Ricardo's burger. They're both equally good, which begs the question ... who actually won?

"So who won this cooking match?" Ricardo asks, beating me to it.

"I don't know," Laura says.

When we look at Margaret, she just shrugs and smiles. "I'm enjoying both."

"What do you like best, Carl?" I ask.

"Well ... I dunno. They're both good."

"Yeah, can I have more?" Bruno asks.

"I don't care," Diego says. "As long as there's more. I'm

damn hungry."

I chortle from his comment. "So what's the verdict?"

"Tie," Laura says, smiling stupidly.

"I agree; you both did amazing," Margaret says.

My fork drops onto the table. "Really? That's the answer?"

"Yeah," Diego agrees.

"Seriously?" Ricardo raises a brow. "No way. Those burgers have to be better."

"Nope," Bruno says with a grin, eating both foods at the same time.

I laugh. "Well, at least neither of us lost." I hold out my hand and wait until he takes it. "We fought well. Let's bury the ax."

"Fine. But my burgers are still the champion."

"And nothing tastes as good as my noodles," I muse.

"Are you two done now? I wanna get back to eating the food," Diego says, making us all laugh.

***

When everyone's full, I help Laura and the kids bring the plates to the kitchen while Carl and Ricardo chat with Mother outside. Laura's washing the dishes on her own, so I see it as a perfect time for something else.

I wrap my arms around her waist and whisper into her ear, "Hope you liked dinner, but I've got something else in mind for dessert."

"Hmm …" She chuckles. "Does it involve some type of delicious cream?" she muses. "If so, I'm game."

I grin as I press a kiss to her shoulder. "Oh, yes, and I

don't intend to wait, so dry off your hands."

"But we have visitors," she hisses, glancing over her shoulder. "What if they see?"

"I'm not doing it *here*," I say, my fingers slithering up her shirt.

She writhes under my touch. "Well, we can't just leave them there. What if they notice we're gone?"

"It'll only be a couple of minutes, tops," I murmur, taking her earlobe into my mouth and sucking on it.

She groans. "Oh, all right ..."

"I know; I make it so hard on you," I joke, dragging her with me to the bathroom.

When we're inside, I lock the door and immediately smother her with kisses. She giggles as I grope her everywhere, making sounds I'm not supposed to make when you have guests who could hear you at any moment. But that only makes it all the more fun.

"You sure we can do this quick?" she asks.

"Babe, I can make you come in less than a minute," I moan, smashing my lips on hers.

I pull off her shirt, and she tears at mine, throwing them both to the floor. I grab her by the hips and pull her up, perching her on the bathroom counter. Pressing my face between her tits makes her squirm, but not as much as ripping down her zipper and pulling down her pants does.

"Shhh ..." I place a finger on her lip, and she immediately sucks it into her mouth. "Unless you want them to hear."

She raises a brow at me. "C'mon, Frank, you said you could make me come in less than a minute ..."

Narrowing my eyes, I say, "Challenging me, huh? I'll

show you what my tongue can do."

Ripping her panties out of the way, I don't give a shit they're torn at the seam, and I bury my face between her legs. She moans softly as I lap her up, letting my tongue roll all over her pussy and clit. I know she likes what I do; I've been doing it long enough to know precisely how she likes it.

What I have to do to make her say my name.

I lick harder, and her head falls back on the mirror. She closes her eyes, and her knees fall sideways so I can properly suck her clit.

She grabs my hair and pushes me down. Greedy girl. She knows just how to push my buttons and give me a boner from here to Timbuktu. I pull down my zipper and rub my dick while I lick her, enjoying the sweet taste of her wetness.

Groaning against her pussy lips, I brush along her sensitive nub, making her quiver.

"Fuck, Frank … I'm so close."

I grin and dive back in, making sure to give her everything she needs to come. Furiously jerking off, I listen to her sounds and feel her body heat rise until finally she bursts and the wetness pours out.

Panting, she reaches for my hand and pulls it to her tits.

"Fuck me, Frank. Do it hard and fast."

Fuck me.

That'll get me going, all right.

Bobbing up and down, that is.

She grabs my dick and rubs it along her slit, making it nice and wet. Biting her lip, she pulls me closer, so I thrust into her while smashing my lips to hers.

I kiss her senseless while fucking her at the same time. Pounding into her, I make sweet fucking love to her, while our mouths collide, breaths mingling with saltiness and arousal. If God is watching us now, I'll probably need to repent for days.

I fuck her so hard, the sink is making noise, and it might alert the guests. But who gives a shit. As long as I can fuck my girl and give us both pleasure, I'm more than happy.

And I'm definitely feeling the high right now.

Fuck, her pussy feels so good.

She rubs herself right in front of me as I ram into her, giving me something to watch.

"You like this, don't you?" she mutters.

"Reminds me of the confessional. And fuck was that sexy," I growl, burying myself deep inside her. "Just like this."

"Dirty preacher," she jests.

"I'll show you just how dirty I can get."

Right before I come, I pull my dick out and squirt all over her. Tits. Belly. Face. Mouth. From top to bottom, I leave nothing untainted. It's even going down her throat, and she gurgles from the surprise.

When I'm done shooting my load, she gasps. "Frank!"

"Told you I'm a filthy fuck," I muse.

She playfully slaps me on the shoulder while biting her lip. "Now I've gotta clean it all up."

"Oh, yeah, babe ..." I mutter as I pull her off the bathroom counter and force her to her knees. "Clean it all up."

She narrows her eyes and makes a funny face at me but then proceeds to lick me anyway.

God ... that feels so good.

So damn good, I get hard again.

"Oh, my God, Frank," she murmurs, giggling. "Is it ever enough for you?"

"Your tongue? Never," I reply, grinning like a motherfucker when she puts me in her mouth.

She licks the full length of my shaft, making sure to go over that good spot before taking me all the way.

Fuck.

My dick bounces up and down in her throat, and she gags.

"Keep going," I say, grabbing her chin with one hand to make her look at me.

She sucks beautifully. Obediently. Like she's a hooker for my cum, and I love it.

I fucking love her to death.

And when I hear that sucking sound and feel that tongue go round and round, I just wanna come all over her again.

Maybe I'll do just that.

"You wanted cream," I muse. "I'll give you cream."

"Fuck, yes," she murmurs, still rubbing herself as she licks the tip. "I wanna taste you."

I arch my back and grab a fistful of her hair, forcing her to take it all the way. That gag ... Fuck. Me.

After I give her a few seconds to breathe, I thrust in balls deep.

"Take it down your throat like a dirty girl," I growl, holding on tight.

Her eyes are all teary, and her face is covered in my cum, and it makes her look so damn appetizing. But I already had my fair share of her deliciousness ... now, it's her turn.

Once more, I grasp her head and make her give me head all the way to the base. My balls slap against her chin as she struggles to breathe, gagging a little.

"Shhh," I murmur. "Don't want the guests to know you're getting fucked hard in here."

She grins as well as you can when you've got a truckload of dick stuck in your mouth.

"Now take it ... I'm about to come," I groan, thrusting back in again.

Her tongue rolls around my length, and a burst of ecstasy shoots through my body, followed by the release. I let it all out, jetting it down her throat, making her swallow it all. I love the sound she makes when she gulps, knowing I'm giving her all the cream she could ever want after a good meal.

When I'm sated, I pull out, allowing her to breathe once more.

"Goddamn," she mutters, out of breath.

"Yes, indeed," I muse. "That's what you call a good creaming."

We both laugh out loud.

I help her up and hand her a wet cloth so she can clean herself. Funnily enough, she actually ran her finger up and down her body and licked up all the cum that was left. I don't know why, but it's the sexiest thing I've ever seen.

"God, I love you so much," I mutter, wrapping my arms around her again as she's busy cleaning up.

She smiles, wiping her face with the cloth before saying, "I love you too, Frank. More than I wanted."

I laugh. "That's what you get when you stumble into a

fuck and then fall head over heels into a relationship that's messed up to begin with."

She sniggers too. "Guess we're that fucked-up couple everyone always mentions when they watch a movie."

"A beautifully fucked-up couple." I kiss her on the cheeks. "And I wouldn't trade us for the world."

She turns around, biting her bottom lip. "Are you sure you're happy here? With me?"

"Why wouldn't I be?" I place my hands beside her on the bathroom counter.

"I don't know … with your past and everything …" She swallows. "Do you ever still think of *her*?"

"Not in the way you think." I lower my head to better look her in the eyes. "I loved her too. Just as I love you. But those two can co-exist." I put my finger underneath her chin. "That I once loved her does not change anything about the way I feel for you now. She's gone. You're here. That's all that matters."

She nods and hugs me tight, and I don't let her go either. "Let's go back," she says. "Everyone's waiting." She pulls from my embrace, but I hold her hand.

"Wait," I say.

I don't want her to go like this.

Without being sure that she knows how fucking much I need her.

"For what?" she asks.

"I meant to give this to you sooner, but I couldn't think of the perfect time. So …" I pull a necklace from my pocket and hold it out. "Here."

Her eyes widen, and she reaches for the necklace with the cross. "That's … my mother's cross."

When her hand is underneath the tiny cross, I let go and let her hold it. "I searched for it back where your dad tried to bury me. Took me ages to find it, but I knew it was important to you."

Tears well up in her eyes, and for a second, I think I may have done something wrong.

"I'm sorry. Maybe I should've given it to you sooner. I knew I should've just—"

Her mouth interrupts me as her lips crash on mine with full force.

Her smile so bright, it could outshine the sun.

"Thank you," she mutters as our lips momentarily unlatch. "I thought I lost it forever."

"Well, I'm glad I could do something to make it up to you."

"Thank you. I mean it. This means the world to me." She squeezes the cross and brushes her tears away.

"So does that mean I'm forgiven?" My brow rises. "Am I allowed to stay?"

She playfully slaps me only to peck me on the cheeks. "You were always welcome here, silly. Even when I said you weren't."

"Oh, so you're a liar now. Hear that, God? It's time for another confession, I hear."

She rolls her eyes at me, but when I grin, she can't help but laugh either.

She kisses me again and again, and I'm lost in her everlasting warmth that keeps pouring out of her, giving me hope for a future.

A future with her, Bruno, and Diego. All of us, together.

A future where I finally belong.

THANK YOU FOR READING!

Thank you so much for reading FATHER. I hope you enjoyed the story!

For updates about upcoming books, please visit my website, www.clarissawild.blogspot.com or sign up for my newsletter here: www.bit.ly/clarissanewsletter.

I'd love to talk to you! You can find me on Facebook: www.facebook.com/ClarissaWildAuthor, make sure to click LIKE. You can also join the Fan Club: www.facebook.com/groups/FanClubClarissaWild/ and talk with other readers!

Enjoyed this book? You could really help out by leaving a review on Amazon and Goodreads. Thank you!

ALSO BY CLARISSA WILD

Dark Romance
Delirious Series
Killer & Stalker
Mr. X
Twenty-One
Ultimate Sin
VIKTOR
Indecent Games Series

New Adult Romance
Fierce Series
Blissful Series
Ruin

Erotic Romance
The Billionaire's Bet Series
Enflamed Series
Bad Teacher

Visit Clarissa Wild's website for current titles.
http://clarissawild.blogspot.com

ABOUT THE AUTHOR

Clarissa Wild is a New York Times & USA Today Bestselling author, best known for the dark Romance novel Mr. X. Her novels include the Fierce Series, the Delirious Series, Stalker Duology, Twenty-One (21), Ultimate Sin, Viktor, Bad Teacher, RUIN, the Indecent Games Series, and Father. She is an avid reader and writer of sexy stories about hot men and feisty women. Her other loves include her furry cat friend and learning about different cultures. In her free time she enjoys watching all sorts of movies, reading tons of books and cooking her favorite meals.

Want to be informed of new releases and special offers? Sign up for Clarissa Wild's newsletter on her website clarissawild.blogspot.com.

Visit Clarissa Wild on Amazon for current titles.

Made in the USA
Columbia, SC
16 May 2017